08-15-17

Dear Phil,

Wishing you peace always,

Dal Boracci

Fatima and the Sons of Abraham

a novel by
Val Bonacci

This novel is fiction. Any mentions of historical events, real places and real people are used fictitiously. Other events, places, and people are solely the author's creation; any similarity between them and real events, places and people—living or dead—is purely coincidence.

Cover design by
Steve Zorc, Val Bonacci, Julia Zorc and Paula Zorc

Cover photos by Steve Zorc

valbonacci.com

ISBN 978-0-9987671-0-9
ISBN 978-0-9987671-1-6 (ebook)

Printed/Manufactured in the USA
Signature Book Printing,www.sbpbooks.com

For Italian Jesuit Priest, Father Paolo Dall'Oglio, a rock star of the highest celestial order, whose heart beat a mantra for interfaith dialogue and peace-building from the community he established at the ancient monastery of St. Moses the Abyssinian near Damascus, Syria. He was last seen in Raqqa, Syria, July 29, 2013. ISIS claims to have executed him, but the proof has yet to be found.

Paolo

CHAPTER 1

Paolo • Calabria, Italy • August 2014

Sunlight smiles through my Valentino shades as I pump my lungs with sea air—a medicinal cleanse after an evening of abuse. The muscular slap of the Tyrrhenian Sea breaks at my back. *Even the waves want to spank this bad boy.* But I won't allow them their pleasure today. I'm here to darken my tan lines.

Il Sole is already glowing high above the emerald hillsides beyond the flat coastline. Their lush forests are studded with fiery terracotta roofs and remnants of turret-shaped stone fortifications of centuries past. If those brooding walls could confess their tales, I suspect they would wail a history ironically similar to today. We're besieged with invaders once again—only this time they come in the form of refugees.

Damn. Here they come with their fresh stock—a sweaty swarm of foreign vendors packing burdens of beach goods for locals and tourists alike. Since the Arab Spring, they're multiplying. *Madonna mia,* their stories are horrifying. The newspapers cry daily of migrants who don't survive the voyage, but what are we supposed to do? Don't they tell you on a plane to fasten your oxygen mask before helping someone else? There aren't enough jobs in Italy for the natives!

Whooping and laughter interrupts my mental rant. A clique of German youngsters surf the frothy edge of the waves as they break on the pebbly shore; while, further inland, Italian teens imitate their A.C. Milan favorites.

Oh my God, check out this salesman walking away from a family stretched across superhero beach towels...he could pass for Eli Kohn's twin...which reminds me, I need to call that bastard. *Do I still have his cell in my contacts?* I hope my iPad doesn't die in this heat before we connect. FaceTime might be a good idea. Eli should see this guy. I'm surprised that the dude doesn't have any trouble communicating with the leggy lady in between us. I'm guessing she's Swiss, judging from her beach chair sporting the country's flag: red with white cross. I'm close enough that the waves don't drown out their voices, and I'm definitely hearing German—from both of them. *That's odd.*

The woman's daughter is a little cupid, struggling to walk in rubber water shoes, one triumphant pair of steps at a time. She lifts her curly blonde locks toward the young refugee and beams the kind of smile that could melt the most frigid of adults.

In an affront both to the ears and to the pleasure of the camaraderie playing out before my eyes, a garish man in a stained pink T-shirt and lime green shorts steps into the frame, preceded by his hairy paunch. He curses the vendor, who is still playing with the Swiss baby. *The bastard's tirade is better than mine after a called third strike.* This bald-headed, shadowy-chinned, pimple of a man means business. The vendor grabs a chunky necklace from his showcase and offers it to the woman, with pleading eyes.

"Time is money," says the *padrone* in Italian.

Apparently she understands and buys it without haggling. The seller's face beams relief as he bows to her with a hand over his heart, before trudging toward a nearby cluster of middle-aged women gossiping in Dutch.

Ooh. Little Curly Cupid is not pleased. She made a friend and doesn't want him to leave. She moves toward him in that stilted way that 15-month-olds do, loses her balance and falls on her padded bottom. She wails, in protest more than pain, raising her little fists in the air, but just as quickly becomes distracted with smooth rocks to either side. The mother drags her seat closer to the babe, who suddenly decides to stand. She carefully waddles away while glancing backward, as if to say 'look at me' and 'let me go' all at once. Cute—but back to business. I punch in Eli's number.

What's happening here? Why do I hear shrieks and yelling all of a sudden? I hope some lunatic isn't waving a gun.

Sunbathers are peeling off in every direction, in a rhythmic ripple vaguely reminiscent of a Radio City Rockettes performance. I blink wide when I spot the cause—a huge, hideous, wild boar! I have a flashback to the first time I went mushroom picking near Mt. Etna with my father. Papa never hunted, so when he took a rifle with him on our trek, I wondered why. But when we came into the path of a similar beast, I quickly learned that my father was a wise man—and one helluva shot.

But today's intruder is even more frightening, not just in size, but in frenetic mood. Maybe it's rabid. Who knows? Who cares? It's crazy and vicious—a deadly combination that spreads total chaos.

Yet I'm transfixed as the activity around me seems to unwind in slow motion. The boar's attention is locked on Oblivious Curly Cupid, like she's lunch. The mother gasps in numb panic, totally freezing. *Pick her up! Run!* I want to shout.

I should be racing toward that kid, but my attention reverts to the stud vendor. I note the graceful unfolding of his lean, 6'3" frame, rising from a squatting position in front of the Dutch gaggle. A serious expression strains his features. At the sight of his right hand, I catch my breath. Long, sinewy fingers curl round a large stone in a spectacular grip. His pose reads fearlessness, strength, and relaxation all at once. *Where have I seen such grace before?*

A switch flips inside my head. I flinch at the realization...Michelangelo's David...the perfect athlete...the one I never encountered in real life—until maybe now.

His stride is catlike, with a speed and force matched flawlessly by his arm action. Even without a windup it rips through the salty air in a hitchless, free-flowing zing of movement so lyrical I imagine the ping of a violin string. The stone rockets from his hand at a rate my practiced eye needs no radar gun to affirm triple digits.

The thud is thunderous. Those behind me collectively inhale like a stupefied chorus of stage actors at the climax of a melodrama. The animal slams into the shore ten feet away from Little Miss Cutie Pie, alone and blissfully ignorant of the theater around her. Hot Swiss Mama nearly faints, drops to her knees, gathers herself, then rushes to her babe. She touches the little doll's face and hair as if recognizing her progeny for the first time.

The reincarnation of David nailed the wicked beast at the temple. *Was it pure luck?* The strange excitement surging in my gut says, no. Only then do I notice that my free arm is raised in a fist. Did I yell something?

"My caller ID says it's you, Paolo, but I don't hear your voice. What the hell is going on? I feel like I was riding a tidal wave. It was a little bumpy and shaky, but did I just see what I just saw? That dude was awesome!"

Apparently in my state of visual intoxication, I flipped the iPad. *Weird.*

I flip it again.

Seeing Eli's face after all this time provokes a strange two-step in my belly. His hair is shorter than that of the refugee-turned-beach-hero, and the shape of his face more angular, but there's no mistaking the resemblance.

"Did that guy look like anyone familiar?" I ask Eli.

"I couldn't see his face, but I have to admit, he's pretty buff."

Call waiting shows that Silvana Giobatti is trying to reach me.

"I have to call you back Eli. My mother-slash-boss is on the other line." I switch to her without saying good-bye.

"Paolo!"

I catch her *bellissima* frown only a moment before watching the scene around the dead boar further unfold. "Did the shipment leave for Rome before you left?" she asks, jerking my attention back.

"Of course not, Mama; you know nothing happens on time in Sicily."

"Well it better start if we're going to compete with the wine-makers in the rest of the world. The grapes can keep their own schedule, but once they're in a bottle it's our job to deliver as promised."

"*Tranquila*, Mama. They're on their way as we speak. Fatima called an hour ago to tell me she handled everything."

That was your responsibility, not your sister's. You know she wants no part of the family business."

I do know it, but little does Mama know that, frankly, neither do I. Besides, Fatima knows more about the business than I do.

"Sorry Mama, but I needed to buy a wedding present before the bachelor party last night. The best man couldn't arrive with empty hands, could he?"

"Where are you now?"

"The beach in Falerna. I thought the sunshine would help me recover my senses. We numbed ourselves with Zio Peppe's finest red until dawn. As Calabrese grapes go, it was pretty good. You can tell Nonna her brother can still drink everyone under the table."

"Don't condescend about Calabria's vines. The world may soon discover them and forget our own in the process. As for Nonna, I'll do no such thing. He's a priest. Show a little respect."

Ah, *Dio mio*, she's relentless. Ever since Papa died she's a changed woman. I miss the old Mama—the one who used to laugh that laugh that made everyone else laugh. I don't think I've heard my favorite sound in over two years. Nonna and Fatima pray for her all the time. That's a one-two power punch as prayer goes, but no change. What are you waiting for, God?

Mama's cell is ringing. *Good.*

"I need to take this call," she says. "*Ciao*. See you at the wedding tomorrow night."

I breathe a sigh of relief. Too bad nobody else chose to come with me this morning: They're missing a tremendous show. It'll be a hanging-on-the-cross contest later at the wedding rehearsal: "Oh, poor me, Nonno put me to work picking olives like a peasant. Oh, even poorer me, my girlfriend won't relent with her cross-examination about last night. Oh lucky Paolo, he relaxed, alone, in peace, all day at the beach." *Little will they guess all the excitement they could have enjoyed!*

Ouch! I should have kept my eyes on the stud vendor and the people crowding around him, instead of turning toward the voices nearer me—everyone is settling back into their sun-soaking routine. Some of those routines I could do without. There ought to be a law against the view to my left: no topless sunbathing unless you've surgically repaired those things falling into your armpits. *Help! I need to get that image out of my head.* Where are all the belle donne today? I see only families and friends in all shapes and sizes—though mostly XL. It's a cardiologist's Disneyland.

They're here for a version of la dolce vita that's more raw and less tame than that from Rome north. If those destinations resemble a refined Mona Lisa, then this zip code is reminiscent of a young Sophia Loren, who, with a slap of the cheek, invites passion and a sassiness all her own. *What I wouldn't give for a vision of her in her prime right now.*

"*Comprate?*" the youngest seller I've seen yet says to a couple on chairs to the right of mine. He does a game-show-babe wave, up and down, left and right, around his four-foot-square display board, proudly showcasing his wares: beaded jewelry in ruby reds and shiny black, pearly headbands, and sea-shell-patterned, imitation-silk scarves. He smiles a comic, semi-toothless grin.

The woman points to a paisley scarf in hues of autumn gold and navy blue.

"Is beautiful, yes?" he asks anxiously.

She fondles the material before tying the scarf around her shampoo-model hair. "I'll take it," she says.

"Wait a minute, my love," objects her husband. "You haven't heard the price yet."

"For you, pretty lady, is only 20 Euro."

The husband checks the tag and says, "Made in China. Take it off and give it back. I'm not paying 20 Euros for that."

Pity breaks her wide open. To call this kid a young man would be a reach. At close range, evaluating his manner, he can't be more than twelve. "I'd also like that white one with the purple and orange."

Her husband quickly assesses where this is going. "If you overpay you'll be inviting a steady parade of these guys the rest of the afternoon." He turns and barks to the boy, "Twenty Euros for the pair. This foolish woman has no money. You have to deal with me."

"OK," the boy answers swiftly, knowing it's still a good price.

The husband pays while furious female eyes shoot fire.

"He probably comes from a country where women have no power," he says, justifying himself. "I just spoke to him in words he'd easily comprehend and paid him a price that was still generous without turning this little oasis of ours into Grand Central Station."

The husband's accent is definitely that of a New Yorker. I remember it too well...their fans brutalized me...which reminds me of my nemesis, half a world away, in Cleveland. I punch in his number again.

"Paolo Giobatti, long time no speak," Eli says sarcastically.

"Before five minutes ago it'd been a whole year, and not a single get-well card in all that time?" I answer. "I thought airmail was invented in the U.S. But hey, that's OK. I'm not hurt or anything, emotionally *or* physically, for that matter. In fact, I'm 100%. That's why I'm calling. I figured if anyone knew what was going on with the team's brain trust, you would. I sent a video of me working out with some coaches here. The back's good as new."

"A back is never good as new once it's been injured, Paolo. They've seen the tape. How many times did you have to ice between takes? You forgot to wear the same cleats throughout."

Damn!

"Look, I feel for you, man. A back injury before signing a contract extension is a real curveball. But you got to remember that you pissed off a lot of people while you were here. Those temper tantrums of yours have become legend. Leyland is your best hope, so ripping him like you did the last time doesn't help your case either."

"I figured our beloved agent would confide in you."

"He was kind of hurt, Paolo. He had to kiss a lot of butts for you the last two years, what with all your hissy fits. You could show a little gratitude."

"OK, OK, you've got a point. But tell me the truth: You miss my bat swinging behind you. That kid Rodriguez can't hold my cleats, let alone fill them."

"We're not the same team on the field without the old Paolo, it's true. Rodriguez is still learning. He gets better every day. But in the clubhouse it's as loose as that redhead you used to chase. She's engaged, by the way."

"Hey, better her than me, man. This Casanova takes his job seriously. Monogamy for me would break too many hearts."

I knew that would make him laugh. I need to lighten up this conversation. He'll be no help to me otherwise.

"Where are you calling me from, anyway?" he says. "Is that Italian ocean I hear or somewhere closer to Cleveland?"

I flip my iPad again as Hot Swiss Mama returns to her seat.

"Wow. Nice digs. Did I mention that Switzerland is my favorite country?"

I snort a short laugh before he continues, "So—did you talk with our future ace between calls, or was your mother giving you an earful all that time—I mean, after you hung up on me?"

"No, I haven't met him, but I hate to admit you might have a good idea there." *(How did he know Mama was giving me a hard time?)* "He's being kept pretty busy by all his new admirers. But let me try and meet him and I'll buzz you back in a few minutes. *Ciao*," I say, this time.

"*Va bene*," he says in a mock accent before I hang up again.

The wicked *padrone* has returned. What a prick he is. I can hear his big mouth shouting orders over the roar of the waves.

CHAPTER 2

Darius

I cringe at the sound of his voice. My break from reality is over.

It was nice while it lasted. Sunbathers who'd seen the shot gather around me, slapping my back in rousing congratulations. A group of Italian men start arguing over the dead boar (likely thinking ahead to the sumptuous supper it could provide in the hands of an expert) when the pretty mother with her child in her arms rushes toward me. She showers me with tears, calling me a hero. For a moment I don't know what to do before my arms embrace them, the beautiful woman, the beautiful child. I haven't felt that kind of warmth in months, so I squeeze tighter. Smartphones in hand, onlookers snap photos of the three of us before proceeding to the carcass.

But now my perpetually angry boss bursts onto the scene, shouting like he owns this speck of earth. The tide breaks over the animal—ghastly and surrealistic—like all the other death I've come to know. My *padrone* waves off all would-be takers from the wild boar, claiming it as his own. "The boy works for me," he growls at the arguing men, and, to me, "Get back to work! You suddenly have more fish than your net can hold." Then he yells at what is by now a crowd, "If you think he's so special, show your gratitude with a purchase. *Comprate, comprate!*"

He calls some of our gang, ordering the scrawniest member to guard the wares before positioning the others around the dead boar. "*Uno, due, tre,*" he counts, and with that, they heave the animal into the air. They carry it to the parking area in the sand, close to the road. His truck is at the far end of a row of tiny cars under the shade of a mesh canopy.

Meanwhile I accept congratulations in the form of a flurry of sales activity. It isn't long before my burden is emptied. I motion the line that's forming to the displays my emaciated colleague is protecting, and I continue selling from those. My compatriots return and I lose myself in a false sense of normalcy.

"Smart kid," I hear someone say. Then an Italian around my age, maybe older, approaches, carrying an electronic notebook. He's as tall as I am but is thicker-built. He offers his hand.

"Paolo Giobatti."

This is weird. I feel respectable for the first time since...

"Darius Salamah."

Intense, caramel-colored eyes peer at me from under a pile of wavy dark hair.

"That was an amazing shot. Where'd you learn to do that?"

It must be 90 degrees today, yet a cold chill passes through me, like an arctic ghost.

"Trying to protect my family. When you have no gun, you do what you can. When it was no longer safe to go to school, I obsessed over practicing with my arm instead of my brain. My father was against violence. He refused to carry a weapon, and wouldn't allow it of me either. But rock throwing did us no good in the end. I'm all that's left of my family."

The handsome Italian's intensity mellows. He's lost for words.

"You saved a life today," he then says.

"The animal had no gun," I respond

"Where are you from?" he asks.

"Syria."

"How long have you been in Italy?" he asks.

"Almost one month, but it's been much longer since I left my home."

This Paolo now morphs into a gracious host. "Come and sit with me. Have something cool to drink. Relax. Your boss will be gone for a while. He needs to get that boar to a kitchen before the meat spoils."

I remain guarded, but I'm dying of thirst, and so I follow him.

"You don't sound like a refugee," he says.

"How should a refugee sound? Like an imbecile?"

"I'm sorry. I didn't mean it that way."

Yes, he did; but he appears sheepish. I shouldn't be rude. I don't need to burn the first bridge I've come across since landing here.

"My parents were language teachers," I tell him "I was their only child. They poured all that they had into me. They made sure I learned to speak as many languages as possible. In fact, when I was young, they even took me on a trip to Italy. Would you believe I was once a tourist upon these beaches?"

I stare out to sea and back in time to another shore. It's hard to believe that only a month ago I landed on a beach not far from this one. My head becomes a blur of memories, each bumping and spinning into a visual string that snaps like a whip woven of sorrow...*backpacks falling like anchors...bodies reaching toward each other...that boy screaming for his mother...*

Is there no justice left in this world? I can't help but beg for the answer. But Allah no longer hears me, so I shout inside my brain, where no one is listening but me: *They didn't deserve such an end!*

I feel this Paolo beside me, anxiously waiting for me to return from my memories. Anxiety and panic wash over me. *I can't think of this now. I just can't.* I force a memory of my rescuers instead, not the ones who saved my body, but the ones who saved my hope—chubby, dimpled Sister Colleen, and her tiny friend with the big heart. Deep inside me I whisper her name, like a bandage for my soul.

"And what's your story?" I ask Paolo, forcing myself back to reality.

"I'm living in Sicily, where my family owns a winery. I'm in Calabria for a wedding."

My pulse begins to race once more, but this surge is one of excitement. Didn't *she* tell me that her family owned a winery in Sicily as well? Before I can ask Paolo if he might know her, a stranger interrupts and asks him for his autograph.

"I didn't recognize you at first," the man says. "You kept your hair so short when you were playing baseball in the U.S."

Paolo smiles, rather absently, and signs his book.

"Will you return to the game soon?" the man asks.

"I'm working on it."

The man wishes him well, then turns to me. "Everybody on this beach is talking about what you did. You could be a pitcher with an arm like that! Wouldn't you agree, Paolo?"

The man taps at his phone. Suddenly I'm watching, transfixed. The video jiggles a little, but it's the child, the boar, the shot. I threw a million chunks of rubble—once the buildings of my neighborhood—but I never actually watched myself doing it. I'm fascinated. I ask him to play it for me again.

Paolo nods politely and dismisses the fan with a little wave, leading me away by the arm. "This same idea has occurred to me as well," he murmurs. I watch as he taps the screen of his notebook. It does a quick dissolve to a face with enough similarities to my own that I nearly gasp. Paolo laughs. "They say everyone on this earth has a twin. Some of us just know ours from birth."

"Hello," the face says, in a hushed tone. He looks as uncertain as I feel.

"Eli Kohn, meet Darius Salamah."

The pause is eerie.

"I saw what you did—deadly accurate."

His words give rise to a wave of nausea. Sweat beads at my temples, my adrenaline fires, my heart palpitates, and the scream feels trapped in my throat forever. *Must I fight this every day? If I run into the waves will they save me or reject me, throwing me back into this pit of despair?* Then I get a grip on myself. I'm good, I'm good. I've made it into the afternoon before the first attack. That's progress. Progress, yes. I'm better. I'm getting better. Focus. Focus. Yes—channel—yes. I smell the salt air all the way to my toes. It passes.

"Are you, OK?" they ask in unison. Their voices blend, as if in a song. It gives odd comfort.

"Yes, yes, I'm fine. It's been a strange day. I'm just feeling...a little overwhelmed."

"Is Fatima there too?" this Eli asks Paolo.

"No, she and my mother and my grandmother are joining me tomorrow. I'm in Calabria for a wedding. I'm recuperating at the beach after last night's bachelor party and before the rehearsal dinner tonight."

Paolo is saying something else, but I don't hear it. My head is suddenly swimming, like the gull I watch cresting the waves. *Could this really be the same Fatima?* I fish inside my pocket for the card. The sight of her last name causes my hands to shake. I tell myself that Giobatti is probably a common name in this country—trying not to build hope that might only be crushed in the next few minutes.

"You mean to tell me you quit texting Fatima?" Paolo continues, not noticing my reaction. "Good. My sister isn't for you."

"You have a sister named Fatima?" I ask.

"Si. You seem astonished."

"Fatima is an Arab name. Are you a Muslim?" I ask.

"I'm Catholic, like most Italians. Not that I've seen the inside of a church in a while—though I guess I will tonight. Hope the place doesn't cave in."

Eli laughs. "You're lucky you have pious women in your life. They cover your ass."

I tell myself to remain calm. *Let me first see what information they're willing to share.* "Where are you?" I ask Eli.

"I'm in Cleveland, Ohio, in the U.S. How is it that you are in Italy?"

"I'm a refugee from Syria." I change the subject back to Fatima. "How old is your sister?"

"Twenty-three—same as me. We're twins." Suddenly I notice the resemblance. *Oh my God. Her brother. Her twin.*

"Is she named for someone?" I ask, faking calm.

"She's named for Our Lady of Fatima. Don't ask me to explain. You're a Muslim, you'll never understand. To be honest, I'm Catholic and I barely get it—but I know there are millions of people around the world who do. My great-grandmother was one of them; some said she was a mystic. When my sister and I were born, she named her Fatima, because she said that she had the face of the Angel of Peace—the story is really a mystery to me. I never realized it was an Arabic name until now."

"It's the name of the youngest daughter of Prophet Mohammed. She's said to have been wholly devoted to her father, dying at a young age, shortly after his own death. She's revered throughout Islam—as is Mary, the mother of Jesus. And you're wrong to say I won't understand. I heard this story from an Irish nun when I first arrived in Lampedusa a month ago."

"What! I don't know what's more shocking: that Muslims revere the Madonna, or that you know Sister Colleen! That has to be who you're talking about! You probably already met Fatima. I know they were on the island last month, working with refugees."

"Is your sister tiny, with tons of hair and your eyes?" I ask.

"Unbelievable. It really is getting to be a smaller world. I'm not sure how I feel about that." Paolo mutters that last part under his breath. He runs his fingers through his prodigious curls and shakes his head. "I can't believe it," he says.

"Sister Colleen told me the story of Fatima—or at least 'the highlights,' as she called it. I don't know why I didn't put together your sister being named for the event. Perhaps because she never mentioned it. But she did mention what happened to your father. I'm sorry."

Paolo stares at me, momentarily lost again for words. "Thank you," he says at last.

"Speaking of names," Eli says *(I nearly forgot about him)* "how is it that an Arab has a Persian name?"

"My mother was Persian."

"Did Shia marry Sunni?" His tone is incredulous.

"Yes, and paid the ultimate price for it."

"I'm sorry. I'm sure there's an incredible story there. I'd like to hear it sometime, but I have to be getting some shut-eye. It's bar closing time here. Don't let him run away, Paolo, before giving him a tryout. By the way, Darius, you speak better English than Paolo. It's impressive how little accent you have. Oh, and Paolo, tell Fatima I'll call her soon. I miss our chats."

Paolo ignores the language stab and zones in like a hawk on Eli's final statement. "Listen, Eli, there have to be at least three to four billion females on this planet. Now I realize that you believe you're God's gift to every one of them, but my sister sees right through you. She's like that about people. You're wasting your time with Fatima. Work the other two billion, nine-hundred-and-ninety-nine-thousand, why don't you?"

"Does she still want to be a nun?"

"Now see, that's just it. You consider her your greatest challenge. But the chase is all you care about. I'll admit she likes you, but not in the way you hope. She never will. Besides, you couldn't handle her even if she doesn't choose the convent. She's a four-foot, eleven-inch mountain who could kick your ass from here to there."

"She's the smartest person I know. And don't worry, she's got your number too. I know about that prank she pulled on you in the spring. That was the last time we spoke."

"Yeah, yeah. And now you want to talk to her again. Let me guess: That Brazilian model didn't quite work out, did she?"

"You prick."

"I still have plenty of friends in Cleveland," Paolo says.

"Good for you, but remember I'm not one of them. Good-bye, Darius. Perhaps we'll meet someday."

His face disappears. I'm glad to see it go. We may share some physical features, but behind those eyes I saw only a stranger.

Pangs of jealousy kick at my gut at the realization that Eli is interested in Fatima. "So tell me about you and this Eli. And I suppose his given name is Elijah."

"Yes, it is. But he's no prophet, believe me. Are you familiar with the sport of baseball?"

"Familiar would be too strong a word. But I've seen it in snippets."

"Dammit, Eli was right. Snippets? What are snippets, anyway?" Paolo asks.

I have to laugh. "I've seen this sport in online international news. I didn't think they played it in Europe."

"You'd be surprised. They began playing it in Italy after World War II. American soldiers taught it. It's become more popular here of late, thanks to me. So far, I'm the only Italian to become a star player in America." Suddenly he turns to look straight at me. "The way you killed that boar makes me wonder if you might not have a gift for this game. I think you could play the most important position on the team, the one we call the pitcher. It's the pitcher's job to throw a ball past a batter—a ball about the size of that stone you aimed at that beast. It was a miracle a stone that big was even here, but sometimes people build fires on the sand at night and put a circle of larger stones around it. But look. Do you see any others nearby? I only see a few in the distance, closer to the parking area. It's a miracle all right. I think it was meant to be."

Anger suddenly boils over inside me. Who does he think he is to speak to me of miracles and fairy tales? His life is all fun and games, creature comforts and happy dreams. There are no more dreams left for me, only nightmares.

"You're a fool. Miracles are a fantasy. See, the *padrone's* truck returns. He brings more work, more hate, more lust for money. Go back to your child's play while the rest of us do what we have to do to survive in the *real* world."

I leave him with his mouth agape. I want to kick myself for losing my temper with him— especially now that I know he is Fatima's brother. But I couldn't help myself. Now what do I do?

CHAPTER 3

Darius

I have no chance to repent or to make amends. The *padrone* shouts at me to join him at the supply truck. By the time I'm at his side, however, the stock has been distributed to my fellow migrants.

"Get in the truck. I want to introduce you to someone," he orders.

I oblige. He's babbling about me like I'm his new prize horse, but I shut my ears to his self-indulgent discourse. *How did I get into this situation?* I drift back in time to a month ago, to my arrival to Europe...to those three days that will stay with me forever.

I replay the most memorable moments in my head, like the video the autograph-seeker shared of me and the wild boar...

•••••••••••

She anticipates being rid of us—the sea, that is. She breathes in rapid gulps as we approach the shore. That's fine with me. I'm no seafarer's son. Instead, the Sirocco wind brands my cheek with a hot dry kiss, as if to remind me of my desert origins.

The wide-eyed boy in front of me clings to his mother's leg like a lifeline as we lurch for the millionth time in our pitiful journey. I curse God for the jealousy that wells up inside me. He answers me with the smell of sweat and puke. It should gag me, but I'd got over all that the day before. All I care about is that we're a bird's short flight from land. Two days have dwindled to ten minutes, maybe less, hopefully less, less sea and more sand, closer, closer.

But a foolish man on the opposite side of the boat begins to yell. Soon others are waving and screaming. Chaos ensues, along with shouting and shoving. I shake my head in disbelief when the few belongings some have carried are grasped as if their loss would mean something.

"No!" I plead as I grab two others beside me, anchoring them in their places in hopes of balancing our shaky craft. But I'm too late. Like sheep in orange life vests, the fools have shifted our bulk to the tipping point.

The shock of the cold and wet is immediate. My clothes and shoes carry a foreign heaviness. The fact that I can't swim is a faint voice in the farthest reaches of my mind as I close my lungs in the womb of water. We were so close, you fools!

I break into air, sucking deeply. The mother is flailing in unison with her screams, "Ahmed, Ahmed!" I continue to kick while scraping at the liquid surface, jerking my head in every direction in search of her boy. I hear his cry, but don't see him. How did such a mass become so separate so quickly?

The answer slaps me with ferocious force. I lose control of my bladder, but embarrassment is a luxury I can't afford. I choke on the wave. The salt surprises my tongue before I quickly break free again, coughing and shaking. My teeth begin to chatter; I clench them, as if in a death grip. I will myself to focus by remembering all those terrors I've already survived.

She's gone. Ahmed is gone. But the Italian Coast Guard approaches. They lower dinghies into the glistening Mediterranean, itself sparkling in mock brilliance, as if in defiance at the darkness of death all around. Divers swim with life preservers toward those heads—like mine—still bobbing above the surface.

"HOW CAN THIS BE?" I roar, like a lion in some poacher's snare, thanks to the same adrenaline that is keeping me alive. A helicopter lowering a body basket a few meters from me drowns my objection to the heavens.

I can't believe what has happened. What do men and women of the desert know of boats? They survived heinous wars, Mother Nature's wrath, as well as physical and financial rape only to come within inches of a new life before losing the one they'd fought so hard to preserve. Why, Ya Allah? Why? I punch my hands on the back of a sea that doesn't feel the beating. Suddenly a different nausea descends, from my gut to my toes. Could it have been my own fault, God? Did my jealousy for a family that no longer exists sweep them under—a mother and son from Egypt, Somalia, Libya, Eritrea? Are they enjoying the last laugh, together in paradise, while I'm still wallowing here—more alone than ever before in my nineteen years on this earth?

The basket comes closer. My arms feel weighed down, as if by elephants, but I manage to grip it. Some strength from a place I don't know lifts me. Why, Ya Allah? I keep asking, over and over. "What are you saving me for?"

•••••••••••

The *padrone* has finished his monologue. We drive along the coastal road, only to come to a dead stop. A bus has collided with a fruit truck. Produce is scattered everywhere, with cars backed up in both directions. Looks like we might be here a while. Suddenly he turns to me and growls, "You heard me, or not? From now on, you're mine. You owe your freedom to me—and to me alone, remember, or else I'll denounce you and have you on a boat back to Africa so fast you'll wish you were dead. Hear me?"

I hear him and nod, with a secret shudder. Then I tune out the pig's cursing and drift back into my dream of days only a month ago...

•••••••••••

My first step upon the soil of Europe is on the island of Lampedusa, Italy. It turns out to be a true haven—except for the new horror film added to my nightly repertoire. Sleep becomes my enemy. Little Ahmed and his mother begin to haunt me, along with the visions of war I wish I could leave behind. But daylight is a balm. The island is paradise, albeit an overcrowded one, with people of all stripes in the refugee processing center. The processors themselves come in a far wider variety than the Italians I expected. I wonder why Westerners fear Muslim women in hijabs when Christian nuns cover themselves so completely. The one I meet during my first morning in Lampedusa speaks in an Irish brogue. The freckles on her face and dimples on her cheeks make her smile appear childlike, although she's probably triple my age. In no time at all she becomes shocked into silence by my language skills—but there's nothing new there. They've been a curse more than blessing the last year.

•••••••••••

The *padrone* has left the cab. He's in the thick of it, waving his hands and shouting as if that'll magically move all the broken vehicles out of the way. It appears that no one is hurt. I dispense with the stupidity before my eyes and close them instead to my dream of Lampedusa—and of the young woman with the Muslim name, Paolo's sister...

•••••••••••

I see us together so clearly. I stand and bow with a hand over my heart as she walks toward me; I feel it throbbing against my palm. "Good morning, Signorina Fatima," I say.

"Good morning, Darius. It's good to see you smile. Did you rest well?" she asks.

"Well enough," I lie.

"I come to say good-bye. Those of us traveling with Sister Colleen have been on a mission for a month, but we're supposed to return to Sicily today. As for you, mainland Italy will be your next stop for immigration processing, but not until the doctors from Médecins Sans Frontières have given you a physical exam... But don't worry; you look fit enough," she smiles.

It isn't worry she sees in my face: I simply don't want to be left alone again. "I will miss you," I tell her. Maybe it's foolish of me, but the words spill from my lips so easily. "These three days have been far more tolerable than I could ever have imagined, thanks to our conversations."

"I'm glad," she says. She compliments me by saying, "Your Italian is impeccable, a bit formal, but trust me, you'll have no problem assimilating here, if you choose to stay in my country. You even look like part of the landscape! You'll do just fine." Then she gives me a card with her name, address, and phone number, adding, "My family owns a vineyard and winery between Taormina and Catania, Sicily. My mother does all the hiring, but I'm sure she could use someone with your language skills. We export to more and more countries all the time."

She tempts me greatly, not only with her words but with herself. She's isn't beautiful like a supermodel—she's too short and curvy for that—but still, she is utterly lovely in a hypnotic sort of way.

"I made a promise to my parents that I would someday become a doctor," I admit. "I am determined to keep this promise. I plan to work my way north, doing migrant labor. I will find a decent-paying job in the city where I can be accepted into a school." I say it with ridiculous certainty.

"I don't blame you with wanting to honor their memory by keeping your promise," she tells me gently. "And, as I told you when we first met, I'm so sorry for your loss. I didn't tell you then, but I will now, that—although I haven't been through anything like what you've suffered— I lost my father to cancer a couple of years ago. It was a slow, agonizing, relentless assault: first on his body, and by the end upon his spirit. Part of me died with him, I think. But for my mother it's been like losing almost her whole self. She walks and talks like an empty shell of a woman. I've delayed my own plans for the future until I know that she'll be all right."

"And what are those future plans, if I may be so bold as to ask?"

A boyfriend, of course... How could someone so compelling be single? I prepare myself for inevitable disappointment, but her words strike an even greater one: "I want to join the convent, Sister Colleen's order. But I won't leave my mother until she's ready. My brother is rarely home anymore, and our grandmother is getting to an age where she can see heaven's door from here."

•••••••••••

The *padrone* is back in the truck. He wears a black eye. It suits him. He's totally silent. The road is still blocked. I hear sirens in the distance. The sound of rescue vehicles takes me back to Lampedusa.

•••••••••••

On that magical day, the day when we finally speak like true friends, Fatima and I are distracted by a crying Arab baby. Sister Colleen sits the babe on her knee and starts cooing in the child's ear. "Nearly one hundred years a leanbh," she says, "one hundred years since yeer latest troubles began."

I think that the Scots and the Irish have the most appealing accents. She mesmerizes me with hers, and with the Celtic she sprinkles into her speech.

Her brogue grows thicker as she continues. "What, me little a mhuirnin? Ya think yeer struggle is new? Abraham 'twas a migrant to Canaan, was he not? And Jesus, Mary, and Joseph were refugees to Egypt, no less. Why, afore and since the time o' yeer troubles, the world's history's been nothin' more than a story o' territorial control—jus' like that little toy ya tried to wrestle from yeer brother afore all these tears!"

The little girl quits crying, raises her shoulder to her ear, and nuzzles toward Sister Colleen's whispers, as if her cooing both tickles and draws her like a magnet. She makes little baby noises to answer each sentence. Eventually the child turns her face to the Sister's. For the briefest moment their lips brush. (It's a scene so precious that it reminds me of the little one who became my friend on the beach.)

But back to Sister Colleen, "Yeer problems, a chroi, are a direct result of the spoils o' war. Did ya know yeer such a treasure? Yes, you and yeer parents and grandparents afore ya and even yeer great-grandparents, too. Near a hundred years it's been since the Ottoman Turks lost yeer home to the Brits and the French, and the 1917 Irish and Russian revolutions came to pass. Ah me darlin'—'twas the beginnin' of the last act o' this earthly drama we all been a-playin' I fear. It's me own humble opinion that God sent our Holy Mother to Fatima for a wee bit o' stimulation, hopin' we'd be turnin' from our devilry... Time's a-runnin' short, me thinks."

I'm surprised by the name. Fatima. "Do you mean the mother of Jesus, Sister Colleen, when you say Holy Mother?"

"Naturally."

"When did she visit a Muslim girl?"

She laughs a melodious laugh—the kind indicative of a beautiful singing voice. "I should have known, me young friend, I'd be confusin' ya with that one. I'm talkin' of a place called Fatima, not a person... Some people wonder if the mystery of it all isn't about to hit us hard, a hundred years later. I'm no dooms-dayer meself, but I know more than a few who'd be just the type. Maybe it's just the fact we humans enjoy a good boast, now and again. One-hun-

dredth anniversaries get a wee bit more attention from us, don't they? I'm not sure why all the fuss, meself. I'm thinkin' that to the heavenly host a hundred years might be like yesterday."

I'm totally confused but I let her keep talking. Her accent is so beautiful.

"Why, just last night when me head hit the pillow, I dreamed 'em so clear—three little shepherds threading theer charges through an olive grove. The flock was so eager to graze it rushed the field. Ah, but those children had no idea of the significance the place would soon achieve. For them 'twas simply the impoverished hamlet they called home—a place named for the daughter of a sultan—a place called Fatima, Portugal.

Now I have to interrupt. "How did this place come to be named for the daughter of a sultan?" I ask.

"History and legend are the answer to yeer question. The history part is that much of Portugal 'twas under Islamic rule from the eighth century—for over five hundred years. But the history o' war bein' what it is, the Arab overlords were eventually driven south, beginin' in the 1100s, or thereabouts.

"Now for the legend part," she continues, "a lovely Arab lass named Fatima fell in love with a Christian lad, and refused to leave with her father's army. This lad must'a been an important fella to have the name of the town changed for his bride, as a gift for all she'd sacrificed for love... I wonder if the Blessed Mother had this legend in mind when she chose this place for her mystical appearances in modern times..."

"What appearances?" I ask, fascinated but bewildered.

"Ah! Well, 'tis a bit of a long tale, me dear Darius. One I have na' the time for a proper tellin' since we must be catchin' our boat, but let me offer ya the highlights. I warn ya, though, me handsome laddy, it might shake yeer sensibilities.

"Once upon a time—well, 1916, to be exact—these shepherds, aged six, seven, and nine, encountered a marvelous stranger. As the wooly ones was busy a-nibblin' the grasses, the wee threesome huddled together for warmth, while recitin' their daily Rosary. However, kids that they be, they prayed it in shorthand, somethin' like, 'Hail Mary, full of grace, now and at the hour of our death, Amen.' And 'twas then when a young man as white as snow and clear as crystal—their words, not me own—showed up to tell 'em

to cut out the cuttin' out. 'Twas no thunder and hellfire—just a nudge, ya see. But they got the message.

"So this sublime figure, a-callin' himself the Angel of Peace, came to prepare the little ones for the astonishin' visitor to come. Although the children lacked for schoolin' their wee minds were as brilliant as diamonds. Under the Angel's learnin' they became died-in-the-wool fervent. I like to suspect that, for the holy angels Gabriel, Michael, and all the rest, these young'uns were tiny superheroes, unafraid to drink from the cup o' sufferin', as it were. A tall order for ones so young, do ya think? But this is how the story goes. Don't believe me? Ye can Google it later, if ye still have your doubts..."

•••••••••••

The *padrone's* cell phone rings. It must be his wife—though he talks to her no more kindly than he does to us. They argue about something to do with one of their sons. I tune them out and gaze out at the glitter-covered blue waters. They take me back to where I'd rather be...

•••••••••••

People begin to gather around. This nun has a way with storytelling. She did the same thing the previous two nights. She's incredibly entertaining—better than any television show that I can recall, before electricity became a scarce luxury in my life. The other nights she had told tales of her favorite saints, but her last tale is the one I'll always remember best.

"The eldest, Lucia, was theer leader," she continues. "She loved the freedom of their work, and the freedom to escape from troubles at home. 'Twas wise beyond her years, that one—a dutiful child, with the kind of steely humility that few can understand.

"Jacinta was the passionate one. I can just imagine her standin' with her little hands on her hips, scoldin' Francisco as to how he'd be burnin' in hell for his foolish pranks. Such mighty words from such a wee child, to be sure, but they say as how Jacinta was like a spunky, diminutive grandma. I love that.

"Francisco couldna burn in hell: 'Twas said he sported quite the guilty conscience. But he was still a lad, like any other. If not for tormentin' his cousin and sister his adrenaline would probably a-burst. They musta been precious, the three of them.

"Beginnin' in the spring o' 1917, Mary, the mother o' Jesus, gave the trio a gift and a curse, showin' 'em visions, both o' heaven and hell. She appeared on the 13th of every month, from the warmth of May to the brisk winds of October. She came to warn the world of worse horrors than World War I—but they were too young to understand. Such words were meant for future popes.

"One month, however, our Blessed Mother waited till the 16th to appear to her young'uns. Why? Because they were in jail! The rulin' authorities, in their infinite wisdom, determined that, if they could skeer the pants and skirts off the wee kiddies, then they'd come clean an' swear the story was only a fancy o' their imaginations—an attention-getter. A shepherd's life can be awful solitary, as y'know.

"Although they were separated and threatened with the worst possible punishments, each of the three stuck to their story—the same story, as it was. Amazin'.

"A furor ensued and the children were released. They returned to the Holm Oak in the hollow, which is where the beautiful lady came a-visitin'—the one as called herself the Queen of Peace.

"Angel of Peace, Queen of Peace—you get the gist by now, to be sure," she says with a wink and a nod.

"Jacinta and Francisco were told they'd soon be leavin' this earth, but na to worry a bit, as a non-stop ticket to heaven awaited 'em. They didna seem to mind this prophecy, which came to pass in the influenza epidemic of 1919–20. Lucia, however, was told that she was needed to live a while longer. And so she carried with her three secrets no' to be revealed afore 1960—secrets still the center of much debate. She died at age 97 as a cloistered nun only two months afore St. Pope John Paul II in 2005. Coincidence? Maybe—an' maybe not. He believed Our Lady of Fatima saved him from an assassin's bullet on May 13, 1981."

I don't know how much of this story is true or is just Sister Colleen being Sister Colleen, but I'm fascinated.

"So heer we be at the threshold o' that magical number: 100. Due to its milestone status, a great noise swirls all round the

world. Prognosticating, pontificating, and predictions pile and pollute. Fear and fanaticism foment."

Some clap at her clever use of language. One of the doctors yells, "I think you might have found another calling, Sister!" We all laugh.

She finally places the baby back in her mother's arms and stands, circling like an actor on a stage. "So what are we to do? Should yeer soul shiver? Should ya pay as much heed as ya doctors would to a stock tip?" More laughs. "Or should we pretend the movie's got too fearsome and change the channel to cartoons?"

She waits for a response, but, with none offered, says, "Well, I have an answer. It's all in the tale just told. Forget yeer fears and live in hope. And—should we all be spared—think o' me come May 13, 2017 and do what I'll be doin'. Rubbin' me Rosary beads in a prayer for peace while recallin' the heroics of mere babes. Just consider this tellin' a parting gift to you from me, for us...we."

She curtsies like royalty. Whistles, claps, and cheers tickle my ears. It's a blessed sound. The charisma oozing from this woman is electrifying. How I will miss her!

A man whispers to Sister Colleen. She nods, then claps her hands for attention.

"I'm afraid it's time for us to go," she says. She hugs me first and says, "God bless ya, boy," before reaching out toward others in the crowd all around.

"I hope we meet again," Fatima says to me.

My stomach aches, all of a sudden. "I hope so too."

She's so tiny that her hug is barely above my waist. But that bouncy hair of hers hits me in the chest. I long to bury myself in it. These Italians are so demonstrative!—I've never before been hugged by a young woman who isn't related to me, but it feels wonderful. She smiles her big smile and waves, a little twirl of the wrist, before turning toward the Sisters, moving in that strange, walking-on-water way of hers. For some reason I sense that we will meet again.

•••••••••••

Finally, the road has cleared. We drive for another five minutes before the *padrone* stops the truck behind a resort hotel. His explanation is quite gracious, for him at least: "The head chef of this place is a good friend of mine. He wants to meet the David that slew dinner for his guests with one stone." Instead of irritation, a strange sense of peace overwhelms me. Sister Colleen had told me, on my first day on the island, that, "*Destiny summons us all, but only those willing to listen to her siren call will find theirs*." I could almost swear that I'm hearing such a siren now. I decide not to chastise myself any longer for insulting Paolo. If Fatima and I are destined to meet again, then it will happen. The only bad part might be dealing with her brother and that Eli in the process...

Chapter 4

Eli • Cleveland, Ohio

Blistering sunshine and black leather seats are a match made in hell, even if my convertible has AC for the butt cheeks. A scorched ass serves me right. I'm late...again. But if I hit every light green between Shaker Boulevard and The Clinic, I just might make it on time.

Doesn't the wind ever take a break in this town? I should have gelled my hair before I left the house. Maybe I'll put the top up, if I hit a red light.

Red light, green light; make up your mind, asshole. Yeah. Go ahead. You can curse yourself, but it won't change the fact that you're late because you lost track of time shopping for more clothes that you don't need—and the watch—don't forget the watch... What a farce: yet another watch for a guy who's never on time.

Oh no, here it comes! An imaginary conductor waves his baton before my car radio, cueing the sports talker to burn my already-red ass. "Eli Kohn was a monstrous disappointment last night in Cleveland's loss to Detroit."

It still feels just so damned weird to hear your name on the radio. I can't get used to it.

Come on dude, cut a guy a break. So I was hitless, but I blocked the plate not once, but twice! Twice, dude, I put my body on the line to cut down a run—twice, for all the good it did us! A catcher's job is a thankless one. Nobody cares about great defense anymore. All the fans want are home runs.

Uh oh, shouting at your radio in a convertible is probably not advisable when you're in the middle of three lanes, one way, at 30 mph. *Oh, maaaaan! Almost made it, but I have to hit the brakes for this one or I'll run it red, for sure.*

I feel her eyes before I turn to see them. In the lane next to me, perched in her own sporty little number, is the reincarnation of Marilyn Monroe. Oh my God, she's leaning over the passenger seat to say something.

I smile with my perfect orthodontics. "Good morning."

"It's afternoon. And thanks for ruining my night. I bet on you guys. You'd think you could've squeezed out one single."

Green light. Gone Marilyn.

"But I blocked the plate twice," I yell, at her taillights.

I douse the radio and switch to my iTunes mellow tracks—a more appropriate mood, since I'm on my way to visit sick kids. I know I should feel good about this, but I don't. I do good out of guilt. How come at their age I was showing signs of becoming a future baseball star instead of signs of cancer? Lucky me! *What kind of twisted love is that, God? Why am I so special?*

At least that's how it seems these days: everybody wants a piece of me. Later this afternoon I have a magazine photo shoot. Then I'm supposed to schmooze a couple of corporate sponsors during batting practice (which, after last night's debacle, should receive the solo focus of my attention...but no, duty calls). I'm meeting my agent and a new sponsor tomorrow, at Cleveland's latest trendy restaurant. Meaning—great—another bombardment by autograph hounds.

I know I should be grateful. I dreamed of this my whole life. But I never imagined that it'd be like this. I wasn't counting on all the demands. Right now, as I drop my car with the hospital valet (another bizarre thing I can't get used to) I wish everyone would forget about Eli Kohn for a while.

•••••••••••

I hear the step-click of heavy canine paws on slate. A mild bark of acknowledgement follows. "Yes, big boy, I love you too, even though your giant jowls slobber all over my new jeans. You're my black beauty. Yes, yes; I missed you too."

Elvis is happy I'm back at home after the hospital visit and a quick stop to see my agent. His tail wags in earnest. It's time for his bladder release before I leave for the ball yard. He heads for his leash—Italian leather, nothing but the best for my Dane. The lock tumbles with a jolt. The heavy wood door of my English Tudor requires two hands on the brass knob in order to pull it open. Elvis bolts outside as I uselessly object, "Whoa, dude. I need this arm!"

I love my neighborhood: flagstone sidewalks lined with giant oak, cottonwood, and silver maple trees. Each one is probably as old as the town, but none will serve as a toilet for Elvis. Instead, we lumber toward his favorite promenade, Shaker Lake.

By the time we reach the pond, my T-shirt is sopping with sweat. Elvis is panting like a heart attack victim from excitement.

"I've got a spooky story for you, my dark and hairy friend. I just got back from a meeting that ended in a real bugaboo."

"Hey, who's walking who there?"

Dammit. I recognize that funky lilt. I really don't want to face the woman, but common courtesy is bred into my bones.

"How are you?" I say.

"I'd be better if you'd return a phone call now and then."

"Life's pretty busy for me. What can I say?"

"Say yes. Just give up already. I won't let you off the hook until you agree to sign autographs at the next fundraiser I'm chairing. That's why they choose me for these boards: I'm relentless. I always get my man. Now I know I've tagged you for two already, but I promise this third will be the last of 2014, what do you say?"

"What can I say? I'm tired of hitting the delete button every time you message me. I don't know how you got my number, but you're an expert, I'll grant you that."

"Great! I'll take that as a 'yes.' I'll mail your agent the details today, and I'll see you in a month!"

She gives me a wave and jogs away before I can protest.

"Am I a good guy or what, Elvis? I mean, really? Autograph sessions are like water torture. I'd rather chew pine tar and yet, here I am, agreeing to yet another one. OK, it's not like I care all that much about her charities, but—let's be honest, here—neither does she. She likes the recognition and I like calming my guilty conscience."

I scratch Elvis behind his pointy ears.

"Anyway, back to what happened this morning. So this homeless guy, whom I've seen around for quite a while, speaks to me for the first time today. I was kind of thunderstruck. You should have seen him. He has these look-right-through-you, smoky gray eyes and the scariest white eyebrows—like a black Albert Einstein turned Mr. Hyde. But the old man's voice was what really got me. It totally trumped his stare. It was like a jazzy bass covered in molten steel. Chilling! But it's what he said that I can't get out of my bones. He said, *'Do good and forget about it; do bad and remember it for the rest of your life.'* Now what the hell is that supposed to mean? And why did he say it to me?"

Elvis stares at me with his gooey eyes, as if hanging on to my every word.

"You're such a good boy; you listen almost as well as Fatima. Anyway, I've seen this guy a dozen times or more. He usually parks his sad self in front of the building downtown that my agent and his partners own. I admit I never offer him money, but then, the guy never asks. I usually avoid looking directly at him by hustling in the revolving door. It's uncomfortable, you know? I just don't want to see him there, wrapped in his filthy blanket, summer or winter just the same.

"But this time was different. I was reading this note that Leyland gave me, not paying attention, when I bumped into someone while heading out the door. The note slipped from my fingers; I fumbled for it like a passed ball. But as luck would have it, it floated right into the lap of the old man, as if destined for that spot.

"It just didn't feel right to reach in there without looking at him, and that's when he spoke. Was he warning me? Was he reprimanding me? Was he judging me?"

Elvis is suddenly distracted by a squirrel near the water, barking furiously before giving chase. I release the leash, knowing that one of the nearby trees will soon be a haven to the squirrel. Sure enough, Elvis is left barking up a tree—the wrong one.

Barking up the wrong tree. "That's it! Elvis, you're a genius. You've given me the answer—I'm barking up the wrong tree. I'm thinking that guy was talking to me about me, but he was talking to me about himself! I'm telling you, Elvis, if there were awards for pets, you'd prance off the stage with top honors in the category *My Dog Is My Shrink.*"

I can't calm down, and I can't figure out why. *What is it about that grizzled veteran of the war of life that's gotten under my skin?*

I stop for a moment and stare at the lake. It's peaceful here. Fatima comes to mind; at moments like these I always think of Fatima. Whenever I'm confused, or in search of an answer to a question I can't quite formulate, I wish for my tiny Sicilian friend with the crazy hair. Her way of thinking is so foreign to mine. She says things that jab me, burn me, or simply stop me in my tracks, but never in insult, never in anger, and never without giving me the sense that she cares. If she was here, I bet she'd tell me to reach out to that old soul.

I squirm, just thinking about it. A guy like that—probably a mental case—he'd be totally outside of my comfort-zone. But he'll probably still be there when I go to Leyland's office tomorrow. Oh, what the hell am I thinking? There're shelters and things for people like that! That's what we pay taxes for, right? I'll throw him a few bucks, for a change, whether he asks me or not. That'll do.

Chapter 5

Fatima • Calabria, Italy

Mama and I squeeze into the ancient piazza of San Tomaso Church. Two old crones whisper in dialect, “The daughter is more the mother—she wears black that doesn’t deceive, but the mother’s dress reveals a bosom in want of a husband.”

The truth is, my mother is stunning and their ugly spirits are jealous without cause. They don’t hear her choking with sadness in her empty bed. As for them, their own daughters have grown fat and their granddaughters look like whores. *(I’ve shut off the part of my brain which sensors my thoughts.)* Thank God Nonna’s half deaf, or she’d curse them with the evil eye for sure.

The church’s castle-sized doors are closed to the crowd. Beside them, the bride’s tall grandfathers resemble dwarves. They raise their right arms and with closed fists knock in unison with heavy thumps. They repeat the process twice more. Finally, the entrance opens, with a grand creak.

The groom smooths his impeccably tailored ebony tuxedo and silken neck scarf. Zio Peppe smiles broadly in front of the marble altar. Guests stream into cherry-stained wooden pews.

My gaze is drawn to the focal point of this *chiesa*. Suspended near the ceiling, just behind the altar, is a gigantic gold-leaf crown, symbolizing the crown of thorns Christ wore at his crucifixion. Instead of a cross, a sculpture of a weathered pink, almost princely, cape hangs from the crown, draped wide as if hidden arms are drawing us into its embrace. Flowingly crafted, it causes most people—at first glance—to assume that it is made of cloth; the fringe looks so touchable, so real. Its classic style drips lavish Renaissance wealth. This is one of my favorite little churches in Italy.

Near the base of the cape is perched a quintessentially Italian statue of the Madonna in peaceful repose. “The lactating Madonna,” as she is called, holds the baby Jesus in her right arm, her open left hand resting casually on her exposed right breast. In most countries this would be shocking, a sacrilege—or a wardrobe malfunction, as Americans might joke. But this is southern Italy where milk mothers are revered almost as much as birth mothers.

Her auburn dress is softened by a royal blue, head-to-toe veil. More gold crowns atop her and her babe's heads were not enough for the local townsfolk: 24-karat gold earrings, necklaces, and bracelets have been attached to their fixed poses. The chubby cherubs at her feet are carved to look as if utterly bemused by the holy pair.

The tender music of a mandolin is usurped by the twitter of trumpets. One of the groom's brothers appears at his mother's side and escorts her down the short aisle. The maid-of-honor glides to her place, but it's the groom's niece and nephew who steal the show. Moving at a deliberate pace, a tiny *principessa* reaches into her woven basket for a single petal. She releases it shyly onto the white carpet of the center aisle. Everyone is amused, except for her miniature escort. He whispers loudly for her to hurry, but when she continues in her slow motion with another single petal, he impatiently grabs a handful of the colorful array and flings them like an angry artist toward the ornately frescoed ceiling. My great uncle, the priest, shakes like a wind-up toy. He dabs his eyes with his handkerchief. His giggling is infectious: laughter ripples into Pachelbel's *Canon*. When the father of the bride, his daughter on his arm, meets the priest and groom, he lifts her lace veil to reveal her radiant face. Then he clasps her delicate palm and places it in her groom's.

The grin in his voice is audible to all, "This is your last chance to renege. I warn you, she's more demanding than you know!"

Laughter erupts again, but I'm quiet. I had heard that the family of the groom had wrangled Calabria's best tenor to sing for the occasion. His version of the *Ave Maria* is said to bring tears—but mine arrive early. My mother's emotion is also palpable. I look at the groomsmen and see Paolo smiling at her. He can be so mean at times, but right now I love my brother.

An hour and a half later the bride and groom are seated in a balcony above their guests. The turbo-charged gastronomy commences.

"It's about time," says Nonna, "I'm starving."

At 86, Nonna Marietta speaks as she pleases, her haute chin raised like that of a triumphant general. I admire her so. I never met my grandfather Multicino, but photos show that he too cut a commanding figure, though a good four inches shorter than

Nonna. It is said that I inherited his stature, and his mother's nature, but this is not totally true. I can still be Nonna Marietta's granddaughter in moments of frustration.

Nonna's pure hair looks so elegant today—instead of the usual matronly bun on the back of her head it's sculpted as if she's competing in an octogenarian beauty contest. She's lean, with fingers as gnarled as her oldest grapevines. Her hazel eyes have faded to grey, but they can still cut as clean as a fine stiletto.

Mama is a 50-year-old version of Nonna with a more genial disposition—though perhaps Nonna was more genial before her son died. My mother became an only child when Zio Enzo was caught in the crossfire of a Mafioso hit. He was then fourteen; Mama four. In Sicily the loss of a husband is as the rain: eventually, it comes. To lose a child, however, especially your oldest son, is a storm cloud that can shroud you forever.

The waiters arrive, dressed in starched white and carrying sapphire blue bottles of mineral water to the tables seating 500 guests. They complete the look of Neptune's heaven: white marble walls and modern leather chairs, a glittery blue-tiled floor, and tables of white linen embellished with blue hydrangeas the size of melons.

"Oh my God," Paolo says.

His expression is one I've never seen before. "What is it?" I ask.

"Don't turn around," he says, "but the guy I told you about is here, the one who killed the wild boar. What I didn't tell you is that I really pissed him off before he left the beach."

"Shocking," I deadpan.

"It's no joke. I need this guy, Fatima. If I can't get back to baseball as a player, maybe I could as a scout. And I just can't shake the feeling I have about this dude. He's the real deal, I just know it."

"So! Go and apologize then, and talk to him."

"There's something else I didn't tell you."

"What?"

"You already know him."

My eyes grow wide with surprise before I turn. *Dio mio!* I can't believe it's Darius. He's pouring water into glasses at a table three away from ours.

"Come with me to help smooth things over," Paolo begs me.

I give him the pissed off look that I've given him all our lives; then we rise from our seats and shift around chairs toward our quarry.

When Darius sees me, he freezes, before eagerly crossing to meet us halfway. "*Signorina* Fatima, how good to see you again! I had a feeling our paths would cross once more!"

Me too, actually, but I don't admit it, except to myself. "This is a wonderful surprise! You look well," I say. He does, actually—until he sees my brother, who is trying to hide a scowl.

Paolo's never been good at apologizing. I elbow him, perhaps a bit too sharply.

"Ah, Darius, you know, about yesterday on the beach. I didn't mean to upset you." Paolo moves his right arm, as if about to try to shake Darius's hand, but in typical Paolo fashion thinks better of bending that far. "You're a busy guy, working the beach as well as waiting on tables," he says instead.

The apology appears to have been accepted: Darius shrugs.

"This is only my first day on the job. The head chef is a friend of the *padrone*. The boar was butchered here, and the chef wanted to meet me, after hearing the story. Fortunately, I made a good impression...however, my training has been negligible. I hope I don't disappoint," he says to me.

The three of us move toward our table. Darius politely pours water into Nonna's glass first while Paolo explains who he is. Darius's hands are every bit as magnificent as Paolo had described: it's odd that I never noticed them before. I smile at him as he pours for me. Staring at me, he forgets to watch what he's doing. Water spills over the glass.

"Oh, *signorina, mi dispiace.*"

"Don't worry. It's only water." I wipe at the dribble with my napkin. "What can you expect on your first day, and with so little training?"

"I've been pouring drinks into glasses since I was a child. I can expect to know that much." He gives a little bow before filling my mother's glass. I recall that same gesture from when we were in Lampedusa together. It tugs at my heart. Suddenly it occurs to me that he looks a bit like Eli, though he doesn't act like him. *Now why am I even thinking of Eli?* Perhaps it's because we haven't talked in so long. I hate to admit it, but I've missed our chats... Snap out of it, Fatima. Concentrate on the guy in front of you.

"I think saving a life in the way you did yesterday is a more critical skill than serving dinner guests." I say. "Paolo told me the story, but never named the hero."

"You're very kind, *signorina,* but the child was blessed. Allah was with her. I was simply his instrument." There's humility in his voice.

"That's not what my brother thinks—and he's quite an expert in this area."

"I've heard something of your troubles from my great-nephew," Zio says, as Darius fills his goblet. "Jobs in these parts are not plentiful, but I'm certain that anyone with your language skills would be welcome in any number of places."

Darius shakes his head wistfully.

"Not if they fear that I might be some kind of a terrorist. Many are kind, but others spin fear. I hope someday, somehow, to become a doctor. But at the moment this is a dream so distant I'd need a space rocket to reach it..."

Chapter 6

Darius

Even though I felt that it might happen, I still can't believe that I'm with her again. She smiles at me with that wide grin, which balances her sturdy nose. As for her hair, I've never seen anything like it: I marvel at it once more. It's curly, in loose ringlets, and there's so much of it, even though it's bobbed. Yes, her eyes are indeed the same caramel color as her brother's, but hers are warm. I feel inextricably drawn to her. I've only been in her presence again for a moment, and yet I can see why that Eli guy likes her too. She's kind, but not in the delicate way one might expect; she's kind in the way that a powerful wind is kind on a day that suffocates.

Suffocate! Oh no. *Breathe, breathe. It's all right. It's OK. Focus on the job. Focus.* Where did I leave off? I've filled every glass at this table. I'll get another bottle. Careful! These tables are too close together, yet how else could they fit 500 people in this room? Smell that food, yes, yes. That's a good smell: ground yourself, focus. NO! Forget bad smells. Focus. Wow. This kitchen is ordered chaos. Chaos! No. No. Good chaos. It's all in order. That's the word—orderly. These Italians know how to serve a meal. Time to deliver the antipasto; I'll bring them the bottle of water later. I can do this. Focus. I load platters of fresh seafood salad, varieties of olives, and vegetables pickled traditionally. I hope they let us eat the leftovers.

As I serve Fatima's family, I realize that I like these other women and the old priest, who is soft-spoken and wise. His sister is regal, strong— and totally unfiltered. I have to bite the insides of my cheeks when she verbally assaults Paolo. (Though he's cocky: he deserves it.) The old woman's daughter—Fatima's mother—seems both elegant and self-assured. They're all very gracious to me, but Paolo is acting—in fact, he's overacting. He's up to something. If only I could talk to Fatima, but I'm so busy.

"I'm sorry, but I have to move," Fatima says.

She stands. The top of her head is level with the top of the hair of her seated grandmother. The funny picture they make makes me smile.

"I can sit eating for only so long before I feel as if I'm about to burst," she tells them.

"Eating!" her grandmother scoffs. "You call that eating? Birds could do better. Paolo ate five times as much."

She kisses her grandmother on the cheek. "Paolo is twice my size and in a constant state of conflicted energy. What do you expect? I could have stopped after the antipasti, let alone round two: *penne* with San Marzano marinara, orecchiette with mussels in a seafood brodo (she punctuates the recitation of each dish by slamming a finger into her opposite hand), pappardelle with shredded rabbit, and gemelli with an egg yolk of pancetta carbonara. Each a meal in itself!...And now this main course: chicken cacciatore, wild boar, sausage and peppers, steak Florentine. They're going to kill us before they cut the cake!"

She slips out the room in that ethereal sort of way that I'm coming to love.

Now is my chance. I follow her; two steps for her is only one for me. *Is it my imagination, or do I feel her brother's eyes burrowing into my back?*

"*Scusi, Signorina* Fatima."

She turns to me in the corridor, beyond those thousand eyes. Her face reveals no surprise.

"I was hoping we'd be able to speak away from the others," she says.

My stomach does an unexpected bounce against my heart as she continues.

"Paolo told me who your *padrone* is. He's not really a dangerous man himself—but he makes himself available to those who are. So that, I suppose, does make him dangerous... You must be very careful, Darius. The sooner you move on to another line of work, the better. This place is owned by someone far more ethical: perhaps you could become full-time here? You speak the languages of all the usual tourists, and it would be so much safer. Promise me that you'll try... My uncle could speak to the proprietor for you. Zio is a man of great influence. Everyone in the area listens to him."

Her obvious concern causes a lump to rise in my throat.

"Don't worry about me, *signorina*; I have worked for far worse characters."

I probably shouldn't have said that, but she seems neither shocked nor frightened. Instead she asks, "Are you serving at the beach party later?"

"Yes." My heart leaps again.

"Good. The atmosphere will be more relaxed there. We'll have more time to chat."

I watch her go.

Before she cuts left toward the resort lobby, she turns and catches me staring, and gives me a little wave. *How did she know?*

Chapter 7

Darius

Fatima was right. My only chore at the beach party appears to be to keep the bartenders stocked with clean glasses. The band is playing what I assume is a Calabrese folk song—although the dance itself seems more like an endurance competition. Everyone is in a circle, clapping and hooting, with pairs of partners taking turns in the center. I wait to see if Fatima will try.

Paolo has his hands on his hips in a sturdy pose while kicking his legs in rhythm to the music. A blonde witch has him under her spell. She's tall and buxom, but overly made-up, with a nervous screechy laugh that I can hear over the strains of the band. Then the old priest grabs Fatima, shoving his nephew off center-stage.

Unbelievable! I hope I can still move like that when I'm his age! Fatima, though, has no rhythm. Each kick is half a beat too late, something she doesn't seem to notice. Her uncle, finally worn-out, feigns a heart attack and is quickly replaced by Paolo and Fatima's mother. Faces grow close to whisper at this; some old ladies shake their heads. One, wearing black, covers her mouth in shock. Most people smile, however, with a few patting the grandmother on the back, nodding and winking to suggest her widowed daughter has mourned enough.

The pin lights strung around the cabana are dim, giving me a clear view of the full moon's spotlight on the sea—a moment's peace outside this noise. It's hot even at this hour, and more humid than I'm accustomed. I wipe my forehead and neck with a napkin.

The music stops. I look toward Fatima and wave a glass of water. She nods, and stops a moment to gulp a breath before proceeding to the bar. I tell her, "That's the best entertainment I've had since Sister Colleen's storytelling."

"We call it the *tarantella*. Do you like to dance?"

"Music is forbidden in our religion, but many of us still enjoy it, although men dancing with other men is the norm."

"I didn't realize; I can't imagine life without music and dancing. I simply assumed Syria was...is...a more secular culture. Sorry: I'm unsure how to speak of your country since it has become so divided."

"That's OK— in some ways, it was never my country. Between you and me, I'm actually Palestinian. I grew up in Yarmouk Camp, on the southern outskirts of Damascus, where my grandfather fled after the 1948 war."

"A camp?"

"It eventually grew into a vibrant suburb while under the protection of the United Nations. We had a good life before the revolution—at least, as good as a people without statehood could have. People here don't often realize how westernized Syria used to be, how well-educated most of its people are. The *padrone* even asked me once if I missed my dress—He seemed to think that I come from the border of Pakistan and Afghanistan! But truly, my world was far more like yours than like theirs. Women mostly wore trousers, except for the oldest, or the most devout. Their *hijabs* were more like scarfs, almost a fashion statement, not worn to cover every lock of hair! You possess more creature comforts and—if I am honest—topless sunbathing came as something of a shock for me, but actually, the biggest adjustment has simply been not having my family." Just mentioning them makes me have to stop and take a deep breath.

"Has Yarmouk survived?" she asks.

"Yarmouk is mostly rubble now. People without enough means to leave are starving."

"But you escaped. And then you skirted Immigration Services once you landed in mainland Italy after Lampedusa didn't you?"

"I did," I admit to her. "And now I'd do almost anything not to be sent back. Millions of poor Syrians are trapped in pitiful camps in Lebanon, Jordan and Turkey, while those with money and contacts are coming to Europe. But we Palestinians, being technically under the direction of the UN, seem to be on the road to nowhere."

She is thoughtful a moment, and then, "So, what will you do?"

"I'm not sure, but I refuse to travel in circles. I intend to go from nowhere to somewhere, from being nobody to being someone with a forgotten past, a real present, and some kind of hope for a future... I'm done with death and its perpetrators."

I swallow hard. Such an ugly story is not one to be remembered on an occasion such as this."

"I'm sorry," she says intuitively.

"Please: don't be. I love talking to you."

Her cell rings. Apparently I'm not the only one.

"Eli! Are you all right? Oh *grazie Dio*...Of course I was worried—it's been so long since we spoke...I worry about all my friends."

She's trying to sound casual, but her face is flushed; I catch myself clenching my teeth. Luckily, the band resumes, and she says, a little more loudly, "I can't chat now, though. I'm at a wedding, and the music just started up again... I'm so sorry, as I've really missed our chats. Call me tomorrow? ... *Ciao!* ... Excuse me, Darius, I didn't mean to be rude. I just thought that I should take that particular call."

Oh great, she gets rid of one and here comes the other.

"Mind if I join you?" says Paolo, and does, without waiting for a reply.

Yes, I do mind. I was just beginning to enjoy myself, for the first time in a month. But perhaps it's just as well. I'm not sure that enjoyment is something I have a right to, at this point.

Fatima gives me an odd stare, as if reading my thoughts. Suddenly her eyes roll up and her head tips back, as if she's staring at the wooden slats of the ceiling...or beyond it, perhaps. Her facial features slacken and she takes on a barely perceptible aura.

I look to her brother for help, but he waves off my concern. "She's fine. She does this. When she comes back to us, I'll ask her to explain."

Is this some kind of a fit—or a vision? What kind of woman is this?

It's a full minute before she gives a slight shiver, then smiles more brilliantly than I've ever seen her. "What just happened here?" I ask, stunned.

"I have these moments. Some might call them mystical, but I just call them a trip to my happy place."

"Did you see anyone this time?" Paolo asks, almost jealously.

"I saw a beautiful Muslim woman. Although I felt at complete peace, it was clear to me that she was not."

"Did she have a young boy with her?" I suddenly ask.

"No, but I felt that she need not be afraid."

"And that's it? That's all you recall?" Paolo prompts her.

"Sorry, brother, you know how these episodes go with me."

I'm completely astonished. Had I not known her previously and watched her at work on the island, I'd imagine she was some kind of a lunatic. When I hint as much, she nods, rather sadly. "I don't know if it's truly a gift or a curse... I would say a gift, if it weren't for the way people treat me sometimes, as if I am some kind of a witch or something."

"No, never—not you," I say.

"Careful, Darius, you don't know her like I do. I've seen the witch spring out of her more times than I can count!"

"Never when you don't deserve it," she flashes back, eyes snapping. "You just hate it when a person treats me like I'm some sort of saint, because of the visions. Well I don't like it either. I never professed to be one."

"At last, something we can agree on," he mocks.

"I know something else we can agree on," she says, suddenly calm, and glancing toward the dance floor. "I don't think we need to take turns with Mama anymore. She finally seems to be having a good time."

"You have a wonderful family," I tell Paolo. "You're very lucky."

But Paolo has something else on his mind.

"Speaking of lucky, I still can't believe that throw you made yesterday was luck. I just can't stop thinking about it. So listen, Darius: I have a proposition for you."

He certainly knows how to bring any conversation around to one more to his liking.

"My uncle—the one over there, the priest—was once a baseball player, a pitcher, in fact. He learned the game from American soldiers on an Air Force base, where he used to sell goods from the family farm. He still lives in that same town, just over the mountain, maybe fifteen minutes from here. I'd like him to watch you throw off the old mound he has on his property. You could have dinner with us: Sunday nights are pretty slow around here. Are you working on Sunday?"

"Not at the resort, but at the beach until the evening. But, what does it mean, to 'throw off the old mound?'"

"Good question! In baseball, the pitcher stands on ground that's piled higher than where the batter stands, several meters away. Not like when you nailed that boar."

This guy—Fatima's brother—must be crazy.

I tell him patiently, "Listen, when I was a child, I loved to play what you call calcio, you know, or American's call soccer. Every one of us thought we'd be a star—until we learned what the competition was like! I'm no athlete, believe me."

"You're built like one, and like a pitcher at that. Put out your arm."

Why I oblige him, I can't say.

"We're nearly the same height, but look at your arm compared to mine! It's an inch longer and your fingers are longer too. Natural tools are where it begins."

I laugh, embarrassed. "And, for me, also where it will end."

"Let Zio and me be the judges of that. Zio was the first bona fide star of the Italian League in his day, but he quit for the priesthood."

"That explains his dancing. I never saw such an old man move so well." I'm trying to change the subject, but he won't let me.

"Look, Darius, you have nothing to lose and everything to gain. You say you want to be a doctor; but do you have any idea how expensive med school is? You could earn the money for college and—for that matter—you could even take classes while playing baseball, if you really wanted to."

His words are bewitching, but he's ill-informed. "The U.S. would never allow me to enter so easily."

"What do you mean?"

"Simply this: they have the most stringent security measures of anywhere in the world, especially where Middle-Eastern Muslim males are concerned. I assure you, I will never be allowed to go to America."

"The owner of the Cleveland team is well-connected. If his people tell him you're their savior, he'll find a way."

Fatima has been listening intently. Now she says, "That's not true, Paolo. You mustn't get his hopes up. Mr. Powers would have to battle public opinion more than the politicians in his pocket... You're not being realistic."

"If Darius is the reincarnation of Cy Young, public opinion will be 'bring him on!'"

Before I can ask, "who is Cy Young," Paolo says, "Darius, do you believe in fate?"

The word is only four letters. It's just a stupid word, spoken by a stupid person. Breathe. Breathe. Focus. Quit letting thoughts of the past you were fated ruin the present. Look at her. Her hair. Her eyes. She looks at me as if intent upon reining me in. *Help me, Fatima. I'm lost again at sea. Don't let me drown.*

"I believe in fate, indeed."

"Then you've got nothing to lose. If this sport is not your fate, we'll quickly discover it. And if it is, then just leave the details to me."

"We could talk more if you come to dinner," she suggests, with that electrifying smile.

What's happening to me? I would follow her back to the desert if she asked.

I yield.

"All right. Tomorrow then. You know where to find me."

Chapter 8

Paolo

I bolt upright in bed. A shrill, mechanized voice is squawking about today's fresh catch specials, straight from the sea. *What the hell? Can't they tinkle little bells or play cutsie music like the ice cream trucks I remember in Ohio?* But I'm not in Ohio anymore. This is San Mango D'Aquino, in the province of Catanzaro, Calabria. Here the grocery store comes to you.

Calming down, I begin to remember why I'm here. These wedding festivities have been quite the little affair. At the rehearsal dinner, Zio Peppe was on his best behavior after having poured too much wine at the bachelor party, so the rest of us followed his lead and behaved like choirboys: I suspect he wanted to keep his head clear for the following day's ceremony. Or maybe it was for the one that evening. That whole "blessing of the marriage bed" thing is a custom that gives me a nervous cringe. The old people still want to encourage us younger ones to start families straight out of the gate. Still, the bride and groom seemed happy enough, which I suppose is all that matters.

That honeymoon suite was just a snippet—*yes, I like my new word*—a snippet of the myriad renovations made to that old villa I always admired. I plan to take Mama there tomorrow, just to check it out. It'll give her some good ideas for her plans with our own property. Tourists would love it. I can see our new brochure now:

Your days will meld into an endless clear blue sea dappled with brilliant sunlight—a sprightly ballet, beckoning the soul to join the dance. (A little wordy, but not a bad opening line.) *By evening, dewy dusk will warm the vista of vineyards, fruit trees, and vegetable gardens as you wend your way from Taormina and Catania's beaches to the foot of mysterious Mount Etna.* (Tourists love volcanoes.) *You'll pass prickly pear cacti, poppy fields, and groves of fig trees where dollhouse shrines stand sentry—the saints within offering prayers for a bountiful harvest.* (Everybody turns religious—at least for a moment—when they see conas.) *At night you'll dine at Agriturismo di Multicino. Her stone façade, featuring turquoise shutters and violet vines, will wrap you in her cozy hug before sending you off to sleep in a featherbed carved from local olive trees.* (They cost a freakin' fortune. Nonna didn't speak to Mama for a week.) *In the morning, the rooster will summon you to a gentle wander over a hillside where hens and goats roam free. There you'll find an uninterrupted view of the valley below to the Ionian Sea.*

Stick to baseball I tell myself, and immediately my thoughts do a backflip to what happened at the wedding reception. *Darius Salamah, why can't I get you out of my mind? The first time I met you I felt so agitated that six speeds weren't enough to fly me up this mountain. I'd have been brooding ever since, were it not for seeing you again at the wedding.*

The wedding. How strange it had felt to attend a Mass again.

Not only did San Tomaso Church not crumble when I entered its hallowed precincts, but I think it did me good. I had a vivid recollection of the day when my parents renewed their vows there for their 20th Anniversary. *Good thing they hadn't waited for their 25th.*

They had joked about how different their wedding had been compared to more recent times...

I'll never forget it. It was the first time I felt they saw me and Fatima as grown:

MAMA: Nowadays they schedule Mass for eleven, which means noon, Italian time. This gives friends and neighbors more time to party outside the bride's house before she makes her grand entrance. It's crazy! The bridal party serves shots of liqueurs and special occasion dolce before escorting the queen for a day in a parade through the cobbled streets to the church. The train of her dress is filthy before she ever says 'I do!'

PAPA (SHAKING HIS HEAD): Basically, everyone gets hammered before the ceremony even starts. Why didn't we do it that way?

MAMA: You're exaggerating, but we couldn't have had such fun. Do you remember the priest who married us?

PAPA: Father pain-in-the-ass! How could I ever forget? He made Mussolini seem like Mickey Mouse. He insisted I first go to confession, remember, and he wouldn't let me out until I admitted that we'd already done the deed.

MAMA: Cuore mia, quit crying, little baby. What do you think he did to me? It's always the woman's fault, you know. All you had to do was to admit to it—then, boys will be boys—it was I who got the lecture!

By this point Fatima's face had turned redder than Nonna's prized tomatoes—while I was laughing so hard that my sides ached.

Damn, but I miss you, Papa...

I open the mahogany armoire, one of only three pieces of furniture in this whitewashed room. My tuxedo and shoes have already been replaced with my normal clothes, which have been cleaned and even pressed. *The old housekeeper has been here again. Does she sneak into Zio's room too?*

Mmm. I smell the espresso and forgive her. I remember an old cartoon where a dog watches his nose grow into a ship's prow that leads him straight to the smell he so desires.... I could be that dog, right now.

Memory tumbles me again—Papa in his tux. In America I learned a useful phrase, "There's no crying in baseball." I should apply the principle to life, and do what Sister Colleen told us she does and pray for someone with worse sorrows than mine. Darius would be a good candidate, but I've forgotten how to pray.

Instead, maybe I'll do us both a favor. He could be my ticket back to The Show. Thank God I stumbled on him again! I'll never be satisfied until I learn whether that strike was dumb luck, a miracle, or genuine skill.

•••••••••••

I smell him before I see him. Who else could perpetuate the stink of a cheap cigar in this paradise? I ignore the scumbag, scanning the beach for Darius from the rail of the cabana.

"The boy you seek has been...how shall I put it...detained," the *padrone* says. He's seated alone at a white plastic table and chairs. I turn to find him screwing his neck for a longer look at a scantily clad woman, just wandering past. She smiles at me as she steps down to the sand, hand lingering on the railing, allowing me the long look she'd shun from the *padrone.*

"Ah, *Signore* Giobatti, it's good to be young, no?"

I forget the woman and silently kick myself for thinking he wouldn't know me. But I don the cock-sure expression I've been trained to wear against opponents. *What does he mean by 'detained?'*

"Join me," he says, waving casually at the opposite chair. "Let's drink to a happy marriage for your cousin." He tips his glass of vino, ordering the boy behind the bar to bring another for me. Then he continues, "My friends at the resort tell me you've become acquainted with my prize pupil, young Darius. I was surprised to learn your identity, as I hadn't recognized you out of uniform. I watched you play a few times, but baseball bores me. Too bad *calcio* isn't your game."

I smile thinly. I want to spit in his face!

"But enough of these pleasantries," he says, waving away air like a flying insect. "We need to do business. Like me, you see a profit in Darius's skills: that was quite a strike he made the other day. Word of it has spread throughout the whole region. Of course, I would hate to lose the hottest horse in my stable."

"He has no contract with you; and he's under no obligation to remain your employee. Migrants move from job to job every day."

"Ah, but where is he? That is the question."

A sick clutch in the pit of my stomach makes me want to gag. The *padrone* smiles.

"These are interesting times, my friend. One must be quick to snatch opportunities when presented. People talk. Perhaps they jump to conclusions, perhaps not, but it appears that you're anxious to make use of this foreigner for your own purposes. Why should I not do the same? If you want him, then you must pay. I'm a reasonable man: I do not expect millions. I recall an article suggesting that, although you have yet to play long enough to land a major contract, your endorsement deals are good. Ten thousand Euros will satisfy me."

"You cunning son of a bitch! I have no intention of negotiating with the likes of you!" I push back my chair and force myself backward, mostly in order to prevent myself from lunging across the table and strangling the bastard. "This game isn't finished yet; you've merely made the first move. I warn you, *Signore*, I won't lose!"

The smug *padrone* merely sips from his glass.

I leave him. I leave the cabana. I leave the beach. But where is Darius?

Chapter 9

Eli • Cleveland, Ohio

I scan the street for an available parking meter; as it's lunchtime, my chances are slim. But today's my lucky day: a van pulls out of a space large enough to make the parallel parking I hate relatively easy.

The old man is there, sitting on the concrete, staring into loneliness, waiting for death to call his number. The breeze off of Lake Erie takes the edge off of the humidity. *How can he stand that disgusting blanket on such a day?*

Still, true to my purpose, I squat down beside him. The breeze pushes me: I have a vision of Fatima nudging me likewise. Instead of reaching for my wallet, I wait for some acknowledgement of my presence, but he keeps staring straight ahead. So I speak the words—his words—and wait for a reaction.

It comes in the form of a tear. One solitary teardrop, that runs slowly down the black, dust-covered cheek of the most forlorn face I've ever seen. The old man doesn't move a muscle. He just sits there as if that one teardrop could cleanse his very soul if he waits long enough.

"Can I buy you lunch, sir?"

"You can buy me lunch, and dinner, and breakfast tomorrow, and the day after, and the day after that, but it ain't gonna make no difference, not to either of us."

I don't know what to say at first, but then I remember the advice my father once gave me. *When in doubt, speak from the heart.*

"Sir, you're probably right. But it'll make the next 60 minutes different from the same 60 minutes you lived yesterday, and the day before that, and the day before that, too."

The old man tilts his head, purses his lips and nods ever so slightly. "You got a small point there, boy. I like Big Macs and fries. How 'bout you?"

"I was thinking hot corned beef on rye, but a Big Mac will do."

"Corned beef on rye! I suppose you'd like a cup of matzo ball soup with that?"

"Sounds good to me."

"Well it don't to me, Jew-boy. Take your do-goodin' down the block to the next Job. I ain't havin' lunch with the likes o' you."

His verbal punch in the gut stuns me into silence.

Then he turns back toward me and smiles a coffee-stained grin. "Hurts, don't it? Words can kill a man's soul just as sure as a gun can kill a body. There's days when I wish someone would just shoot me dead. They'd be doin' me a favor – releasin' me from all the words that tear like bullets—words I can't never get free of—words dancin' 'round my head like they's havin' some kind o' party at my expense. People say the darndest things to the likes o' me. Nice young man like you'd be surprised. But the worst is knowin' the things I said that I can't never have back. Them words...and deeds too...is what ultimately put me on this street. Serves me right, I s'pose. Big Mac or a hot corned beef on rye, it makes no difference. I just want the likes o' you, Eli Kohn, to know better. Oh, yeah, I know who you are. They got a big-screen TV down at the shelter. We watch you boys 'most every night."

I stand and stretch out my hand toward him; he grasps it. I hoist him off the sidewalk and into my life. *Holy crap, he's as tall as me!*

My face must be easy to read. "I was built like a brick shit-house when I was your age, taller too. I shrunk an inch or two in my oldness."

We stand eyeball to eyeball for a moment, silently measuring each other. "Why'd you speak to me?" the old man asks, at last.

"Guilt. I'm riddled with it."

"Well, I don't need your pity, but I do need to eat. Let's go."

First I text Leyland that I'll need to reschedule our meeting. *He'll be pissed, but hey, he'll get over it.*

I hear a low, appreciative whistle when he sees the car. People on the busy street slow their pace to stare at us. A woman in a beige business suit gives me a sly wink and a thumbs-up with the hand not wrapped around the handle of her briefcase.

My favorite deli is on the East Side, far enough away for the old man to enjoy the feel of the fresh breeze through his curly gray hair. The sun beats down on his black clothes. Finally, he relinquishes the blanket, his jacket as well. We ride in oddly comfortable silence, like old acquaintances.

Once in the deli, however, a few customers move uncomfortably away from us. Though—soon enough—a couple of the employees recognize me and we chat amicably about the ball club. After we take our seats, a couple of executives in slick tailored suits come over to ask me to autograph their napkins. Eventually, people leave us alone.

"So, you know my name, but I don't know yours," I say.

"T.P. Smitt," he says. "And don't ask me what the T.P. stands for, 'cause it don't stand for nothin'. My pappy had an annoyin' sense of humor... What's Eli short for? Elijah?"

"You got it."

"No wonder you're chock-full o' guilt. With a biblical name that famous, expectations'd be sky-high. So is this your way o' tryin' to live up to your name?"

"Maybe—but mostly what you said to me yesterday kept bugging the hell out of me. I needed an explanation."

"Ain't much to explain. Life sucks and it's all my own fault, refusin' to let go o' my bad habits. The bottle got a grip on me like a monstrous vise. My family got tired o' me making their lives a mis'ry, so I ended up on the street, maybe 14 years back. Finally gave up the drink, but my kids don't want me; they've moved on. 'Sides, they take their cues from their mama...can't say as I blame 'em. They don't want their own kin knowin' me as grandpappy. Anyways, I'm too old to start over. This life on the streets got regular. Some idiot doctor told me I had depression; I knocked him on the forehead and asked how much he had to pay for the fancy education that taught him that one."

"What'd you do before you ended up on the street?"

"I was the pro at a country club down south till the race riots back in the 60s. Ain't that a hoot? Civil Rights finally come along, an' I lose my dream job."

I almost choke on my ice tea. "You must have been one helluva golfer to have been the pro at a white men's country club!"

"I was indeed. And young and good lookin' just like you. But I lost my dream and took consolation in the bottom of a bottle of whiskey. And the rest, as they say, is history. I bounced around after that, at jobs, and places to live. When my kids got older, and educated, mostly thanks to my wife, they turned against me. So I sit on that sidewalk, thinkin' on all the things I done in my life to end up here. I could blame the ways of the world, but my kids've heard that excuse more times than they can count, and they quit buyin' it a long time ago."

No wonder he's depressed. "How do you survive, then?"

"There's shelters and soup kitchens and nights under the stars. I still got my wits about me. Lots o' folks on the street are just plumb crazy, poor bastards. Many are drug addicts. I ain't never been a smoker, so I don't need to beg. Used to when I was on the bottle, though."

"How did you quit?"

"I got sick enough once that St. Vincent's took me in. I was in the hospital with pneumonia. Once I got out, I figured if I could last a whole month without a drink, then maybe I could do it for another month. Felt so good not to be beggin' for booze that I just kept goin'. I don't know any other way to explain it... Called my oldest daughter after I'd been dry for three months. Kept leavin' her messages on voicemail. She never came lookin' for me though. So then I tried the rest of my five kids one by one. Last I knew my wife was still in the Carolinas. I finally gave up on 'em." He sips his iced tea. I can't think of anything to say, so I stay silent.

"Due to havin' all my marbles, I'm kinda an unofficial assistant over at the shelter at nights. That's all as keeps me goin.' Can't do nothin' for my family, so I do what I can. The worst part is havin' nothin' and nobody to talk to. I can't take the crazies for too long—the nights are bad enough—so daytimes I keep to myself. Which gives me time to remember all the things I'd rather forget, too much time, maybe. 'Cause, at 81, I ain't got no more dreams to dream."

I watch T.P. eat, trying to think of what to say or do. Suddenly it hits me.

"A couple of us on the team are stinking it up pretty bad these days on the golf course. Golf is pretty much our number one pastime when we aren't at the yard."

"Woulda thought chasin' women would rank as number one."

"OK, number two then, although, to be honest, there isn't that much chasing required. We're a bit like kids in a candy store... But I'm serious, about the golfing, I mean."

He gives a short snort then says, "You don't need to assuage your guilt to that degree, son. And don't look so shocked at my use of the English language. I got me an education, even if I don't always talk like it... Anyway, you can consider yourself officially off the hook. Thanks for lunch. I won't forget it."

"This isn't about guilt... I want to use you to improve my golf game. I shanked so many balls last time out that it was beyond putrid. So, what do you say? Are you game?"

"I'm a bit short of the proper accoutrement."

"Wow. You trying to get uppity on me with that fancy talk?"

T.P. gives me that leaden stare again. My heart beats nervously. I immediately regret the joke. Then he lets loose a howl that turns every head in the deli: "Gotcha!"

"Holy shit, you scared the crap out of me with that look. Would you allow me to take you to a barber on the way back into town? You're killing me with those eyebrows. And don't you worry about the proper accoutrement, either. I have a pair of nice sweats that'll fit you, and my Dad left his clubs behind last time he was here, so you can use his—at least, you can if you're a righty."

"I am. What color are the sweats?"

"Seriously?"

"Seriously. I'm feelin' about as uppity as I've felt in years, and I'm likin' it so much, I think I'll keep right on feelin' it, thank you very much."

"They're Tar Heel blue."

"Perfect. I was afraid you were gonna say red. I look like shit in red."

Chapter 10

Fatima • Calabria, Italy

"What is it, Fatima? You're pacing like a caged animal," Zio says.

"Something's wrong. I can feel it."

Mama and Nonna trade nervous glances; the veggies they're chopping momentarily forgotten as they recall my odd powers of perception. Just then Paolo's Alfa Romeo screeches to a halt, with an audible grind of the clutch. A breeze sweeps through the French doors, carrying the scent of the potted flowers on the balcony.

The smell gives no consolation.

Only one door slams. Paolo's Guccis click, too swiftly, on the cobbles. My premonition is correct. He bounds through the door, looking far more of a caged animal than I.

"Darius has been kidnapped," he says flatly.

"I was afraid of something like this," says Zio, squeezing his temples with one hand.

"Why afraid? Two can play the *padrone's* game. He needs him—plus, he can't keep him locked up forever. He didn't think his strategy through."

"I'm afraid it's you who needs to think," Zio tells him. "The human-trafficking business is pretty lucrative in these parts—and not only in sex slaves. It's a very short trip from here to Libya, where militias are always in need of people willing to kill in order to stay alive. When Darius struck the boar, he proved that he's nerveless enough to bring a worthwhile price. Also, you shouldn't underestimate the *padrone's* guile. He's probably very well aware you're my nephew and that I'd explain such things to you."

"So what can we do? We aren't exactly the Navy SEAL Team Six! How can we find him, let alone free him?"

Zio now tweaks his chin, lost in quiet reflection. "I'm not certain. First, let me make a few phone calls. Some of my most ardent churchgoers come to Mass on Sundays to—how shall I put this?—to play for the tie. There's no guarantee, but I'll see if I can prompt a confession of sorts, just to find out where the boy is hidden."

"The police—" Nonna begins, but he cuts her short.

"I'm guessing that neither the *polizia* or the *carabinieri* may be particularly helpful, given the choice between a refugee and a fellow who no doubt treats them well. We'll probably have to settle this matter ourselves."

"It's too dangerous, Peppe," she objects. "Surely there's someone you can call?"

"No," I say. "He's right." (Knowing as I do that Darius skirted "full process" with Italian immigration means that—at this moment—he runs the risk of being saved, only to be condemned to a life he can no longer bear.) "At least, let's see how much influence an old priest still has first."

"I'm not sure I heard a real vote of confidence in that remark, my dear, but still, I'll take it," Zio says, but then he becomes serious again. "Once we know where he is, if the odds don't seem too long, we can devise a plan. The *padrone* is a man of great ego who likes to flex his muscles. Let's hope that there isn't more to this than that. But vengeance is breath for such men."

My brother and I share a look. My sense of unease intensifies.

"Come, *cara mia,*" Nonna tells me. "Let's pray a Rosary together and try not to worry too much about this young foreigner. I'm sure he's suffered much worse: he's likely devising some escape plan of his own. It was clear to everyone at the wedding that the boy is no fool."

She's right, but still, I find it hard to concentrate, which is rare for me... I spend two hours every day in prayer or mediation, including Mass and reading scripture. I began this routine at an early age, by my great-grandmother's side: this is how I learned how to quiet my mind. But not today. Today, once again I'm debating *the call* in my head. How could someone who wants to be in total control become a nun? Have I been playacting? Do I think hanging around Sister Colleen will magically change me?

Nonna is always telling Paolo, "You come to resemble the people you hang around with." She says this with disdain, because she suspects that many of his friends are phony. They do nice things when it suits their purpose; but their idea of right and wrong appears to be dictated by how they look in the eyes of others, or by what kudos and admiration they might receive. Perhaps this is why I've become his polar opposite, seeking out self-sacrificing colleagues instead. But they're not perfect either, so why should *I* try to be? It's as if I've been entered in some kind of a piety contest, or as if I'm still trying to live up to my great-grandmother's expectations—or at least, what I perceive them to be—even though she died when I was only six. Simply because I have the same mystical gift doesn't mean I resemble her in every respect! After all, she lived through some of the hardest times in the history of the world; life was scary then, and people pray far more when they're scared... But right now, I'm scared too. I'm scared for Darius. I try harder to focus on the words I'm mouthing with Nonna, and to put my fears aside.

Zio returns before we finish counting our beads. He calls out to Paolo, busy watching a match in the parlor.

"I have good news," he says. 'Darius is apparently being held in a shed on a family vineyard abutting the property of a very old friend of mine, Palmida Fiore. I phoned her and—within minutes—she called back to tell me that there appear at least to be only two men on guard. I suppose that the *padrone* can't make as much cash if he busies too many men with guard duty. She noticed no weapons, but, as we know, the locals always carry knives, and guns are easily hidden."

"So, what's the plan?" we ask.

"I'm going alone. I don't wish to put any of you in harm's way. These men will likely know me and will anyway hesitate to hurt a priest."

"Good," says Nonna, satisfied. "You're finally talking sense."

Mama also looks relieved, as Zio continues, "Continue praying, and I hope to return in a few hours with Darius."

As my uncle leaves, Paolo, frowning, returns to his TV entertainment. Nonna and Mama begin to prepare the eggplant and zucchini—not even a word passes between them, but I can see that their lips are moving. But I can pray no longer. Instead, I strut into the parlor and turn off the TV.

"What are you doing? The score's tied, and there are only two minutes left!" Paolo says.

"How can you be so callous? The fact that you hope to use Darius for your own selfish ends is what's led to his being in this mess! Thanks to you, he has far more to worry about than a tied score. The least you could do is come to the church and to pray with me!"

"Why? God doesn't hear my prayers—and anyway, he helps those who help themselves. I hate it when you start your sanctimonious bullshit with me. *Basta:* enough! I'm going to the farm to pick some figs."

He storms out of the house. I tell Mama and Nonna not to delay dinner for me, and sprint after my brother.

"I knew I could push enough of your buttons to get you out of the house. What in the world is wrong with you? How could you let an old man go off, all by himself to clean up your mess?"

Paolo only frowns.

"Scusi, signores," I say to two old men sitting in the shadiest part of the tiny piazza. *"Dov'e la Contadina di Palmida Fiore?"* They tell me how to take the overland route toward Zio's friend's farm.

"What are you thinking?" Paolo grumbles, after I thank the men and we walk away. *As if he didn't know.*

"We need to help."

"Are you crazy? You heard him. It's too dangerous!"

"If you don't have enough between your legs to help, then go pick your figs, little girl!"

The rage in his face tells me who's winning, and as I turn and run toward the outskirts of town, I hear him sprinting, just behind. We pause at the family farm only long enough to disguise ourselves with ratty old clothes, and to fill two wineskins with water and strap them across our shoulders. Once on our way, we switch between running and walking until we spot Zio in the distance, wearing his straw hat and using a walking stick.

When we catch up with him, he scolds us—but only a little. I sense he's happy that we're there. We make good time trekking across the hills through fields of vines, sunflowers and fruit trees, choosing the footpaths, as Zio suspects that the roads might have "eyes." Part of the hike is sheltered by columns of chestnut trees, giving welcome shade from the fierce August sun.

Zio Peppe has no problem keeping up: indeed, he sets the pace, having lived his entire life striding up inclines.

"Are you sure you aren't part-goat?" Paolo jokes, as we rest momentarily in an olive grove. I can tell that he's disgusted to be breathing more heavily than Zio.

An hour's trek brings us to the door of Palmida Fiore's farmhouse. Rocking on her front porch, fanning away the flies, and smiling, is the proprietress, eyes fixed on Zio. My uncle reaches out to her, half-lifting her from the chair. He touches her hand to his lips and kisses it lightly. "It's been far too long, Palmida, but time has been kind to you."

"*Grazie.* Hopefully, I'll live to see another harvest."

"Are you sick?" he asks, clasping her hands tenderly.

"No, no, just old!" she laughs. She pats his hands saying, "We can chat later, once the boy is safe. *Andiamo.*"

Peppe escorts her like a queen down the wide stairs. We circle the house to where a three-wheeled Fiat motor-cart for shuttling produce is parked. "She's old," Palmida says, tapping the hood, "but she still has work left to do; not unlike her driver."

Palmida wears a tired, sleeveless, black, mid-length dress and orthopedic dark shoes without socks. Her head overflows with once-dark ringlets. Her sinewy figure climbs into the tiny cab with a fluid motion that suggests she's done it a million times.

"She still has quite a head of hair," I whisper as we climb onto the attached flat bed.

"And all her teeth," Zio says with pride.

"What is it between you and this woman?" I ask.

"First love."

"No, really?"

"Fatima, you know that I love the priesthood, but I am still a man, after all. However, Palmida was promised to the oldest son of the family that owned all the land you can see—so, that was that."

"And that was that. Really? Just like that?" I sing-song it back to him, like a Dr. Seuss book.

Zio puts his hand on mine and repeats, "Yes, Fatima, that—was that."

I can tell he doesn't wish me to dig any deeper, and fall silent.

"Can we dispense with the trip down memory lane and go over our plan?" Paolo asks.

The matted dirt road peters out before the tiered hillside of Palmida's vineyard. The property line, with its broken fence, is a steep 30 metres higher. Palmida tells us that beyond it, perhaps another 15 meters, lies the neighbor's shed. Pointing to a spot nearby, she adds to my uncle, "There's where I've seen the two of them."

Zio treads lightly a few meters sideways and sits down on the dirt. He starts to hum an old Calabrese folk tune, simultaneously wriggling his walking stick along the ground in as close to an undulating motion as such a stiff instrument can manage. To my amazement, he seduces a pair of vipers to the surface, almost as if he's conjured them out of thin air.

This is quite a day for revelations. I had no idea my uncle the priest was such a charmer—of snakes or of women...

Zio coos and whispers to his creepy friends as if they understand him and, within minutes, he's holding one in each hand. "All right, let's move!" he tells us. Palmida waves farewell and walks toward her home, leaving us the Fiat for our getaway, its keys secure in Paolo's pocket.

Paolo walks next to Zio, completely unbothered by the writhing snakes, though their proximity make me shiver. "C'mon, Fatima, what's your problem?" My twin's challenge sounds like a hiss itself.

"I have two problems, to be exact, and Zio's holding both of them,"

Paolo and I climb to the peak of Palmida's property. We tend to the last row of vines, chatting in dialect like farmhands. For show, Paolo even tests a few grapes and debates their readiness with me.

Glancing down, I notice that the shed is of stone, perhaps five meters square and windowless. Its heavy wooden door appears rough and worn but substantial, with an iron exterior latch and a tiny window—more of a glorified peep-hole. Its shutter is mercifully open, presumably to provide Darius with air. Thank God it's a windy day—but how hot it must be inside! The men standing guard are whittling olive branches. Like most men of their age, they're skilled with a knife in more ways than one.

A single line of barbed wire separates the two vineyards, sagging in one spot, where a post has been broken. The guards glance up upon hearing our voices; but, seeing what they assume is a couple of harmless farmhands, they soon return to their projects.

Meanwhile Zio crosses under the wire, just beyond the guards' sightline. He slips behind the shed with his latest prized possessions, pausing at the rear corner nearest us, where he nods his readiness.

Paolo calls out to the men, faking curiosity for their handiwork. Stooping under the jagged divider, he strolls toward them, casually chatting about our grandfather and how skilled a craftsman he'd been with a knife: I follow him. He asks if he can compare the men's work. At close quarters, the *padrone's* bullies appear to be aged about sixty, but in good shape. One of them proudly hands over his creation.

Gushing with admiration, my brother engages the bruiser in rapt conversation, urging me to shake hands with the next Michelangelo. I draw closer, pull off my straw hat and shake my hair alluringly at the second guy, who appears struck dumb with admiration. While I chat with him about the condition of the vines—he is too charmed to say much in response—Zio unobtrusively works his way around to the other side of Darius's jail. Once Paolo spies that Zio is in position, he starts to rave about the guards' *bellissimi* tools.

The first man hands over his shiny stiletto and begins a long, dull tale about how he came to own it. Meanwhile, I continue to tempt his colleague, complimenting him on the strength of his leathery hands.

"You are single, *signorina*?" he asks. I nod, asking if I can admire his knife as well. *Grazie a Dio,* he lets me.

That's when Zio Peppe tosses the snakes at the men's backs. The hissing is loud, immediate—and, for me at least, chilling. Paolo and I, both prudently hanging on to the knives, begin to sprint back up the hill. The guards step away from the agitated snakes, bug-eyed.

"Run, *signori*, run," Paolo shouts to the bastards, waving the knife menacingly—but the men are already running, toward Palmida's vines.

With the quickness of a youngster, Zio rounds the shed and flips the latch, sneaking inside; the squeaking door barely heard over our shouts.

Paolo yells and curses the reptiles, rather enjoying himself, covering Zio's efforts to tease the slithering monsters into the shed.

Soon the snakes are at the door. One slithers up toward its opening. "Look! They're going inside," I shout.

The snakes squirm quickly, the second following its leader up the door and through the old wooden portal's miniature window. Per Zio's plan, Darius screams a blood-curdling yelp like a horror film star. Paolo, not to be outdone, gives an Academy Award performance of his own. He acts shocked and indignant, demanding for Michelangelo and DaVinci to come clean. "Who's in there? Why do you just stand here? Hurry! We must help that poor soul."

He leads the charge down the hillside while the *padrone's* men keep motoring all the way to their car parked below.

"Come back, you cowards," Paolo yells for good measure.

Now that I'm inside, I see that Darius looks frazzled. He alternates between pacing, running his fingers through his hair, deep breaths, rubbing his hands up and down his thighs, and clutching his neck while craning his head like a blind man.

Paying no attention to the reptiles, he glares at my twin. Jaw clenched. His body still. He snorts like a raging bull. "This is your fault!"

I swallow hard and jump into the fray.

"You can't blame Paolo for the *padrone's* schemes. The man would have sold you to the highest bidder, perhaps to mercenaries in Libya!"

Darius looks at me. Those deep eyes hold an encyclopedia of information, not to be told—or not yet, anyway. I refuse to look away. Instead, I walk toward him, praying for him not to snap.

The top of my head barely reaches his chest. I look up with a face that pleads for calm. And it works: he glances down, raises a hand and touches my hair, as though it's a gift. "Thank you for coming to my rescue," he says to me, with all his customary chivalry. "And you as well, *Signore*," he says to Zio.

Zio smiles, and then holds out his arms to Paolo, a wriggling demon in each hand. Instinctively, I wheel backward, but Paolo wields the guard's stiletto with expert precision.

Back inside the little truck, I ask my uncle, "Are you keeping those two as prizes?"

"I promised Palmida I would get rid of them. But I told her I'd never have the heart to leave them to the vultures."

"You're kidding. You're really that fond of snakes?"

"No—but I am fond of the delicious soup they'll make in the hands of an expert. Palmida's preparing the broth as we speak."

I laugh at the joke, but this little exchange isn't enough to cut the tension between Paolo and Darius. It's as if Darius sees Paolo himself as a snake, just awaiting an opportunity to strike.

Which he is, of course. He wants Darius just as much as the *padrone* does but, while the *padrone* is just a local tough taking his chances, my brother sees Darius as a path back to baseball—even to a future in the sport after retirement.

A prize indeed.

Eli

Chapter 11

Eli • Cleveland, Ohio

It was the collision from hell. My head feels like loose gravel under the tire of a 100-ton truck. Gradually different voices around me come into focus. Glancing around, I seem to be in a grown-up version of the pediatric hospital room I visited recently. Our team physician is speaking to a nurse—a male nurse—just my luck.

"Hey, he's awake! How do you feel?" the doctor asks.

"A little fuzzy."

"That's perfectly normal on the pain meds you've been prescribed. Do you want the good news or the bad?"

"Both."

"OK. The good news is that you don't have a concussion, but the bad news is that your collarbone's fractured."

I suppose it could be worse.

"I'm glad it isn't my throwing shoulder."

"Everyone's glad about that. Try to get some rest. They'll probably be able to release you tomorrow."

"What, no vacation in the islands with meds in umbrella drinks?"

He's about to answer, when Leyland steps in, slipping his phone in his jacket pocket.

"You're in one of the best hospitals in the world, Eli," he quips, "isn't that enough for you?"

The doctor wishes him good luck as he leaves. *Hey, shouldn't he be wishing me good luck?* Clearly, it's not my day.

"Did you think to bring my cell?" I ask.

My agent hands me my phone with a look that says "Did you really have to ask?"

Then his own phone rings.

"Sorry, gotta take this." He heads back to the hallway.

I check the clock. I could catch a pre-season game of Sunday Night Football, but somehow I'm not in the mood. I've witnessed enough brutality for one day—up close and personal. It's 2 a.m. in Italy: she'll be sound asleep. *I'll just text her.*

OMG, she's up! 'Can I call u?' I punch.

Yesssss! Maybe my luck is changing.

"*Ciao*, Eli. *Come stai*?"

"Not so good. I'm in hospital."

"Oh Dio, what's happened? Are you all right?"

"I broke my left collarbone in our game this afternoon. Hurts like hell, but I reckon I'll live. My season is over, however."

"I thought you were calling me on your way home from a bar. I almost didn't pick up, but something told me I should."

Her straight talk doesn't sting as badly as it used to—plus, that accent of hers that ends every word with a vowel is the best medicine I've found yet.

"What are *you* doing still up at this hour?" I ask.

"Not much, just chatting with Darius Salamah. You won't believe what's happened since the incident with the boar."

She tells me. *It sounds like something out of a movie.*

"...Anyway, Paolo and Zio Peppe intend to watch him throw off a pitcher's mound tomorrow. Zio says, no matter what the result is, he'll do what he can to help. Thankfully, my uncle's still quite a powerful man around here."

I don't care for her enthusiasm. Who knows who this Darius really is, anyway?

"You need to be careful with this guy, Fatima. All of you do. You know very little about him."

"He told me his story only tonight—it was beyond belief. Horrific is the only word. Perhaps he'll share it with you someday."

I'm not sure I care.

"It could have been lies, for all you know."

"It was the truth."

Dammit. I wish I was there. I can't believe how swift she is to defend him...

"Fatima, I'll admit you've surprised me on more than one occasion with your uncanny intuitions, but these are unique times. Jihadi's are everywhere—maybe even under your roof."

"They're not everywhere, and the Muslim under Zio's roof is a refugee who deserves a life, just like you or me. I suspect he's suffering from Post-Traumatic Stress Disorder. I've seen him fight down anxiety more than once."

I take a deep breath. "You are one stubborn Sicilian—worse than your brother, in some ways. Remember the Boston Marathon bomber, the one who survived?"

"I know the face of evil when I see it, Eli, and his just doesn't fit."

"Yeah. Well, people change."

Dead silence. Great.

"And, who knows, maybe that arm of his is for real," she tells me.

She's been talking to that brother of hers. Might as well change my tune or this'll be a short conversation.

"Yeah. Well, anyway, I wanted you to be the first to know that I petitioned the league to allow me a reprieve on wearing the team's red-faced cartoon Indian logo called, Chief Wahoo. I've asked for two years, beginning next season."

Her voice is tweaked with amusement. "I didn't figure you for a guy with a death wish," she says, only half-joking, "but really, I admire your guts. I still remember when you and Paolo were quoted in the press as representing the two opposing points of view about this logo. I was embarrassed by his quote: 'Who cares what a bunch of people on a reservation think? I just think it's juvenile. I'm from the country that sets the fashion for the world.' Eli, between you and me, sometimes I can't even believe Paolo and I are related, let alone twins. You're far more my kindred spirit than he is."

It's as if I've been hit with a great, warm spotlight, or announced as an award winner. My heart is pounding. *It almost scares me that her approval means that much.*

I tell her: "I've promised to underwrite a series of lectures that will hopefully enlighten fans in just the same way that my Native American roommate at Stanford enlightened me. The team isn't very pleased, but they aren't going to fight me, either. I'll know by Spring Training whether or not the league will allow it."

"I remember you telling me about your roommate and his pragmatic voice for those annihilated by war," she says. "What you seem to have forgotten and what I recall is that he told you 'genocide won't end with a logo change.' I understand this all so much better since I've joined the ranks of those trying to help here. It's not just in the Middle East—although that's what makes the news—what's happening in Sub-Saharan Africa is just as frightening. But I'm proud of you, Eli, really, although I feel a little nervous for you as well. Even if the league agrees, I'm sure the fans won't. I worry about the abuse that will be hurled at you. But I know how strong you are."

My ticker is about to bust out of my chest.

"I wouldn't bother if I didn't think it possible to open their minds to an alternative perspective," I admit. "It's not political correctness. The fans really don't think about native Indian tribes when they see that logo—they're just thinking baseball. But at Stanford I learned to think of it as my father and grandfather taught me to understand the Holocaust. If the team and league don't agree, I can live with that, but I'll be a free agent by then and able to go elsewhere."

"You're an interesting man, Eli Kohn," she says, after a moment. "You're an odd combination of tremendous—how shall I say this kindly—self-assurance—"

"You mean arrogance," I interject.

She laughs and continues, "Well, a bit of that, but you also seem to carry a conscience that must be a heavy burden at times. The two don't seem to go together—yet they do in you. Oddly enough, I've seen the same combination in more than a few priests."

"Your uncle?" I ask, surprised.

"Oh, no. Zio Peppe is a true shepherd. He would deny it, but humility—the most powerful virtue of all, I think—is abundant in him. Maybe he was different as a younger man, I don't know, but for me he's just the best."

"I remember overhearing Paolo on the phone with him last season, before your brother injured his back. I felt instantly curious about him, and also amazed by his baseball acumen. I can appreciate his desire to watch Darius throw off a pitcher's mound, too. The fact is, every once in a while a real prodigy comes along, and if that's the case with Darius, even Andrea Bocelli could scout him... But there's a lot more to pitching than arm strength, not the least of which falls between the ears and in the heart."

"I believe you."

"Of course, anyone fluent in so many languages is no dummy, and as for the strength of his character, well, he's probably survived more than most Big Leaguers."

"I think you are right," she says softly.

She likes this guy. I hear it in her voice. Dammit, I wish I was there!

"Well, I've got a prodigy story for you, too." And so, I tell her about T.P.

She's a noisy listener. Just what I'd hoped for—lots of oohs and ahhs and even a fair sprinkling of praise.

Nurse Dude arrives to take my temperature, followed by a few of my teammates.

"I gotta go, but call me some time," I say, as casually as I can manage.

"I realize you've suddenly got a lot more time on your hands, Eli, but I don't. Boatloads of refugees are arriving, as the end of the summer is near. You just wouldn't believe the things that I see."

I'm sure I wouldn't, but I have to end this call before the guys start kidding me.

"Get some rest and I'll call you soon," I say.

"You're the one who needs the rest. *Ciao.*"

"Bye."

A trip to sunny Italy might be just the prescription for my broken shoulder...and it might not hurt my broken love life either. Her influence may have played on my guilty conscience enough for me to reach out to T.P., but this Darius guy is a whole other ballgame.

Chapter 12

Darius • Calabria, Italy

The rooster has been clearing his throat for almost an hour. My accommodations in the priest's house are both comfortable and uncomfortable. Oh, there's plenty of space, and the four-poster bed sweeps me into a much-needed, dreamless sleep. A wooden door with a dozen window panes, all covered in lace, opens onto a tiny balcony. What more could anyone ask for?

Yet there *is* more, there's also the view... A spectacular green mountain opposite this one is terraced with vineyards, with only a trickle of a river in between this perch and that one. It travels westward toward the sea, out of which juts the volcano they call Stromboli. I should feel as if I've died and gone to heaven, but, well, it's a Christian heaven. The holy statues, crucifixes, and giant rosary beads made from chestnuts are a little unnerving to me. *But really, who am I to judge? I left my prayer rug in the desert, and Salat five times a day with it.*

The wickedness I've witnessed in the name of religion assaults my faith. In my mind's eye, each memory is tinged with blood. I had hoped that these attacks were becoming less frequent but, after yesterday, they're back with a vengeance. I have to control myself almost brutally: *Breathe. Think. Stop seeing desert where there are only grapevines.* A sudden gust of breeze fires me up instead of soothing: I'm reminded of the shivering blast of a bomb.

I can't think of this now. Breathe. Breathe. Smell the wet in the air. Admire the pattern of the cobblestones below. Memorize this picture postcard view.

It's beyond beautiful here, so lush and green and full of flowers, as lovely as my mother's smile—*Oh, Allah, how I miss her. Focus. Focus on the scenery. Keep breathing. Think of Fatima instead.*

And there she is!

"*Buon giorno, Signorina* Fatima. Where are you coming from, so early in the morning?"

A reckless kid on a Vespa dodges her. She waits until the revved motor grows faint.

"The cemetery. I always try to visit, at least once a trip."

I shouldn't have asked.

The woman next door emerges to retrieve her laundry. She gives me a curious glance.

"*Buon giorno,*" I say to her just to test the waters.

Frigid. Precisely what I was afraid of.

"Meet me by the kitchen door. I could use some help at the chicken coop," Fatima shouts.

I skip down the stairs. The heavy door is propped open. A sense of safety I realize I've forgotten tries to break through the wall of fear I've worked so hard to construct.

"Nothing like eggs still warm from the hens," she tells me, as we walk around to the back of the house. When she puts some in my hands she starts to laugh.

"Your hands are so big I don't need to carry any."

I follow her inside, where the smell of coffee, fresh bread and olive oil compete for my nose's attention. I feel happy, then guilty, then angry, all in a split-second. She's staring at me.

"It's all right to be happy, Darius. It's how life was intended to be."

"What are you, some kind of a mind reader?" I ask.

"Yes, so be careful what you think," her brother says, reaching for the coffee. He pours espresso into demitasse cups for himself and his grandmother.

"Fatima's not a coffee drinker. How about you?" he asks.

"I'm like Fatima."

"I'd like some coffee," the priest says, taking a seat beside his nephew.

"Where's Mama?" Paolo asks his sister.

"On the phone. Someone has to work in this family."

"Don't start with me, Fatima," Paolo says.

Her grandmother hands her a plate of fried eggs, and a look that says, 'Don't go there.'

Church bells begin to toll. I must admit I like their sound, but without the call of the muezzin life has lost its rhythm for me. The clock on the stove reads 8:45 when the priest stands.

"My wakeup call," *Signore* Peppe says. "Now Paolo, the basket of balls and old mitts are still in the wine cellar, as they've been since the last time we played. The rakes are in the shed. I'm guessing you'll have the mound in some kind of shape by the time

I finish Mass." He swallows the dregs of his coffee as if drinking a shot of liquor and grabs a cookie on his way out the door.

"I'm coming with you and Nonna, Zio," Fatima says. She lingeringly wipes a dollop of egg yolk from her plate with her last bite of bread. I get the impression that, if I wasn't around, she'd lift the plate to her face and lick every last trace.

"Well, like it or not, it's just you and me," Paolo says, and we finish our eggs in silence.

He drops his plate and cup in the sink near the end of the L-shaped marble counter. I follow his lead. Then I watch him lacing up his shoes. "Too bad we don't have cleats," he says.

We exit the house, stepping down an incline to the street. There, Paolo unlatches antique doors that open outward. Wooden barrels and assorted wine-making equipment confirm what my nose told me the minute he cracked open the door. The musky sweat of pressed grapes is thick in the air.

"In the old days, this is where those lucky enough to have one kept their donkey. Since people now get around by car or motorbike, mostly they're used as garages," he tells me.

In a corner we find a large woven basket, full of grimy once-white balls. I pick one up and roll it across my hand. The faded red stitches interest me; I palm and finger and squeeze.

"I take it these stitches affect the trajectory of the throw."

"The pitch. Yes. Wow, you're quick."

Then he hands me two lumps of worked leather. One has five huge fingers, rather like the hand of an ogre. The other is heavily padded, with just a separation for the thumb. I can guess at their use in conjunction with the ball.

He picks up the basket and we begin our journey together. Several neighbors wave or call out from their balconies or storefronts: Paolo is clearly popular. After only about 150 yards, we arrive at the edge of town. The blue expanse in the distance is breathtaking; I make a mental note to return at sunset.

We trudge downhill, through a poppy field that gives way to an olive grove, pausing at a little fountain with a hand crank. Paolo pumps and slurps, invites me to do the same: an oasis of spring water dribbles down my chin.

This area is filled with fruit trees. Figs, oranges, and some kind of apricot, I think, flank our left. On the right is a vast vegetable garden, carved in perfect rows, ending where the grapevines begin. A shed is in our path, once painted yellow but now faded cream by sunlight. We each take a rake and walk toward an open space, backed by a bump in the ground.

"Well, this is it," Paolo says, at last. "When I was young Zio tried relentlessly to train me to be a pitcher on this spot, but I was always more interested in swinging a bat. Finally he gave up and started pitching to me instead... My Calabrese great-grandfather was old and very sick in those days. On weekends I'd come with Nonna on the train so that she could help take care of him. The kids Zio paid to chase balls eventually tired of the sport so he framed a giant fish-net for me to aim at instead. His patience was endless, his technique impeccable. He taught me to swing with my lead arm only, in order to strengthen my left wrist. Look!"

He shows me how his left wrist is larger and more muscular than the right. Then he explains the science of shaping the mound, and together we set to work.

Time passes, in serene slow motion. I have no idea how long until someone's piercing whistle, as if summoning a dog, snaps me to attention.

"That would be my dainty sister," Paolo says. "She can fold her tongue in half; it's the weirdest thing. But it creates quite a noise."

Fatima and her uncle approach, side by side. As I watch her come toward us, hands clasped behind her back, I imagine crazy things: a fairyland of butterflies, throaty birds in vivid colors, children laughing, and sweet peace. I shake my head. *This place must be hypnotizing me.*

Paolo sets the basket of baseballs near the freshly-groomed mound. *Signore* Peppe reaches for one like a child choosing a favorite toy. Rubbing it hard between his palms, he climbs the hill to its peak. "This old pitching rubber's pretty warped. If need be, I'll make a new one out of wood."

He places his right foot alongside it and asks me to watch him from behind.

"Come halfway toward the mound," he tells Paolo. "This old body needs to work up to the full distance."

The *signore* winds and tosses a pitch that sails perfectly into the target area. They continue tossing the ball back and forth, gradually moving further apart.

"Tell me the truth," Paolo says to his uncle. "You've been staying in shape throwing at your old bounce-back pitching net since we last did this. I saw it in the shed."

"I haven't."

"A priest isn't supposed to lie."

"I'm not lying. Being old doesn't have to mean being out of shape, especially for people who still work a farm. See that pile of wood over there? Who do you think split that?"

This man is a specimen they should freeze for science.

Fatima emerges from the shed holding an old walking stick.

"OK, Zio, I'm the batter."

"*Cara mia*, your strike zone is too small for me to aim at."

"What's a strike zone?" I ask.

"Hand over that stick for a minute," Paolo tells her. He uses it to explain the basics of pitching versus hitting for the next half hour, even going so far as to trace a batter's box and home plate in the dirt.

The basics out of the way, he hands me a ball. We toss back and forth just as he and the *signore* did, except that I'm on flat ground.

"Do you think you killed that boar with the strength of your arm?" Paolo asks.

"I don't know how I killed the boar. It was instinct."

"Well, in a way that's good, because skilled athletes never think about what they're doing with their bodies while they're doing it. The trick is to teach your muscles the proper movements, so they know what to do on their own. I suspect that the strength and positioning of your legs had just as much to do with your effectiveness as your arm. But your legs and your arms weren't alone in that dance. Do you know what else played a role?"

"I do recall considering which rock to choose."

"Uh huh. And why did you choose the stone you threw?"

"Because of its size and shape, I suppose."

"Why that size? Why that shape?"

"It just felt right. Like a stone I could control. One that I could make do what I wanted it to do."

"Bingo," Paolo shouts, raising a fist in the air.

"Is bingo good?"

"Sorry. It's a word Americans use when something is correct, on the mark, hits the target. It comes from a game you'll learn about 50 years from now. But anyway, I'm excited to know that you *think* like a pitcher. What you unconsciously did was to choose a stone that would roll off your fingers, giving more speed in the air and consequently more force at impact while at the same time allowing you to control the trajectory."

"I admired the Palestinians who fought Israeli soldiers with nothing more than stones. I even emulated them when the Syrian conflict started to move closer to Damascus. With so many factions involved I figured it was inevitable it would soon be at our doorstep... But in the end I was a fool. Stones can't fight guns."

"Channel that anger into your workout," he says.

I didn't expect sympathy from him: still, this annoys me. Fatima and her uncle, on the other hand, offer apologies. *I should just shut up about it. It's done. Nothing can make it undone. There's no sense in making her and the priest uncomfortable: they aren't to blame.* As for all this—the ball, the pitching—why do I even bother with this nonsense? I don't want to be a professional athlete; I want to be a doctor. Athletes have only a few years before their bodies require them to give up the profession, but a doctor could work another forty saving lives.

"Your arm has to be warm by now. Climb up the mound and let's give it a try."

"Not so fast, Paolo," the *signore* says. "Darius, do you like to dance?"

"This family must be crazy about dancing. Fatima asked me the same question just the other night."

"Well let's hope you have more rhythm than she does." He winks at her to soften the blow. "Paolo, come over here and play the role of pitcher for a bit."

He does, while I imitate a whole series of motions that Paolo performs.

Finally, they ask me to try for real. I'm surprised by my nerves. I tell myself this isn't life or death, that it's just a kid's game.

But she's watching.

Paolo explains that a catcher usually wears various items of padding for protection. "So throw only half-strength," he advises.

I do. But the slope of the mound causes me to lose my balance and throw over his head.

"That's OK; I expected that. While I get the ball, work on your dance steps from that perch."

I face nothing but fertile fields. The others are behind me. I decide to momentarily forget them. I close my eyes and imagine a Bollywood number from a movie I used to enjoy; I stop thinking of baseball and dream of music. I lose myself in the rhythm in my head.

"OK. You seem under control. Now try it again with a ball. Remember, only half-speed."

I oblige Paolo.

Then I hear a thump.

He hasn't made a move, but the ball is in his glove.

Paolo remains squatted for a moment, only moving his head toward Fatima and his uncle. She claps and jumps up and down. *Signore* Peppe folds his arms across his chest and nods, his head to one side. "Again," he says.

Again I oblige, with another perfectly placed thump.

Each time Paolo throws the ball back to me he asks for another.

"Take your time," he says, once or twice. We continue this game for ten minutes.

"I want to see more speed," Paolo says. "Zio, did I see a rope and an old blanket in the shed?"

"I like the way you're thinking," he answers.

They set to work, stringing a backdrop from a smoke pipe atop the shed to an olive tree several yards away. A dusty white blanket is draped over the rope. Paolo carries a bottle from the shed, uncorks it with his teeth and takes a whiff.

"Vinegar," he says, making a face. Then he pours it on the blanket, creating a rough, geometric, violet stain.

"This is your strike zone. Now you can throw as hard as you like."

Fatima feeds me the balls while the men watch, from every angle.

I get through both dozen balls in the basket.

"Nineteen out of 24 strikes," Fatima says, grinning.

The *signore* tells me, "I'm amazed at how consistently you release the ball at the same point. Shocked might be a more precise word. But let's not tax your young arm. Time for a rest. Let's pick some fruit, but only the ripest. That's the way we like it."

After we've filled our hands with a juicy variety, we eat a couple. They're too ripe for my taste. *Signore* Peppe hands me a peach and suggests I throw it rather than eat it.

"OK. You're the boss."

I palm the peach gently and begin my windup. As I'm about to release it, it squishes in my hand and squirts into pieces, flying every which way.

Paolo and his uncle howl while Fatima sprints to fetch a rag from the shed. She hands it to me: "Hopefully we have enough of these for one afternoon!"

"Did you trick me to make a point, *signore*?"

"Yes, and I'm not the least bit sorry for it. You need to learn the musical interplay between power and finesse if you're to become a professional. Listen to me very carefully: a pitcher is not a thrower. Or, to put it another way, throwing is a craft but pitching is an art."

"You see, Darius," Paolo says, "for a pitcher, a baseball is like a fine woman. You want to show her your strength, but also that you understand that she's a delicate creature. Touch her with the proper combination of strength and delicacy and she'll go wherever you ask."

"Is that the way they explain it in the big leagues?" Fatima asks.

"That's the way we explain it in Italy. Get over it. I didn't invite you today. You want to hang out with the boys then deal with it."

My face probably matches the shade of the tomatoes growing nearby.

The priest suggests that the brother apologize to his sister. "A little crude," he tells me, "but hopefully you get the point."

I do.

Chapter 13

Eli • Cleveland, Ohio

"My name is Eli Kohn and I'm a control freak. There. I said it."

Albeit I'm confessing to a dog, but Elvis is like my shrink.

"Aren't you buddy? Is it really so bad to want what I want when I want it and how I want it. But all because of a damn broken bone, I have to do what I don't want to do—when others want me to do it and how they want me to do it."

Elvis licks my hand. He always licks my hand when I'm down. I'm holding his leash, but I'm parked on the steps. I really should carpet them and buy an area rug for the foyer. My voice echoes in here. Elvis is usually anxious to dash from the foyer out the front door, but he knows I'm not ready.

"Is it because I'm such a control freak that I hate answering questions I don't want to be asked? But Leyland Tilson is a good agent: he'd already told me what to expect and what to say. I mean, it's great that the league ruled on the matter so fast, but the fans aren't exactly sympathetic toward my stance on the team logo. Hope I can get the worst of the fallout behind me before Spring Training, but I won't be holding my breath. Frankly, Elvis, good buddy, the reaction has been far tougher than I expected."

Seeming to feel the need to comment, Elvis barks.

"Fatima called me after she saw the news about the press conference. She was impressed, anyway. Every piece of crap I've had to put up with seemed worth it, after that. She again reminded me my old roommate's words, 'Genocide won't end with a logo change,' then added, 'but only with a change of heart. At least you're beginning the process by trying to initiate a thoughtful discussion.' I wanted to jump through the phone and squeeze her. Yet it bugs me that her praise means so much.

"But now, questions have started about my friendship with T.P. I'm getting grief about him becoming my chauffeur. People are suggesting that I'm treating him like my personal slave. What they don't realize is that the guy *begged* to drive my car; he loves driving a stick, especially one with as much juice as my little Beemer. So we go for his driver's test and turns out he's a better driver than me. Not that it takes much. I'm a little reckless, as you know."

Elvis, sensing that we might be here awhile, sprawls into his sphinx pose. *Good dog.*

"So, I didn't tell you, but I rented him an apartment downtown and hooked him up with the Boys and Girls Club. It made perfect sense. It's the league's go-to charity and they've been after me to join since forever. I've thought about it, but I wasn't too confident about how good I'd be with kids: their problems so often relate to a family life foreign to mine. But T.P.'s perfect for them. It's a win-win, don't you agree?

"Anyway, now here we are well into September, and it's become clear that this season's over for the club: whatever chance we had at the playoffs broke right along with my collarbone. So I'm considering a vacation in Sicily. What do you think, Elvis? Should I go for it?"

Elvis lifts his monstrous head and lets loose a single yelp.

"I'll take that as a yes. Between you and me, it's partly that I just can't tell if Fatima only pities Darius Salamah or if the tone I hear in her voice is serious affection. It's driving me nuts. Plus, I can't stop thinking about her. She's the only person who truly gets me... Well, yes, you get me, but you're not really a person."

This time Elvis' bark is more like a whimper.

"So, OK, I admit it: I've become insanely jealous. Her eyes slay me and I don't know what's more lush, her hair or her lips. She's sassy and sweet, insightful and brutally honest—but in a good way. Elvis my friend, I always hate to leave you behind, but I think a road trip is in order. She's pretty adorable, you have to admit, especially next to you."

I show Elvis my latest screensaver: a picture of her standing beside him, from last season. He gives two loud barks, stares at it another second, then barks again.

"You remember her, don't you, buddy? I went from champ to chump whenever she was around... But I promise I won't kennel you while I'm away. I'll get that Romanian dog sitter you like so much. The one with the blue streak in her hair and the nose ring always accessorizes with leather—you know the one I mean. What the heck was her name? Natasha, Boris...whatever. Apparently you find her hot in her hardcore kind of way. You'll be fine.

"Paolo claims that this Darius's talent is for real. A prodigy. But I don't care how good he is, with the way things are right now, I can't imagine U.S. Immigration even letting him near the country. But you know Paolo: he can be mister nice guy when it suits his purpose."

The mere mention of his name gets Elvis growling. I can't help laughing.

"I know, buddy, I know. He bugs the living shit out of me, too. He only cares about one person—himself. He's figuring that he and Darius could be a package deal, even though it's a package that could deliver disaster. It's one thing to have Paolo back terrorizing the clubhouse; it's another to have a guy on the inside that might terrorize the whole ballpark.

"Fatima put Darius on the phone with me the other day. Did I tell you? She thinks she's Camp David.

"The more questions I asked him, the more evasive he became. He's seen a lot of violence; that much is clear. But at whose hands? I sense that he was in the thick of it. He said Daesh, the term he uses for ISIS, was isolating communities and starving them, in order to recruit additional fighters. When I asked him if he was one of those guys, suddenly he couldn't hear me anymore... Supposedly, something went wrong with our connection. *Pure bullshit.*

"Every time I warn Fatima about him, she says that, if I knew his story, I'd feel differently. But when I ask her to share it with me, she always says I'm not ready to hear it.

"She blanked out on me again for a minute yesterday, while we were on FaceTime; I get the weirdest feeling when she does it. The look that comes over her is like an instantaneous lift of light. Her head tilts back, her jaw slackens, her eyes roll up almost inside her lids, but the overall impression is of total peace. I'm not doing a very good job of explaining it, but I'm telling you, you'd be drawn to it. It's like this magnetic field shoots out of her, effortlessly drawing you in. *I can even sense it on FaceTime: imagine what it'd be like, if I was there...*

"So I said to her, 'There, you did it again; where were you?' She calls it her happy place. If it wasn't that she's probably the most rational person I know, I'd think she was some kind of a mental patient.

"When she was here last season she tried to explain it to me. Her great-grandmother had the same ability: people used to say she was a mystic. Fatima described it as being spoken to, but not with a voice. She said it was like an injection of love—that no other joy could compare to it. She also wishes that she could harness it on demand, when bad things are happening, but she has no control over her gift. If I remember correctly, she likened it to the innermost sanctum of her soul melding into light... I was fascinated. Had I never witnessed it, I'd have guessed she was faking, but this was no act. It was otherworldly. I need to rocket my way into her world—and soon."

Chapter 14

Paolo • Sicily

If I have to talk to one more dealer about one more wine shipment, I think I'll slit my wrists. I have about as much interest in this as in cleaning toilets. I wish Zio could get away to Catania. Why can't he just retire like any other priest? But San Mango isn't a bustling city. Why force a young priest to shepherd so few sheep, is probably what the hierarchy is thinking... Like all the other picolo paese in the south, it's turning geriatric.

Ironically, some of these ghost towns are resurrecting themselves into havens for refugees. It's so strange to think that, perhaps a hundred or so years ago, Sicilians, Calabrese, and Neapolitans began migrating in vast numbers to the U.S., Canada, and Australia in search of a better life. While, of the families who stayed, the young people mostly escaped for better work to the cities north of Naples. Now migrants are fleeing to abandoned villages here—and for the same reasons!

But when I was only ten, 9/11 happened, and the world completely changed. Boatloads of Sicilians, some of them Mafiosi, had no problem relocating to America during my great-grandfather's generation: America needed the labor, back then. But now, no matter how pathetic your situation may be, if you're a young male Muslim, well, good luck getting into America.

I'm all for it, to be honest. I want Muslims in Sicily about as much as my island did when they first overran the place, 800 years ago. All I'm asking is for American Immigration to look the other way in this one, particular, very rare instance... Selfish? Maybe—but why not? Ex-cons still play professional American football, don't they? Whatever it takes to win, in my opinion... Fatima claims that Darius is innocent, but frankly, I don't care if he is or not. What's passed has passed. All I really want is for the present to turn in my favor.

Italian Immigration Services have agreed to register Darius, but they've given him only a limited amount of time to move on. The very idea of his ending up in America is utter lunacy, they tell him. Germany or Sweden are his best bets, and the sooner the better, as he has cousins in both places, refugees who've already been accepted. They could vouch for him, but if he delays too long, he might well get shut out from Europe altogether: all the bleeding from Syria is in need of a tourniquet.

Fatima has friends in immigration. She believes that they should themselves hire Darius because he speaks fluently—or at least passably—almost every language they might need. Besides Arabic and Italian, he speaks 'broken' Pashto and Urdu, potentially assisting those fleeing strife in Pakistan and Afghanistan. And besides English he also possesses almost accent-free Farsi since his mother was Iranian. But he can get by in German, French and Spanish, a bit of Dutch and marginal Swedish. His Greek and Russian are halting, but his Turkish excellent. He says he tries to learn a new language every year. He wants to try Mandarin next. I remember when I was told that St. Pope John Paul II could speak that many languages. I found it hard to believe until now.

"Paolo, your cell is ringing. You left it on the table." Mama waves it in her hand. She's flanked by glorious pink oleanders at the edge of the brick patio. What a picture they make. We just finished lunch. I wasn't ready to leave this brilliant sun anyway for the dank cellars of the winery, so I walk back toward her.

She looks at the caller ID. "It's Eli, shall I answer for you?"

"*Si, grazie.*"

She likes Eli, too. What can all these women see in him? I'm especially sick of all the oohing and ahhing over his most recent stunt, the one involving the team's logo. I don't care if the team dumps it or not. I don't find it particularly inspiring to go up against powerful opponents wearing a cartoon, but if Eli's got anything to do with scrapping it, then count me out. *Between all the fawning and fuss over Darius and this kiss-kiss crap with Eli, I'm ready to lose my—really excellent—pasta lunch.*

I know I told Eli that my sister sees right through him, but that isn't really true. If I'm honest, she seemed attracted to him from day one and—I think—has been battling that attraction ever since. I overheard her talking about it once with Sister Colleen. I used to like that nun, who's an honest soul, until she told Fatima she needs to 'prayerfully discern her feelings.' They kill me with that stuff. Why waste God's time with what you already know?

"How's your father getting on?" I hear Mama ask. Abe Kohn was instantly attracted to my mother at Spring Training last year: though, to her, it seemed to barely register. Papa's death was too fresh; not that the sorrow doesn't crush her at odd moments, even now, but, in those days, I think life was pretty much a blur. I'm surprised and irritated that she even remembers him. Don't tell me that, even if I do make it back to Cleveland, I'm going to have to deal with a possibility I've never even wanted to contemplate. She's smiling, dammit, as she hands me my phone.

"*Ciao*, Eli."

"Hello, Paolo. Thought you'd like to know I've pretty much convinced Leyland that a trip to Italy to scout Darius is in order. But...he's still looking for an invite from you. And he wants to bring his wife, who needs a vacation. So do I, so I was just telling your mother that my dad has business in Rome the first week of November and that we're thinking about flying to Catania once he's finished. She just invited us to Villa Multicino. What do you say about setting up an exhibition?"

Mannagia! Couldn't my mother at least have asked me first? I need his help, but I don't need him under the same roof with my sister, not to mention the nausea of having to witness a contest between the champions of social justice. *Where's a barf bag when you need one...*

"To be honest, I think it's too soon. He only has a fastball—though Zio tells me he can put it where he wants it 75% of the time."

"Have you tried hitting it yet?"

"Look, I realize you know little about our business, but we only just finished the grape harvest. I'm stuck in Sicily right now and my uncle is stuck in San Mango. Otherwise, that would've happened by now, for sure."

"How far apart are we talking?"

"Four hours by car, plus the ferry from Sicily."

"Well, I don't know how rigorous his training schedule is, but you made it sound pretty intense. If that's true, couldn't he at least manage a curveball by early November? That's over a month away."

"Maybe. I do have a couple of friends who might be interested in playing an exhibition. There's a field just south of here, near Paterno, where the old Catania Warriors used to play. I think I could make it happen on my end, but I'd have to defer to my uncle's judgment."

"Well, do that, and let me know the verdict."

"I will." I say.

I suppose I should thank him. Although I'm going to hate every minute of this, I need his help as much as Darius's if I'm going to swing my return to baseball.

"OK, I'll wait to hear from you," he says.

"It pains me to say it, but I guess I owe you one, as far as Leyland goes."

"Guess that's about as close to gratitude as I'll get. You're welcome, Paolo. Talk to you later."

"*Ciao.*"

He didn't ask me to say hello to Fatima. They must be in contact. Damn. He's like an annoying relative who comes for Christmas and stays till Easter. One way or another it feels like I'm stuck with him too.

Chapter 15

Darius • Calabria, Italy

The heavy footfall means more than the usual peeping children are nearby. Peppe's eyes speak the thought in my head. I heard his conversation with the housekeeper last night. Rumor has it that the *padrone* seeks to break my arm. I should be scared, but I'm not. A broken arm isn't a beheading, after all. There's been a recent crackdown on human traffickers, so another kidnapping seems remote, at least for now. But the bastard still wants the last word.

We always walk to the farm, but today we drove Peppe's old Fiat.

"The sun is setting earlier these days, so tonight we begin a new routine," Peppe says. "We'll study the game footage Paolo sent both before *and* after dinner. *Andiamo*," and he gestures for us to go.

I squeeze into the *macchina*. The sun has started its usual magnificent descent as we wind our way up the hillside to town. How could anything be amiss in such a gloriously ethereal place?

"You're early," the housekeeper complains. She hasn't started making dinner yet.

"*Tranquilla, signora*. First we have work to do," Peppe says. "Darius, do you trust me?"

We're walking from the kitchen to the parlor; his question catches me by surprise.

"Of course, *signore*. You're not only my teacher, but also my friend. Not once have you judged me harshly—and nor has the *signora*; she acts as if she works for me as much as for you. You shelter me, you clothe me, you feed me, and you teach me this sport you clearly love. What more could I ask?"

"It's been an absolute pleasure. You can't begin to know how much. And though every other sentence from the *signora* is a complaint, believe me, she's having the time of her life. For a woman who was never blessed with children of her own, your presence is a gift. I've never seen her happier than these last two months. She whistles while hanging out the laundry!"

"I'm also grateful that you haven't tried to convert me."

"What is there to convert? You have no religion, it seems.

Ah, excuse me, my dear boy, for the judgment that slips from my tongue. "

"There's no need to apologize. If you knew my past, you might better understand my ambivalence toward God. But in this place, and during this time with you, I'm beginning to feel that maybe Allah hasn't forgotten me, that it might instead be me who continues to forget Him.

"Last night I dreamed of a horrifying monster. It was sucking everything around into its great maw—I woke up gasping for breath. Then I saw the face of the Madonna, as you call her, in that picture framed in my room. I was suddenly thankful that it was the one image the *signora* didn't remove when making space for me. For the first time, my anxiety didn't spin out of control; my heart calmed. I find this a small miracle."

"She has more miracles to work, trust me. And since you do, I'm going to ask you to do something that may sound a little crazy." His voice darkens. "I don't mean to alarm you, but you need to know..."

"That the *padrone* seeks revenge. I heard the rumor—as well as the spy at the farm."

"Good! Then you understand. I have a plan to force the authorities to deal with him, at least long enough to finish your immediate training—before we move to Sicily."

"What! You're leaving, after all these years?"

"I'm well past my expiration date as a priest. My bosses have had someone waiting in the wings for a time now. Marietta is my closest living relative and she's been begging me for years to come and live with her before it's too late for us to make up for all the time we lost."

"What do you mean, time you have lost?'"

"It's an old story, but let me explain. Much as we enjoy each other's company today, there was a stretch of ten years when we didn't even speak. Marietta was angry with me—with the whole world—when her son, Enzo was accidentally killed. She couldn't take her revenge on the *Cosa Nostra*, so instead, she took it out on me. She blamed me for failing to 'call them out' at Enzo's Funeral Mass. I thought I was being prudent; she thought I was a coward—and she was right. Ten years later I apologized and she forgave me. Mama's negotiating skills, leveraged by her impending death, helped to break the impasse, but we were both fools to let our dispute go that far. Between us, we broke our mother's heart."

I grieve for him, and for his mother, but all I can trust myself to say is: "It's sad."

"My older sister is an extremely superstitious woman. She believes that if she looks after me as she did when I was young, then Mama will bless her when she passes... For really, Darius, Marietta brought me up. During those terrible war years, my father was a soldier and my mother the farmhand. As I grew older, I used to accompany Marietta to the American Air Base over the mountain; there my beautiful sister would entice GIs into buying our garden produce. It was during that time that I was myself taught the game I now teach you! It was also then that my sister Marietta met her future husband. Pietro Multicino and his father, an enterprising wine merchant, also frequented the American military outposts within Sicily and Calabria, and, in the final months of the war, Pietro asked Marietta to marry him...which is how my Calabrese sister ended up in Sicily—and why I will end my days there too in spite of our 10-year battle."

"No wonder there's no peace in this world! When a priest feuds with his own family how can Palestinians and Jews, or Shia and Sunni, be expected to get along?"

Peppe sighs, and continues. "After the Americans suffered 9/11, many of our churches saw an increase in parishioners coming together to pray for peace. I myself attempted to use it as a teaching point to end some of the battles being waged among families within my congregation. Only one got the message, as I recall. We're such a stubborn species.

"Anyway, I appreciate your feelings, and it's precisely that kind of anger I want to use to trap your former employer and his men. When we know our visitors have returned, I'll give you a signal. Then I suggest that you pretend to become frustrated and angry with me. Tell me you've had enough and claim you're leaving town, walking down the hill, away from me. I believe that the plan is to jump us on our walk home, but our bringing the car today probably has them wondering if we might be onto them. When they see there's only you to jump, this may encourage them to attack.

"As you know, my neighbor has the best figs in all Italy—outstanding even this late into their second season. Anyway, every Thursday my neighbor's nephew, the captain of the *polizia*, comes to gather a basket for his family. He'll almost certainly be a witness, along with the town priest and former mayor, of the attempted assault on you—and this time he won't be able to look the other way."

"But how can you time it so precisely?"

"That's where the trust comes in. Do you trust me, still?"

"I thought I did."

The old man grins.

"*Va bene.* OK."

Chapter 16

Fatima • Sicily

I break the biscotti in half and share the cookie with a small Somali boy. The smell of his breath is of the emptiness of his belly: he can't have eaten in some time. Still, his brilliant smile almost overpowers me, as he looks down at the treat, then up at me. His eyelashes blink like the flutter of feathers. My heart does a dance.

Instead of putting the bite in his mouth his bony fingers break the gift in half: he shares joyfully with his little sister behind him. Now there are two smiles. But to my amazement, her tiny fingers manage to snap the piece yet again, to share a fraction with the baby in her mother's lap.

They don't realize that there's plenty more where that came from. They make do as they've done before—maybe as they always have done.

The strapping Irishwoman, Sister Colleen, wearing the white habit with blue trim of the Sisters of Charity, walks with a worse limp than usual today. Sometimes she carries herself so that it's nearly imperceptible, but at others her bones seem to recollect their souvenir from that IRA bomb in her childhood.

As far as the migrants are concerned, people often behave badly even under the best of circumstances, but after suffering Dante's nine levels of hell, emotions are naturally raw. Sister Colleen is sometimes thanked, but mostly badgered: people want help and they want it instantly. Unsurprisingly, they can't comprehend the struggles of those trying to assist. The refugees' struggles can never be trumped.

Sister Colleen never loses patience. If I make a mistake or take too long to do something, she never criticizes. She encourages while reminding me what I've learned, presuming I won't make the mistake again. Usually I don't.

Cultures clash in an environment like this one. Many of the boat people don't know what to make of us. They're especially unsure if they can trust women in positions of power. They ask, "When can my child see the doctor?" after Sister Colleen has already explained—in their own language, half the time—that *she* actually is the doctor...

Some days are crazier than others. We never know how many refugees will arrive. So we expect the worst and hope for the best, but keep setting a new bar for "the worst."

I've spent very little time at home over the last two months. Nonna keeps complaining that she's forgetting my face, but Mama and Paolo both seem too preoccupied to notice—which is just as well, as weird things keep happening to me. I joke that the less it happens around my family the better, but Sister Colleen is worried. She's started insisting that I see a specialist.

It happened again this morning. I'd just finished interviewing a new family, and turned to walk away. It was as though my foot hadn't got the message from my brain that it needed to lift. I was left motionless, like a mime that forgets his next move, left stranded in the middle of a story. It scared the heck out of me. At other times my slow reactions have caused me to fall. My lack of height makes for a short trip, but still, I find myself covering bruises with makeup, and hoping no one will notice.

I'll think about what to do later. I don't have time right now.

My cell rings: I let it go to voicemail. I know it's Eli. He either can't do the time-zone math or else he'd rather not call in the evening, when Paolo might be around. Every night Paolo calls Zio, mostly to get a "Darius Update," then he hands me the phone. He's using me, but I don't mind, if it helps Darius.

Darius must be one of the most focused individuals I've ever met. It's as if he's on a mission to counterbalance all that he's lost. Even according to Paolo, finding Darius was like finding sunken treasure. My brother is beginning to act like a lotto winner. He says Darius has learned to throw what Zio calls a "commanding" fastball and a "wicked" curve. His slider is coming along so fast that my uncle thinks that he can teach him a changeup before the exhibition, which is scheduled three weeks from now.

In short, Darius is a physical and mental prodigy, a polyglot and a pitcher *extraordinaire*. But he's also a PTSD victim with a tale of woe that could flip their sweat equity on its head. Paolo thinks that Cleveland's owner will race to land Darius and move heaven and earth to sign him. But heaven and earth might not be quite enough for Darius. It'll take a universal effort to fill his black hole.

Chapter 17

Eli • Cleveland, Ohio

T.P. shifts gears. He smiles like a man in control of his destiny.

"What you lookin' at, son?"

"Nothing. I was just wondering if I'm ever going to drive my own car again."

"You can drive me anytime. I like bein' chauffeured too."

"Wow, thanks for the generous offer. Where are we going anyway?"

"I told you, I gotta surprise for tonight."

"But we're going toward Progressive Field. The season's over."

"But the neighbor's next door are gearing up for theirs. Someone I met workin' with the young'uns gave me tickets to-night's exhibition game. No offense, but basketball is my favorite sport."

"Hey, I thought golf was."

"To play, yeah—but not to watch."

"But I have access to tickets anytime I want, and not in peanut heaven either."

"Don't be such an ingrate, boy. Just trust me."

The look of control becomes him.

•••••••••••

We tumble the turnstiles. I do the usual sign-and-walk to avoid getting trapped by autograph hounds. I don't mind the kids, but when a middle-aged man shoves one out of the way, I give T.P. the nod. He shames the dude and motions the boy forward, while we keep moving. I turn away from the thug and, smiling at junior, ask him his name before signing his cap. We move at a quicker pace. We hurry through the hallway that separates the concourse from the seating bowl and come to the walkway dividing the lower box seats from the upper ones.

"Which way," I ask.

"Down," says my black Santa. Row by row the alphabet comes closer and closer to A until we step beyond it. Oh, my God. My fairy godfather has granted me a seat in the greatest place to park a fan's fanny in all of sport. Basketball's best will be splashing us with their sweat as they pick and roll, dribble and dunk.

Not my agent, not my owner, not a single brand I've endorsed has ever scored me seats this good. I doubt I could even score them for myself, but the homeless guy pulled it off. *Go figure.*

Awesome. It's only pre-season, but it's still freakin' awesome. Wow. I've met the big man on more than one occasion, and watched him play many times, but never from as close as this.

Once settled in, I glance at my friend T.P. He appears engrossed by the action until he turns to me—and winks.

Life has done a funky pivot. We've come to the place where "do unto others" gets done unto you.

I go with it, snatching my phone to capture the perfect selfie of the two of us. I'm checking the last pose when a big paw wraps my shoulder, drawing me close to him and to T.P. People are clapping. A cameraman gets up close to my up-close with none other than the greatest basketball star on the planet. The two of us become the three of us.

As he stands, unfolding every last inch of his too-tall self, he fist-bumps T.P., who tells him, "Thanks for the tickets."

What the hell is happening here? Everybody's hero walks away. *Where's my fist bump?*

"I'm starting to think T.P. stands for 'too priceless.' How many more surprises can I expect tonight?"

"That's it. I gotta pace myself. I don't wanna spoil you anymore than you already are."

I check my watch. It's well after midnight in Italy. There are plenty of people, both male and female, I could share this moment with: *why is she always the first to come to mind*?

Twenty more days, and I'll be there. *Chill, dude. She's only a friend. Her brother's right. She's not for me.* Anyway, for two people to be together, they should start by being open to the idea of marriage, yet it's not even on her radar screen.

In twenty days I'll also cross paths again with the one guy who most wants to keep us apart—and with another, who seems to want to get just as close to her as me. I'm nervy about it, which makes me nervy for being nervy.

We stand for the National Anthem. I touch my hand over my heart out of habit, although I'm not holding a cap. I think about my

Dad, who immigrated to this country from Israel shortly before the 1967 war. *What if this Darius guy is Palestinian?* His last name, Salamah, could be an Arab name from anywhere, but it happens to be also the name of someone my dad once knew. I found her love letters years ago—typical of Dad not to hide them very well. I never told him what I found; I wonder what his reaction will be when he hears the name. I text him the 'trio selfie' with a little note: c u n 20 days.

Chapter 18

Darius • Calabria, Italy

The cinnamon nodes of dried fig leaves are not enough to calm my other senses. I'm ready for this to be over—yet, in some ways, today is an odd gift. I've behaved myself for long enough: a bit of action would be welcome. Now's my chance to let loose the hate that's boiled too long inside me. At moments like these, I understand why men make war. Hate is formidable. It intoxicates. You feel larger, vindicated, more alive. Hate gives meaning and purpose: a reason to exist. *Or is that love?*

By the time today's performance ends, the *padrone's* pigs will wish they had no ears.

My friend the priest places a finger against one nostril and blows out the other—an odd choice for the signal; still, it begins.

I pound a ball in the dirt for effect and slam my glove to the mound. My tongue releases fire. I babble and blubber, rant and rage, gesture, gesticulate, and generally go berserk.

Just as I'd suspected, it feels strangely good.

Peppe tries to calm me, truly alarmed. He thinks he's created a monster.

I dial it down a decibel before my grand exit. "I've had enough, *signore*. You were kind to try, but this life is not for me. I hate it, and everything about it!"

I do exactly as instructed. I cut toward the road and stomp downhill past the neighbor's farm. I soon hear the revving of an engine. Its whir is muscular. This is no matchbox.

Also, it's getting closer.

My feet head automatically off the pavement toward the safety of the grass. But my body will not run. I refuse to do it. I turn to face my nemesis.

I've seen the driver and the guy riding shotgun before. It's my jailers from two months ago! Hard to believe that the *padrone* has given them a second chance. The driver—I hadn't noticed it before—bears a resemblance to the boss himself. My imagination tricks me, as his partner's head morphs into that of the boar. The man with the boar's head waves a handgun in my face as he leaps from the vehicle, screaming at me to get into the back of the van.

He yanks the tailgates open with a loud creak. But not loud enough to drown his barb—a favorite Muslim slur.

Before I can draw breath a staccato burst of gunfire stuns all three of us in quick succession. The left front tire and left rear tire are in ribbons. The van slowly keels sideways as the driver ducks out the passenger door. The men scramble toward my side. As for me—thanks to habit—my hands are in the air.

Breathe. Breathe. Oh God, I don't need this now. Stay calm. Think. Focus.

Peppe's shouts ground me. Gravel shuffles; more shouts. The posse is rushing down the hillside.

A middle-aged man is leading, not in uniform, but still exuding the kind of command that goes beyond the gun belt around his jeans and the Uzi in his hand. His words, too, carry power. In response, the pigs drop their weapons.

Peppe keeps yelling something, but it takes me a moment to process what it is. ("Get away from those men!") Then he is with me, embracing me. *Oh, Allah, how I've come to love this man!*

The policeman doesn't even look at me as we pass each other. He's focused on the pigs.

I thank him just the same.

•••••••••••

It's hours later. The early evening excitement has given way to a mini-celebration around the dinner table. The *signora* has cooked a meal as close to my Arab palette as she could muster with the ingredients she could find. She appears especially proud and contented this evening. I ask her why she went to such trouble.

"The meal was no trouble," she says—with an accent on the word 'meal,' as if something else she'd done today *was*. Realization creeps across the table, past the pasta and the lentils, the fish and the onions.

I lift her trigger finger to my lips, saying, "But how—"

A sly smile is followed by a soft wink. Her hand cups the stubble of my cheek.

She speaks quietly, in a simple, sensible tone. "No man wants to marry a woman who shoots better than he does."

Chapter 19

Eli • Sicily, November 2014

Our Alitalia flight from Rome dips toward a sun-smitten Sicilian sea. My father, playing tour guide, points out Mount Etna's smoking summit. I marvel. *How do people live so close to a tempest and not worry when she'll blow? Does every year that passes without a Pompeii dull the imagination?* Having grown up in New Jersey, my first earthquake at Stanford scared the crap out of me. But when no damage was incurred, I soon grew as accustomed to tremblers as the natives.

"There's the ancient Greek theater of Taormina, a baby at 2000 years young, at least compared to the wonders of the Middle East."

My father's Israeli accent is almost gone after years as an American, but his bias toward his homeland hasn't diminished. What else can I expect from an architect?—He certainly appreciates structures still standing after thousands of years far more than your average tourist.

"Do you remember that word some of your Italian buddies from the old neighborhood used to use for idiots?" he asks.

"You mean, *stunads*?"

"Yeah. I always liked that word. That's what I think about when I see all the crowds of gawking tourists in Italy. There's so much more to captivate throughout the whole of the Middle East, but too many *stunads* are in charge; they'd rather divide and conquer with fear and destruction than unite, and invite the world to our door."

Hmm. He said "our."

"I hear people all the time say they'd like to visit Israel's holy sites or Egypt's pyramids, but they're too afraid," he continues. "Plenty still go, but what of the lost opportunities? The exotic sites of Persia have been off-limits for years, and now Syria's architectural history from Aleppo to Damascus is about to be erased—not to mention what's already happened in Baghdad and elsewhere in Iraq."

"Maybe you're the *stunad*, Dad."

"Watch your mouth, superstar. You may be too famous for a spanking, but you're never too special for a piece of my tongue." He's only half-joking.

"Sorry. I'm not trying to disrespect my old man. Just making a point."

"Oh, really? And what point might that be?"

"That to some people ideology trumps archeology. And who is to say your opinion is right and theirs wrong?"

"History. Something of which you sorely lack knowledge. I can't believe how much I paid for your fancy education to leave you so bereft of it. Your grandmother always used to say I was a poet with a politician for a son. She used to predict that we'd come to blows."

Bubbie was half-right. I wonder if my status as an only child has forced us to keep the peace? If my mother hadn't died when I was two, would we rarely speak to each other? I'd like to think this wouldn't be the case, but deep down—and I suspect Dad feels the same—we know that we're all we've got.

The pilot hits the brakes, our philosophical argument sticking on the runway. An airbag explodes inside my chest. She said she'd be waiting for us, outside baggage claim.

•••••••••••

The pile of black waves atop her head beckons to me first. Then her smile blitzes me, like the jump to light speed. A strange power reverberates between us, around us, over and under. It's not the first time I've felt this thing she has. Once it hit me before I even saw her. I said "Hello, Fatima" before turning around, and she wondered if I had eyes in the back of my head... I'm not the only one who senses this energy, either. My Dad noticed it too, the first time they met; and he's noticing it again now.

"*Ciao, Signore* Kohn. So nice to see you again." My father bends in half to hug her.

I don't know why, but I pick her up and squeeze. She's like a doll with a fur cap. I set her back on her feet, like a porcelain tea cup, but I can't lose the stupid grin that takes control of my face. I'm not sure I even care.

My skin registers mid-70s and no humidity as we follow her to the car. She leans into the driver's window and asks him to open the trunk of the big black Mercedes.

"I thought you'd pick us up in something more your size," I tease her.

"This has plenty of room for suitcases: Mama uses it for guests at the villa. My feet can't even reach the pedals."

We laugh and get in the back seat together; Dad sits in the front.

Damn. The driver is Paolo.

"Welcome to our home," he says, with false bravado.

Dad leans over to shake his hand. "Thank you. We can't thank your mother enough for this wonderful invitation."

Paolo's trying to hide a scowl that—for a split second—twitches across his face. Dad says, "Eli tells me your rehab is going well."

"I had some setbacks early on, but recently I've been doing far better than I'd hoped. I plan to hit in the exhibition tomorrow. Where are Leyland and his wife, anyway?"

"Change of plan. He ended up having to fly to Germany for a meeting, so he's getting in later in the day," I tell him. "His wife can't make it at all: their youngest took a tumble and broke his leg. The kid's going to be fine, but the Mama Bear didn't want to leave her cub."

"I don't blame her," Fatima says softly.

"Have your uncle and Darius arrived yet?" I ask.

"Mama's picking them up at the train station after her meeting. They might even be there already," Paolo says.

We wind past some of the most gorgeous scenery I've ever seen in my life. It's like the Californian coast on steroids.

After ten minutes Fatima says, "We're here!" Though still we drive on, down a corridor of the pines I call umbrella trees.

At the end of another mile the road opens into a football field-sized cobbled courtyard in weathered brown, embellished with white arches. The villa itself is one of several stone buildings, each covered in purple vines, with a subtle pink on the most distant one.

"The building with the pink vines is the winery."

She reads my mind.

"I'll show you the batting cage later," Paolo tells me, "after your wine tour."

I barely hear him, as my eyes are glued to a piece of history more my speed. Fatima pats it on the hood as we roll our suitcases toward the villa.

"I wish my left eye could concentrate without my right," my father says. "I don't know what's more impressive, the door to your home or Paolo's little toy here."

"It's not my toy, it's my mother's. Well, to be honest, it was her father's, but now no one but Mama is allowed to drive it. She claims I don't have the sensibilities for such craftsmanship. 'A Testarossa is a driver's ride,' she says—Fatima and I don't qualify. According to Mama, all we do is motor our behinds from one place to another, with no appreciation for the journey."

"Is your mother always so passionate about everything she does?" Dad asks, perhaps a little too obviously.

If Paolo notices, he doesn't show it: his sister is quick to fill the silence, "Before our father died, Mama played at life the way these two play baseball. Two and a half years on I'd say she's shifted out of low gear, but still isn't interested in racing to win."

Her metaphor is a cue. A red Alfa Romeo emerges from under the line of trees.

"She's driving my car," Paolo tells Dad.

With Darius in it. Dad doesn't even notice; he's too focused on Mrs. Giobatti.

I'm more intrigued by Darius—the subtle familiarity of his face unnerves me even more in person than it did online. *Will Dad spot a resemblance between us—and, still more importantly—how will he react to Darius's last name? Or am I being crazy to imagine that there might be a connection? It's not as if it's such an unusual name in the Middle East...* Fatima runs to her uncle, while my nemesis waits his turn.

Darius does a funny sort of half-squat, encircling Fatima with his arms. If I didn't know better, I'd guess the uncle/priest/coach to be about 65, but as I get closer the lines of his face suggest a greater seniority. Mrs. Giobatti looks fetching in what I'm guessing is Valentino or Gucci or some other high fashion brand. Her hair is tied at the nape of her neck in finest silk.

Are we in some kind of wine commercial or perfume ad or something? If so, central casting has got Fatima's character all wrong. She seems out of place in this scene, but in reality she infuses it. I can't help thinking that, without her, we'd all fall off the page.

"*Buon giorno; bienvenuto,*" Mrs. Giobatti says. "I'm so happy you're here. All our other guests have left us. November through February is far too quiet at Villa Multicino!" She does that double-cheek kiss-kiss thing.

"Permit me to present my uncle, Giuseppe Colbino," she says to Dad.

My father has to tear his attention from Darius's face to greet the priest.

He must see it too.

Dad and I shake hands with *Signore* Colbino. His grip is thirty years younger than his face. I wonder: *Does he wear that collar when he's coaching?*

Paolo takes over the pleasantries. "Darius Salamah, this is Abe and Eli Kohn."

Oh no, it's worse than I imagined. My father is choking: on air, on saliva, on his past? Concerned, I thump his back: "Dad! Are you all right?"

"Yes, yes, of course I am. I'm fine." His voice is husky; he tries clearing his throat.

Then the weirdest thing happens. My father takes his hand from his throat and extends it tentatively toward Darius, as if afraid to make contact. Darius's greeting is cool.

Dad recovers, but not quickly enough. I'm sensing everyone's curiosity, thick in the air. "Sorry to stare, but you, um, kind of remind me of someone," he says. "Salamah, you say? I knew a family of that name, a long time ago. Are you Palestinian?"

"Half. My mother is...was Persian, from Tehran."

"I'm sorry for your loss. It's unbelievable, what's happening in your country."

"Thank you," Darius returns, his tone not inviting further comment.

The door my Dad was admiring creaks open. It's painted turquoise, to match the villa's window shutters. Out of it comes the *grande dame* of the property. She shuffles in the greatest hurry her old bones can manage toward the priest. I'd forgotten that they're brother and sister.

They hold each other so sweetly. *Who will hug me like that in my old age?*

They aren't the least ashamed of their tears.

"My ears fail me more and more each day. I never heard *le macchine*," she says. "And now I'm late to the party!"

Mrs. Giobatti introduces her mother to us.

Damn. She too has a good grip. Maybe it's the surroundings that are so invigorating? Olive groves, fruit trees and an elaborate vegetable garden pass before my eyes. On the flip side of our entrance, rows of robust gnarls slope in tiers toward a distant view of church domes and bell towers, the whole bordering a vast blue sky and sea.

Mrs. Multicino orders Paolo to take our bags, and suggests that Fatima give us a quick tour before dinner. Paolo squints and presses his lips together—just in time, I sense, to smother an objection. *This woman rules.*

She and her daughter each loop an arm through Mr. Colbino's—Father Colbino's—what should I call him? Dad looks subtly disappointed as Paolo's mother waves farewell; I remember at Spring Training he seemed attracted to her...apparently, he still is. She promises we'll enjoy the walk after sitting so long in transit. "Mama and I need to finish dinner," she tells us.

I watch Fatima gracefully slip her arm through Dad's, as they lead the way. *I wish it was me.* I want to be chosen by her over all others. I especially want to be chosen over Darius. After all, I'm only here for a few days. He'll be here for who knows how long, to walk with her, talk with her...

Dad's clearly as enchanted with the daughter as with the mother. Darius and I follow them like sulky puppies.

•••••••••••

The property is magnificent. My father points to the sky. "Look, Eli, you can see Mount Etna from here. It's not fair to the rest of the world for these people to call this place home." Paolo joins us in time to show off his workout digs. He seems to have everything he needs—except a team.

Having said that, I'm secretly rooting for the old Paolo to magically reappear in the exhibition tomorrow. I badly miss his bat in our lineup even more than I enjoy the new peace and tranquility in the clubhouse. I want to win. Period. I wouldn't admit it to his face, but we need Paolo's firepower to become champions: he's a former Rookie of the Year for a reason.

At the same time, I don't believe in miracles. Back injuries are a bitch. *Maybe his wasn't as serious as originally thought, though; doctors aren't always right...*

Nature's smells are gradually supplanted by cooked ones, as a grape arbor opens out into a covered brick patio.

"They must have needed a forklift to get that stone table in here," Dad marvels.

Trust him to notice the table rather than the assorted delicacies it's displaying.

"Actually, we think it was the first thing built on the property," Mrs. Multicino tells him. "If you look underneath, you'll see that the bricks of the patio were set around its pedestals. It's volcanic, and legend has it that a rock landed here after an ancient eruption and was later sculpted into this masterpiece. The entire property was a *latifundium*: land granted to a Roman noble for agricultural purposes."

"Fascinating," says Dad, as she continues, "Truly, the entire history of Sicily is one of occupation. This property alone is said to have been owned by Roman, Vandal, Byzantine, Islamic, Norman, and Spanish overlords. My late husband's family has been charged with its safekeeping for over 150 years; but we're really merely its latest caretakers."

I know from Fatima that her grandmother ran the family wine business before Silvana took over. I'm even more impressed by the old woman's English than with the table.

"Beautiful," says Dad, running his fingers over the top. "And it's still used today for its original purpose?"

"Precisely," says Mrs. Multicino. "And it's my intention to ensure that it remains so, as long as our volcano will allow. She's still very active, more so, since 2001. Her last major tantrum occurred in 1669, when her molten tears flowed all the way into Catania. Some locals think she's angry that people keep fighting for control of her island. I think she's just getting warmed up to show who's *really* the boss of this place!"

I notice Darius's face as she speaks. He seems to hang on her every word. I suspect volcanic tendencies in him. His eyes are hot.

Chapter 20

Darius

I'm almost at home here. I think I could stay forever. I haven't prayed in months, but this place nearly makes me want to try. I wish I could bottle the harmony that seeps from every beautiful thing I see around me, to drink from it when anxiety starts to scratch at my senses...

Eli flirts openly with Fatima. Beauty is suddenly replaced by an ugly urge to palm his face and shove him off this patio. Instead I speak to Fatima in Italian—cutting him off cold. He's the only blemish on this day. Even Paolo has been tolerable due to his insisting we talk baseball. I'm surprised how comfortable I am with it now; I suppose studying film each night with Peppe has taught me the lingo of the sport. It's been a balm to me, as the best way to fight my nerves is to stay busy, even distracted. As for Peppe, he isn't only a priest, coach, and mentor, but also a psychologist, I think. He's kept me occupied every waking moment since the day he rescued me from the *padrone*. Slowly, I'm healing.

Fatima is the best medicine of all. It's hard to believe it's been over two months now that I've been able to talk with her most nights. I also appreciate the times she's got me on the phone to act as an interpreter for a refugee without Italian or English. It makes me feel useful—and, of course, it's the least I can do, after all that Sister Colleen and her assistants did for me.

Being useful is the key. It's why I still want to be a doctor. Baseball is only the means to an end for me. I could never be like Paolo—he speaks of the sport as if it's life itself! I've seen enough of death to know what for me will bring authentic life... But, we all need to make a living; and, if this game might pay for my education, then I'm in.

I often catch Eli's father staring at me. The weirdest part is that I would like—if it wasn't rude—to stare right back. I'm both drawn to and unsettled by this man: it's as if the nerve endings in my body are getting disorientating signals. Mixed marriages between Palestinians and Jews are rare, but they've been known to happen: this might explain the resemblance. I wonder how well he knows his family tree.

But he can keep that information to himself. Considering the long hatred between our peoples, the last thing I want to hear is that we're any more closely related than age-old DNA would suggest.

"How's the shoulder, Eli? Are you up for catching Darius later?" Paolo asks.

"Oh no, I'm not going to allow any advance scouting," Peppe says.

"But that's not fair! He's watched plenty of old footage of me hitting."

"You've been playing the sport since you were a boy. That's your advantage," Peppe says.

A car engine hums, getting closer and closer up the drive, followed by the honk of a horn.

"Bet that's the infamous Leyland Tilson," Paolo says.

His chair scrapes across the pavers and he's gone. *A little anxious perhaps?*

•••••••••••

Paolo soon returns with a short man whose handsome face makes up for his lack of both height and hair. He knows everyone except Peppe and me, and seems genuinely glad to be here. His handshake is sure and his smile that of a man brimming with confidence. With his arrival we commence eating...and eating...and eating. The *signora* cooks for Peppe and me three times a day, but never as much as this. It reminds me of the wedding where I first encountered this family.

Finally, Peppe recounts the story of the *padrone's* men in San Mango. *Signora* Multicino, however, guesses the ending before anyone. Peppe claps and laughs at the stunned look on the others' faces. They can't believe she's right.

"Of course you would guess, *mia sorella*. I forgot how well you once could handle a rifle." Peppe smiles proudly at his sister. "When we were children we would hunt pheasant with our father; I still have his guns. It was one of them which the *signora* used to shoot the tires."

"How old is this woman?" Eli's father asks incredulously.

"Sixtyish," Mrs. Giobatti replies.

"Why do I get the feeling you also know your way around a weapon?" Mr. Kohn asks Paolo and Fatima's mother.

"Ah, well, if you grow up on a farm you learn these things. A shotgun or a knife are as much tools of the trade as a spade and a hoe."

Paolo, twirling pasta along the side of his plate, tilts his head in response to his mother's words. He looks up to find my eyes on him. It's a noisy table; almost everyone is engaged in conversation. But suddenly the silence between us is even louder than that between Eli and me.

Chapter 21

Darius

Figs have been followed by grapes, then olives and now chestnuts. The season has come for me to bear fruit.

The word is out. The packed bleachers prove it.

Paolo does a few calisthenics near the home team dugout on the third base line. Then he points to Mount Etna in the distance, joking, "My eyes say Italy, but my nose says Ohio. Whose ridiculous idea was it to sell hot dogs?"

His teammates laugh. They're having as much fun as their children, who are giggling while chasing balls in the outfield.

The men greet Paolo like a warrior hero returned to his people.

They only glare at me.

As we cross the diamond to the opposite dugout, Peppe slows his pace. "Hmm. I count three radar guns," he says. Then someone yells a derogatory slur about, "the refugee."

Peppe seizes the opportunity to lecture me: "This day presents a perfect scenario, at this point in your training. So far you've been pitching for Paolo, me, a few peeping children, and the birds and bees of the farm. Today you have the chance to learn how to stay focused in enemy territory. You must establish your command early, stealing the energy from their jeering tongues. All the foolish noise they're making now—listen to it—remember it—because in fifteen minutes it'll be so quiet you'll be able to hear the wind tell you where it's been."

Peppe fits on his glove to begin our game of catch: an easy warm-up, nothing showy. We have no catcher of our own, so Peppe calls to Paolo to send over the designated back-stop.

In the Italian League, a pitcher is only permitted three advance throws before facing the first hitter of the inning, but Paolo offers us the mound for as long as we'd like. Surprisingly, it's he who snaps on the tools and crouches behind the plate for a first-hand review of his competition. The crowd eats it up, dishing up mock accolades for Catania's new catcher. "What's wrong, Paolo?" someone shouts. "Are your young legs too tired for centerfield, that you need to squat behind home plate?"

Paolo borrows the umpire's brush. He bends over to clean the white pentagon, deliberately wiggling his ass toward those bleachers in general and that joker in particular. Another comedian promises to kiss his fine fanny in the middle of Catania's busiest piazza if he can park five homers off "the foreigner."

Paolo shakes his head and pulls the protective mask down over his face. He punches the glove and squats tepidly. I bet he forgot to wear a cup. He's probably praying I'm accurate.

I start at 50% power. Straight fastballs are all I'll offer for now, first, because Paolo probably can't handle much else, and second, because two can play at this game... I scout the stands for Fatima and find her hair. Her mother sits on her left, Eli on her right.

Damn.

The agent fiddles with his radar gun while Eli entertains the women. His father is watching me intently. I hear the rush of the breeze before it chases sand into my eyes. They tear up so much that Peppe insists I borrow his handkerchief.

Someone yells, "Look, he's afraid. He cries before even facing the first hitter!"

A few degrees at a time I ramp up my speed until I hear someone yell, "140." I compute the numbers in my head: 87 mph.

I glance at Peppe, hiding my smile inside my glove. I have plenty left in the tank.

Mystery solved. Adrenaline rush. *I want to blow them away.*

Peppe waves his arms, "Fine. He's ready." He walks to the mound and puts his face very close to mine. "Do not throw any harder than this the first time through the lineup. You can speed up a bit for Paolo, who'll hit last, but otherwise, remember why we're here: We're here for you to test your pitches against live bait. We're here for you to experience moving men off the plate, mixing up your repertoire, hitting your spots for strikeouts, groundouts, and flies.

"We are NOT here for you to blow out your arm. We are NOT here for you to learn how fast the technology says you can throw. And we are NOT here for you to show off to Fatima. Well, maybe that last one, just a little." And with that he winks and returns to the dugout.

"*Comincia,*" he shouts to his nephew, with a wave of his right arm.

Suddenly everyone is laughing and clapping in rhythm. Peppe

curses, not so low that I can't hear him.

And this is why: the first hitter is a 'little person.' I recall a story Peppe told me. The legendary Cleveland owner of the 1940s once signed a dwarf to a contract for one game, hoping to rattle the opposing pitcher by presenting a shrunken strike zone. Perhaps he told Paolo that tale too?

I decide that I might as well have some fun of my own. I pull off my glove with a fake flourish and wave it angrily in the air. Then I shake my head in a grand show, while pacing around my tiny island in phony frustration. The crowd loves it.

The diminutive batter actually has the *coglioni* to mock me, "What's wrong, little boy? Aren't I man enough for you?" I respond with a practiced bow, as from a Sultan's court. *I need time to adjust. This joke has caught me by surprise.* Breathing deep, I remind myself to miss low.

The ball floats from my hand, slowly but perfectly into the mini-wheelhouse. The 200 umps in the stands call 'ball,' but the one who counts gets it right. The crowd, displeased, curse the poor umpire, his wife, his parents and grandparents, his dog—even his car.

I peek at Peppe, who gives a sideways glance that says, *"You've proved your point, now let them have their fun."*

I throw the next one in the dirt, to the relief of the umpire and the glee of the audience. With the next, I do the same. The dwarf has no intention of swinging, so I quickly dispense with the drama with two more around Grumpy's eyes. Suddenly he morphs into Happy and skips to first base under a standing ovation. He blows kisses to his adoring fans, and then feigns a lead from first base. While this improvisation continues behind my back, I concentrate on my first real hitter.

After consulting briefly with my catcher, I keep my speed as ordered and shave the right-hander with a curveball inside. The man throws his arms up and his hips back to avoid castration.

He gets it. I'm for real.

He steps out of the box to gather himself, down 0–1. The catcher signals for a fastball up. The batter swings, but can't get around on the ball quick enough: 0–2. He spits on the ground and whines to the catcher for sucking him in, "Whose side are you on anyway?"

"His," the backstop replies, "or would you prefer I just blab each pitch to you beforehand?"

The batter curses under his breath, then steps back within the white lines. He glares at me, determined not to be fooled again. But the changeup, beautifully executed at perfect speed, he never sees coming. He swings so hard he spins himself into the dirt like a drill bit.

I look at Peppe. Now it's his turn to hide his laugh behind his glove. He's thrilled I now understand my mentor's obsession with this pitch. I recall his words the first time he taught me the favorite of his repertoire:

"I love the changeup, Darius. It's by far the queen of the hive for me. This pitch is like a naughty girl who teases you to come and get her before disappearing from your eyes. It makes chicken soup look like chicken shit." He laughed, adding, "I threw out many heavy hitters, flailing at this pitch. Did they get hot! Once, the star hitter for Bologna, Nettuno's bitter rival, broke his bat over his knee, before turning from the batter's box to the dugout. He was angry with me, with himself, and with life, it seemed. The crowd loved it! Another time I struck out a guy who swung so hard his legs flew out from under him. He just lay there for a moment—completely winded—then he stood up and took a bow, like the great Caruso. The fans followed his lead with a standing ovation. It was hilarious... He even had the balls to come out for a curtain call. The next time he came to bat I plunked him on the ass for that little show!"

I shake loose the web of memory as a leftie strides to the opposite box, while the crowd continues to barrage the previous batter with creative Italian insults.

The next victim gets ready. I read the catcher's signal, nod, and promptly brush back this knucklehead as well.

Was he asleep during the last at-bat? Maybe he thinks I can't do the same from the left-hand side? At least my catcher has a clue.

My next pitch is a fastball up in the zone. I'm amazed at how well my partner knows his teammates. I wonder if he'll ask me to deliver the changeup again for strike three.

Unbelievable!

For a second, I wonder if the catcher is switching sides, but when a mirror image of the last chump happens its clear he's on mine.

Batter number three is perhaps a hair sharper. He challenges me to mix it up a bit more. The guy even manages to foul one off. But, in the end, he too goes down with a thud.

The dwarf meanwhile has been "stealing" bases and, to the delight of the crowd, pretends to snatch home. I play the good sport and wave him off the field. But as Paolo appears, the hush over the sun-drenched field can only mean that the sitcom is over and the drama about to unfold.

My arm feels like it has a life of its own. It's wired. I have the impulse to swoop like a condor. But I'm married to Peppe's instruction and resolve to take myself up only a notch. *But how I itch to unleash myself like a whip.*

Paolo, however, is no idiot. He senses I'm reining in. He also probably remembers that his uncle threw four pitches in his day. He knows which three he's already seen.

Sweat drips into my brow. I wear no cap—mostly because I've never worn one. Unlike the others I have no uniform: instead I wear a white t-shirt, blue sweatpants and castoff cleats from the man I now face. I wipe my forehead with my wrist and look for Fatima. She sits with her arms partially crossed, chin cupped in her right hand. *Who's she rooting for?*

I tap the pitching rubber, receive the sign, nod assent, and let loose. The pop of the mitt is a noise unfamiliar to this audience. They all jerk in unison. A buzz begins to diffuse through the ranks. I breathe deeply: *adrenaline is a tough thing to control.*

Paolo has taken the first pitch fastball, down the middle. It's the right choice, rather like a polite greeting between noblemen; he's willing to waste a strike in order to gauge my speed. Unlike the others, he stands off the plate, giving me my due. Does he know the next pitch will be the deuce? I like this pitch—the curveball—and its nickname, based on the fact that it's signed with two fingers. He probably guesses that it's coming, but isn't sure where. I aim low and away.

Incoming.

He guesses right, catches a piece of it, and turns it into a souvenir. *Wow. This guy is good, really good.* Even though he's down two strikes I sense his danger.

For the first time today I throw the slider.

Paolo turns on it nearly perfectly, spanking it hard. It shoots deep down the left field line, hooking, hooking—foul—missing a trip around the bases by a single foot.

The crowd is on its feet, screaming, clapping, chanting, alive with anticipation.

I know he's expecting the changeup, but, unlike the others, he wisely tries not to do too much with the pitch. His strategy works. He bloops the ball into shallow right. In a real game everyone knows Paolo's smack would have dropped for a hit. It isn't the home run they wanted, but the fans still cheer in appreciation for their country's baseball star. Even Peppe stands and claps, while Paolo touches the brim of his cap in gratitude, smiling at his uncle. The catcher's ten-year-old son scoops up the ball and fires it back at me, as the crowd cheers his effort.

As Fatima sits down with the others Eli whispers something in her ear.

I hate that he's so close to her while I'm so far away!

The little person doesn't return to action, while the three batters that follow are left grumbling to themselves again. Even Paolo is summarily dispensed of in round two. Rounds three and four aren't much different, although Paolo is learning more with each at bat: I have to work harder for both outs.

In his fifth and the final chance of this pre-determined-four-hitters-in-five-innings exhibition (rather than the traditional nine of each), I begin to feel tired for the first time. Paolo had dazzled the crowd in his fourth trip to the plate by fouling off ten pitches before striking out; I suspect that he intends no encore.

I'm impressed not only by his ability to make contact, but also by his keen mind. I find myself shaking off my catcher's signals, knowing in my gut that Paolo would guess that pitch. Cash is changing hands in the stands with every swing. The fans are hooked, noisily willing each outcome to turn in their favor.

I hope Peppe feels I've already exceeded expectations, regardless of what happens in this last showdown of the afternoon. I bet he hasn't had this much fun since the brakes went on his ancient Fiat, causing total mayhem in the produce market before he ditched it in a cistern on the mayor's farm. How I laughed when he described it to me, adding that, anyway, he hadn't voted for the guy.

My darts come and go. Paolo zeroes in on every one. He has no choice; he knows that to miss will mean a bull's-eye for me. *Damn, he's wearing me out.*

It begins in slow motion: the release of each finger from the ball, the spin of its red stitches, my arm feeling like lead, the sphere landing too easily in Paolo's oh-so-sweet spot—the spot that makes chocolate-covered canolli look like dog poo, the one where dripping-down-your-chin strawberry gelato tastes like tofu and, yes, the precise place where Nonna's award-winning pasta sauce is reduced to muck. Sweet for Paolo is sour for me—*boom!*—just like that. NASA couldn't have launched it better.

I turn like a weather vane in a storm, nausea floods into my throat. At that moment I resolve to never feel that sick after a pitch, ever again.

Paolo takes a champion's stroll around the bases, thrilling even those who'd lost their bet. He pumps his fist in the air then gestures upward with both arms, cranking up the applause.

I remain on the mound, remove my glove, and tuck it under my arm. I clap graciously for Catania's hero, Fatima's brother, Peppe's nephew, and—maybe someday—my friend.

One more base and he's home. But instead Paolo stops at the third bag. Rather than jog to home plate he stretches out his hand to me as he cuts across the diamond toward the pitcher's mound. But as the space between us shrinks to a couple of feet, he thinks better of his offered hand and hugs me instead—very Italian, but very phony. He doesn't even make eye contact before quickly returning his attention to the crowd.

Hours later, I learn from Fatima that Paolo had his own side bets going. He was likely hugging me for the money I'd just earned him. I guess he wanted to ensure he got *something* out of all the effort he's expended on me, just in case his plan to bring me to Cleveland goes bust.

Chapter 22

Fatima

It's such a simple thing. Pick up the glass of vino and toast with the rest. But my arm won't do what my brain is telling it to do. Everyone is looking at me, waiting.

"My stomach's a little queasy. I think I'll skip the wine tonight," I murmur. *I pray my face isn't caught in the lie.*

Glasses clink. Paolo can't stop talking. Good. He's distracting everyone, except Mama and Nonna, who both glance at me warily. I give them an "it's nothing" grimace and mercifully manage to pick up my fork. Watching me maintaining an appetite seems to give them comfort.

What's happening to me? I hate to see a doctor, especially one nearby. To keep a secret from the two most well-connected women from Messina to Syracuse is like trying to cap Mount Etna...

I'll figure it out tomorrow. Tonight is for celebrating. Darius and Paolo both proved to Leyland that they can play. Now it's up to him to convince the *real* scouts.

I remember the first time Leyland met with my parents, shortly before Papa passed away. Mama did all the negotiating. I don't think Leyland was prepared for some of her demands—or for her style, either. For example, when Paolo was offered an Italian interpreter for assistance, Mama was emphatic. "Absolutely not," she'd said. "He'll never learn English if he's kept suckling at the tit." Poor Leyland wasn't accustomed to our ways of speaking. He almost choked on our best house red.

Eli's teasing his father mercilessly. "Tell Leyland about that geezer league you joined."

"It's not a geezer league. Didn't I teach you to respect your elders? It's a senior hoops league."

"I'm only busting you because it's a bad idea and I wish you'd quit. Clothes can hide your bruises and your knee brace. That shiner under your eye, however, hasn't completely cleared. Makeup won't cover it."

"Basketball calms my nerves."

"That's why alcohol was invented, Dad."

Mama's laughing in notes I haven't heard in some time.

I'm sure Paolo notices. He's trying to be polite, but I can see the prospect of our mother enjoying Abe's company is a concept he can't accept. At first I thought that there was nothing in it: now... I'm not so sure.

Still, doesn't everyone have a right to pursue their own version of happiness?

"Mama, remember when Papa bought me a basketball and drilled a hoop to the barn in the west fields? I couldn't believe he knew how to play, let alone utterly dominate. He never once let me win."

"How does a child learn how to succeed if his parents let him win? Will his boss be so kind?"

"True, *my* boss isn't," Paolo says.

The more we laugh the more you'd think the atmosphere at the table would slip into neutral: instead I sense we're racing out of control. Darius speaks to me in Italian, effectively cutting Eli out of the conversation. Eli then starts chatting about mutual acquaintances at the ball club, in order to counterpunch Darius. Meanwhile Paolo is copying Darius's language snubbing tactics in an effort to steer Mama's attention away from Abe Kohn while Zio and Nonna are enjoying a bit of age-old sibling rivalry regarding who grows the best tomatoes.

Leyland skillfully steers the conversation around to a more pressing subject: how to obtain a visa for Darius. It's clearly complicated. Immediately, he suggests that Eli lobby his owner and general manager on Darius's behalf. Eli's not unwilling, but he doesn't commit himself, either: "I'll need to catch him myself first."

"Perfect. I'll film the session," Paolo adds.

"Good," says Leyland. "If the team wants him bad enough, between my contacts and Mr. Powers' political clout, we can probably cut through the usual red tape. My PR team can handle swaying fans. Fans are like team brass—they just want a winner. But non-fans might put up a fight, could even get ugly. The key is to reduce our risk."

"Which means, as long as you aren't hiding any skeletons, Darius, we'll be fine," Eli says.

A shadow crosses the room. It isn't the skeleton Eli might be wishing for—it's something worse.

Darius assures everyone that there's nothing to fear from him.

But I fear *for* him. This ghost is satanic.

The shadow is wrestling with my new friend right now. I see it pass between his eyes. This is one of those moments when my gift is also a curse.

I reach under the table for the Rosary beads in my pocket. I take the crucifix between my fingers and make the sign of the cross on my leg, over and over, reciting a well-worn prayer behind my lips.

Its wretched cry is heard only by me.

It's leaving. It smokes the room with its ugly odor, so ugly I can almost taste it.

And then it's gone...at least, for now.

Chapter 23

Darius

The party has broken into sections. Abe and Silvana—they insist I address them as such—are enjoying the evening *passaggiata* in uptown Taormina. Silvana boasts it's one of the best in all Italy with its four amazing *piazzas* to pleasantly slow the trek. She was teasing Abe with images of runway fashion connoisseurs alongside senior citizens, hipsters pushing baby carriages alongside typical tourists, and lovers walking arm-in-arm—unless the arm might be needed to hold pistachio *gelato*, from pistachios grown along nearby Mount Etna.

Peppe and his sister reminisce while Fatima clears the table. Mr. Tilson, I mean Leyland, invites me for a walk, leaving Paolo and Eli to their favorite subject in the batting cage.

"So. Why are you pursuing this baseball idea?" he asks me.

His words are as crisp as the night air. I'm cautious; I measure my response.

"It's the means to an end. I have no money, so I need a job. I want to go to medical school, but first I must be accepted to a university. The school I attended in Syria has been obliterated by shelling. Without the proper transcripts and entrance exams I'm a scholastic nomad."

"Your language skills would have great value to many employers, I'm sure."

It's an obvious assessment, and one I've been told many times. I sense he's testing my commitment. Suddenly that dreaded *whoosh* rushes over me. My ears buzz. My body tingles, as if all the blood is draining toward my toes. *Breathe. Breathe. It's a beautiful night in a beautiful place with beautiful people. This sports agent means no harm. He's just doing his diligence. Smell the whiff of pine on the breeze.* I hate it when my nerves tell me to run away. But I know only too well that bolting won't chase these tremors. Instead, I try desperately to focus on the beauty around me and on the calm collectedness in Leyland's demeanor. But, deep down, all I can think is *I don't deserve this. Too many are dead. Why am I still alive?*

"Paolo tells me his great-uncle is retiring and moving here with the rest of the family," Leyland says.

I picture the one member of his clan that calms me. *Fatima. Yes. Think of Fatima. She's the ultimate antidote to my anxiety.*

"Signore Peppe could continue as your coach while you transition from pitcher to player," Leyland continues. "You need to learn your position in relation to the other men on the field. Paolo has plenty of friends to fill those roles; they could run you through the necessary drills."

I consider, while he notes, "You throw hard enough to excite curiosity in the best ball clubs. However, command of the strike zone is what separates hard throwers from skilled pitchers. You seem to be on your way in that regard. Clearly, you're also extremely bright, with the ability to grasp technique and strategy quickly."

"But," I prompt him.

"But...you need to decide if you really want me to help you. I can't help if you're not willing to be completely honest with me."

I want to trust him. But should I?

"The world of high-profile pro sport is not what you see on television," Leyland adds. "What you see on TV is only the parts that the fans want to see. Without fans the business doesn't exist. And it's every bit a business, Darius. Fans flock to sport to escape the anxieties of everyday life. But for those who work in the sports business, it *is* everyday life—complete with all the stress, drama, anxieties, and physical demands of any other job. In fact, what appears to be the greatest job on the planet comes with far more stress than the average construction job! If you choose this life, you'll need my help for far more than wage negotiation. I'm the one who'll always have your back, no matter what happens."

His words are convincing, but I focus briefly on his eyes as we walk toward the terraced vineyard separating us from the lights of the city below.

"History has a way of repeating itself, with individuals and families just as much as with nations and peoples," he tells me. "So I'd need to know your own history, in order to do my best by you, to protect you from the worst of the business, and help you to make the best of it."

I need to look down to search his eyes again: on one level, he's larger than I am: I'd like to have what he has. The aura of command shines from him almost as much as the moonlight from tonight's sky. *Still I doubt.*

"How did you become a sports agent?" I ask, buying time.

"We're all blessed with different gifts. My gift is the ability to put myself in the shoes of others. When I negotiate, I strive to achieve not just what's best for my client, but what's best for all concerned. Money isn't the only aspect in negotiation. For some, quality of life is strictly defined in dollars and cents, but for most there's more, much more... Athletes only have a short amount of time before their bodies will dictate the need to close the record book and to open a new chapter, for themselves and their families. I see the big picture, and work to create not just the best deal for a client, but the best life for a client. Alienating everyone else in the negotiating process in order to earn the most money usually leads to a lousy quality of life. These players are the exceptions, and my hunch is you're not one of them."

"No, I'm not. I have no desire to be the richest person in the cemetery. I've seen the quality of life of an entire nation disintegrate faster than money can buy it. I had a comfortable home, attended a good school, and had access to markets to meet our every need. Most of all I had wonderful parents. They were smart, loving, hard-working, and respected. Even though my grandparents were angered by their marriage, I still had many loving cousins as well as friends. But now...now almost all those people are dead, and my home, school, mosque, and local markets all destroyed, leaving only a wasteland, created by the delusional. What have the fighting factions won? What is better than it was before? Oh, there are a handful of people who now have more money and power, but they live in confined spaces, with no freedom from being hunted. I have more freedom than they do! It's the opera of the ridiculous—a litany of cultural rape—a dance of drunken ideologues that spin fear, twist truth, and squeeze the neck of freedom, all for their own brief moment on the world stage..."

"What happened to *you* during that time, before you landed in Italy? I don't doubt it's painful to recount, but I must know, or else I won't be able to protect you."

I breathe deeply, trying to trust. *I've told Fatima. She believes me.* This man is different, but he holds out the key to a new future with open hands. I appreciate that he doesn't coerce, threaten, tempt, or tease. He reminds me of my mother after my father and I would argue about joining the rebellion. Every word from her lips was thoughtful, sensible and spoken pragmatically—but in the end, the choice was always mine. It is again.

I take it.

Chapter 24

Fatima

Dr. Dante scribbles on a chart after examining me. His office is crisp and sterile except for some striking prints of African landscapes on the walls. I project myself into the safaris of elephants, giraffes, lions, and rhinos. I've never been to Africa. Why not? It's so much closer than the U.S. But few people from the U.S. are trying to escape to Italy: why visit a land where even the natives don't want to remain? Though it's a big place, and surely these prints come from wild and lovely places that I should wish to see.

Before any question about his safaris slips from my tongue he says, "I want you to have some more tests, Fatima. I promised your father in the last stages of his cancer that I'd never let anyone in his family wait as long as he did to be diagnosed for anything. I'm not suggesting that you have the same disease—not at all. But something neurological may be amiss here.

"I understand your brother has been invited to Spring Training again with Cleveland. A good friend of mine practices neurological medicine there, with access to much newer technology than we have. Regardless of whether or not your brother succeeds in returning to baseball, I think that you should accompany him to the States and visit my friend in Cleveland. I can have my office make the necessary referrals."

It makes sense, but, "I was hoping not to have to worry Mama at this point."

"Don't be naïve, Fatima. This is your second visit to my office in as many months, with tests at the hospital in between. I ran into your mother only last week—she was at a restaurant with some American fellow—and she told me straight out to tell you it's time to remember you have a mother."

"That sounds like something she'd say."

"Listen, you're an adult and can do as you please. But don't underestimate the strength of your mother. I've known her much longer than you have."

"But she's only just starting to enjoy life again. Mr. Kohn—Abe—has been good for her."

"He seemed very pleasant: my wife and I shared a drink with them. Comfortable in his shoes is how my wife described him.

Which struck me as funny, as that was precisely the way that I used to describe your father."

"Oh, I see the similarities too. Mama colors every challenge in black; Papa always used to open her eyes to a wider palette of possibilities. Abe Kohn has the same gift."

"I'm glad to hear it. Your mother deserves every happiness. Ah, um, does your brother appreciate her new friend?"

"Paolo? Are you kidding? But he's convinced himself that such a long-distance relationship can't survive—and besides, he's too intent upon returning to baseball to focus on much else."

"And what about you and your focus? Don't you have any questions for me?"

"Not yet. I don't want to think about it. My focus at present is still with helping Sister Colleen. She appreciates all the time you and many of your colleagues have spent with the refugees, by the way. She says your hospital has the most generous staff of all."

"I can't say this to everyone, Fatima, but I can say it to you. This job pays the bills. That job fills the soul."

Light from the golden sky in the picture of a lion pride behind Dr. Dante suddenly fills the room. I'm gone; he's gone; all the sterile stuff is gone. Even the lions and their four-legged neighbors dissipate into the light as the hazy outline of a smiling face develops. It doesn't need to be motion picture quality for me to know who it is. He's not alone. My father and Bisnonna come to me often these days. They want to tell me something, but I'm not yet able to discern what, though I feel confident that I will, when the time is right. I have no worries when I'm in this state. *Why can't everyone know this feeling, God?*

When I come around, Dr. Dante is holding my hand.

"How long was I gone?"

"I'd say a full five minutes."

"It's happening more often. Do you think it's related to my physical problems?"

"Some might think so, but I don't. I've known you too long, and your great-grandmother before you... Once, when I was only a little boy, she was at the fish market, buying the best of that morning's catch from my father. Suddenly she stopped, and stared out to sea for a minute. When she came back, she said to my father, "Don't take Domenico with you in the boat tomorrow morning."

My father was a strong believer in your great-grandmother, and did as she instructed. The next morning a freak storm blew up, completely out of nowhere. It tossed him overboard, but he was strong enough to climb back in the boat... Anyway, whatever it is that she had, you have it too. As for it's being a physical problem, well, we should all have such problems."

Chapter 25

Darius • Goodyear, Arizona, February 2015

Thus Leyland becomes my new Peppe. I miss my old coach, of course, but I'm grateful for modern technology. The combination of his restful voice and wise eyes is like carrying a slice of comfort food inside my pocket.

The juxtaposition of Fatima with a saguaro cactus is my new favorite cell screensaver. It calms me now, as members of the media file into seats behind the dugout in this new, crisp and shiny baseball facility. It doesn't have Mount Etna in the backdrop, but this grass feels almost cushiony under my cleats. Paolo and I have gone from the outhouse to the penthouse of baseball facilities.

The week I spent in Cleveland with Leyland is about to reach its climax. Mock press conferences, with his staff and the club's PR team acting the part of members of the media, have prepared me; I've been coached on everything from my appearance to my body language to my words. Pitchers and catchers officially break camp tomorrow, but today Eli, Paolo, and I will stage a demonstration to show off my new skills. That'll be the easy part of this dog and pony show. This ordeal by press will be the hardest.

The elderly black man Eli introduced to us before leaving Cleveland is smiling at me from a seat beside Abe Kohn and Silvana Giobatti. Where is Fatima? All three promised to make themselves available for questions...to vouch for my character, even...but only Eli's father and Paolo's mother are here. *Surely Fatima isn't afraid to converse in English. Her accent is thick, but that's part of her charm, and she's easily understood.*

Mr. Powers arrives, and, almost instantly, people stop talking. My new *padrone* is nothing like the old one. It's like comparing a nasty skin rash to the silky smooth face of a cosmetics actress. True to their word, he and Leyland have pulled more strings than a puppeteer to usher me into this amazing country. I've seen so little of it, so far, and yet I'm continually impressed and astonished by the orderliness of so many different kinds of cultures existing under a single government.

Our first stop was two days in New York City, with Abe Kohn showing us everything from the Statue of Liberty to the Bronx. I couldn't stop the tears when I read the inscription at the foot of the statue that has greeted so many refugees to this land. I'd thought it couldn't be true—not, at least for someone like me—but my cynicism is slowly retreating. I've seen Asian faces, black faces, men with heads wrapped in turbans and others under yarmulkes all sitting in the same subway, while Silvana has insisted I taste a different cuisine with every meal.

If the lifestyle in New York was frenetic, Cleveland's was slower, and Phoenix's a mere turtle in comparison. One country, so many different kinds of cities! The Rock-n-Roll Hall of Fame was exactly what I'd imagined of America and Americans, but the more I travel the more I see that, for all the barking in the Syrian press about the U.S. as the land of decadence, that's only part of the story, and not even the largest part. At least the creatures in this zoo aren't trying to eat each other, as in the one I left behind. I'm even beginning to think that, the more similar people are, the more dangerous they can be to each other!

But, in this moment, the last ten days of being a tourist have been a cultural education. Near Tucson I bought a Native American dream catcher and a cowboy hat in the same store where Fatima purchased a figurine of Mary—or as she called her, Our Lady of Guadalupe. From Sedona to the Grand Canyon I marveled at nature, but even more at all the languages I heard speak this country's praise.

Someone tests the microphone on the podium between the dugout and the grass.

Mr. Powers hands me a note, which I'm to read and destroy after we finish this session. It's the price I've been asked to pay for admission. I don't like it, but—for now—I have no choice. I put it in my pocket, still fretting.

Where is Fatima?

The club owner makes the first statement, followed by Leyland, and finally me. I sense surprise as I begin to speak. My script is gentle and unassertive: I smile at the prescribed moments—and then the easy part is over. As expected, the first questions are "How did I get to Europe?" and "How did I learn to speak English so well?" But, as I'd been warned, neither is asked quite as simply as this. The men and women of the press corps do their best to lead me where I don't want to go. But they also appear sympathetic when I speak of the loss of my parents. I take a deep breath of relief when, after 25 minutes, it is Paolo's turn to discuss his comeback. Still no Fatima.

No, wait, how stupid I am! I forgot, she mentioned going to Mass; it's not surprising she's late. *Someone needs to pray for me. I won't do it.*

She slips in at the back, just in time for the fun. The press appears in good spirits, after Paolo has entertained them with his usual crazy bravado and Italian quips. Eli and I warm up together for a few minutes, although we already had prepared, very thoroughly, in the bullpen before the press arrived. That bullpen session was only the second time Eli ever caught me. There was a strange atmosphere between us, and his reaction was not quite what I expected. *Part of him would prefer me to fail.*

Some of the other players, those who've arrived for camp, sprinkle themselves around the dugouts to watch us.

Showtime.

A radar gun keeps track of my speed, for all to see. Paolo makes contact with only three out of nine pitches, but two were fouled backward. One off the end of his bat lands in right field. I throw the last two at 100 and 101 mph. The rest: mid-to-high 90s.

"*Grazie Dio* I won't have to face him," Paolo yells to the audience, and everyone laughs.

The club's pitching coach finishes, throwing batting practice to Paolo and Eli from behind a screen placed on the pitching mound. Immediately, Paolo turns on one: it shoots out of the yard so fast that, at least at first, nobody claps. Shock and awe.

Eli pushes him out of the box after three more: we're being treated to a private Home Run Derby. There's something pastoral about the whole experience. I think I might like this job.Then I remember.

Damn. I forgot I have another one. I read the note and then, crumpling it, return it to my pocket. I can't trash it here...Fatima is watching me, instead of the action. I zero in on her face and let it carry me back to this baseball land of make believe. I refuse to let the reality that chases me ruin today.

Chapter 26

Paolo

After fielding the same questions over and over, the pat answers roll off Darius's tongue as soft as sleeping on satin sheets. Even the "ouch" has exited his demeanor every time anyone mentions his resemblance to Eli. His almost accent-free English impresses even the most sarcastic, while his concerted efforts to speak Spanish to our Latino teammates have already made him a firm favorite among the salsa set.

But this isn't the whole story. Minor Leaguers garner little attention during Spring Training unless they've already captured the collective imagination of the coaching staff. Darius's bio has taken a back seat to his prodigious ability to throw a baseball faster than almost anyone around, and in spots almost no one can hit. There's a certain euphoria in camp. Parallels are even being drawn between Darius and the club's greatest hurler of all time, Bob Feller. Feller, a member of the organization till the day he died at age 92, was a phenom who burst onto the Major League stage (with no Minor League tour of duty) at the age of 17. Darius is slightly older, but could lightning strike twice? Why not? After all, baseball is a game littered throughout its history with tales that begin, "Just when you think you've seen it all...

Darius's tale of loss tempers any doubts about rooting for an Arab Muslim to those who, at first, kept him at arm's length. He experienced racist remarks on several occasions during the first two weeks of camp—no surprise there. From "camel jockey" to "terrorist," the stereotypes were evident. It didn't break my heart as it did Fatima's: I'm as suspicious as anyone else of someone from a culture I only know from television. I think Darius wanted to lash back, but he wisely bit his tongue and took it out on hitters instead. *I should probably take lessons from him; Leyland keeps riding me to stay cool and exude a new serenity: the new, tantrum-free Paolo.*

Yesterday Eli's friend T.P. told Darius the story of Larry Doby and Jackie Robinson. The grace with which these two men battled racism in the American and National Leagues, beginning in 1947 (Larry with Cleveland just a few months after Jackie in Brooklyn), was something Darius probably needed to hear. He listened attentively and said how he appreciated ol' T.P.'s concern.

We both appreciate that dude's sense of humor, too. He invited us to dinner one evening when Eli was alone with his Dad, and Mama and Fatima were in Napa Valley "getting ideas." When I caught T.P. smiling at a fifty-something black woman at the next table I joked, "Too bad she's too young for you."

He said, "Son, when you get to be my age, then you can judge what a man's got left in the tank. You got a whole lot o' livin' to do before you learn that age is just a number." Then he asked us if we ever heard of Satchel Paige. Of course, we hadn't.

"Lord, you young'uns are sorely deficient in the history department. Shame on y'all! Can't you even study up on your sport, at least where your own team is concerned?" *(I love his "manner o'speakin'.")*

Anyway, he went on to explain that Satchel Paige had been a Negro League superstar and eventually a Major League pitching great who, thanks to the casual paperwork of the time, obscured his true age. Many think he was the oldest pro of all time. Paige is also credited with having been the first to say, "Age is a question of mind over matter. If you don't mind, it don't matter."

I like that line. I hope I can still remember it in 40 years.

•••••••••••

Life in Arizona moves in a rhythm I've missed, while the benefit of live games with top pros is immeasurable for Darius. He still struggles with men on base though. I heard him say last night that he hates base stealing so much that he's decided the best approach is to keep batters from getting to the first one.

Thanks to my damn back, Darius is getting more attention in camp than me. I guess I'm not quite as ready as I'd hoped. According to rumor, I'm probably going to have to start the season somewhere south of Cleveland... Haven't they considered the stress of long bus rides in the minors on an ailing body like mine? *Stunads!*

•••••••••••

This Minor League clubhouse at Spring Training is just that compared to ours. However, it still beats the hell out of anything in the Italian League. Darius is killing time with Moki Fukui, a former Japanese League standout: Mr. Prodigy working on his next language, no doubt.

Everyone's predicting Moki will be the team's closer by June. I certainly hope so, because we need a great one, badly. As for Moki himself, he has to be the happiest human I've ever met. *Don't his cheeks ever ache from all that smiling?* Moki's right fingers are talking as much as his mouth as he describes the cutter he's learned from the club's pitching *maestro*, or *"sensei,"* as he calls him.

Suddenly a door slams: Darius flinches. Manager of the big club, Mose Founder, struts into the room and stops cold. Moki and Darius stare like nervous chicks.

Now Mose is the most respected figure in camp, having led the club for 20 seasons. At 70 years young he appears ageless, without a white hair to be found on his head. His poker-straight posture and prominent dimpled chin, combined with his 6' 4" frame, could make him a poster boy for AARP. He sports only a smallish paunch with a well-padded derriere, while his pumped chest balancing his taut back muscles make him look like the swimmer he is. (He claims it's the reason for his evident vigor.)

We all rise as he shakes hands and gives us his famous 'Mr. Mose' smile. We foreigners are especially mesmerized—not just the dazzling white of his teeth against the black of his skin, but also by the fact that many people from our own homelands are missing a few teeth by his age.

"I've been gettin' good reports about you boys," Mose says. *I think his Texas drawl is pure cool.* "Y'all are tearin' it up, I hear. Keep it goin'. Sure could use ya in Cleveland when all's said and done."

Even I'm too abashed to respond, as he adds, "And you young'uns stay outta trouble now, y'hear? I don't need a repeat of last spring's stupidity or I'll have to knock heads for sure."

We all mumble agreement: even newbies like Moki and Darius have heard this story. A pair of twenty-year-old pitchers were caught with fake IDs in a Phoenix strip club. That was bad enough, but one of them foolishly decided to take on the bouncer and tore up his 'million dollar bonus baby' rotator cuff... So far this year he's a mere shadow of his former leftie self.

Just after the big man disappears, *"Il Sole Mio"* blares from my cell. Fatima speaks to me in Italian, even though we've promised ourselves to work on our English. She wants to be sure we remember our dinner reservation for tonight. I tell her I'm also inviting Moki along. It'll give me some distraction from young Darius vying for my sister's attention. He may be my teammate, but family I pray he'll *never* be.

•••••••••••

Saguaro cacti direct us to Camelback Mountain; Fatima calls them desert statues. Mama points to a prickly pear so large it's like a roadside monument. "In some ways Arizona feels like Sicily without the sea," she says. "Oh, by the way, did I mention we're meeting Abe and Eli for dinner?"

Fatima is parked between Darius and me in the back seat. His face looks as disgusted as I feel.

My mother meanwhile routes us through Scottsdale, showing off the glam side of this part of the world to Darius before we spiral to our destination. A blazing red sunset has given way to a starry night. *I swear the sky is bigger here. If only my arms were long enough I could pluck my favorite pin lights out of all that blackness.*

The pungent scent of mesquite permeates the restaurant, while the décor is raw ranch. Picnic tables, gravel floor, and business cards are tacked to pine walls: Country Western tunes twang from the jukebox. We greet Eli and Abe, who tell us that T.P. has tracked down a relative in Tempe to visit for a few days.

The 30-something waitress is dressed in a Stetson hat, Frye boots, and Wrangler jeans; she acts like she won our table in a staff lottery. I like the way she fills those Wranglers, and her little T-shirt too. The body language she's using while taking our drink order is sexy bordering on sleazy, but I can forgive such things.

"So, what's the good word, Eli? What are the coaches saying about us these days?" I have to ask.

He appears reluctant to tell, at first, but when he notices Fatima's interest is equal to mine he admits, "Well, Mose has taken to referring to Darius's changeup as the 'humdinger.' He's been talking my ear off about Darius and Moki all week. As for you, Paolo, he's concerned your back isn't ever going to be 100%. But the trainers have him convinced they can whip you back into shape: wherever you start the season, the staff will be charged with extra work for you. But he also says he sees more signs of the old Paolo every day."

I grab the pepper shaker and sprinkle some into my water glass, then snatch my freshly delivered *vino* and pour a drop into the concoction, making the sign of the cross over it three times.

"What the heck are you doing?" Eli asks.

"You gave me the 'the overlook.' It's bad luck to give too much praise. The exact opposite could happen if I don't do the antidote."

"Sicilian voodoo," Mama teases.

"So, let me get this straight," Abe asks, "if I drone on about how good-looking, or smart, or talented someone is, it could cause them to become ugly, dumb, or a flop?"

"You got it," I say.

"Now explain the evil eye thing to me."

"The *malocchio*? Well, *'mal'* means bad and *'occhio'* means eye. You know how you sometimes see Italians wearing necklaces with a hot pepper medallion?—Well, that's to ward off a curse. There's also a hand gesture; it looks a bit like the University of Texas Longhorns 'hook 'em horns' symbol. You can point that at someone, if you think they're giving it to you."

"OK, so basically, for Italians, whether you're cursed or complimented, you could be in trouble?" Abe says.

"Basically," I reply.

"Wow. Now that's a whole other level of drama queen. That's the major leagues of drama. I bow to you, my friends. Even we Jews don't go that far."

He clinks his glass with Mama's and gives her a wink.

I want to puke.

Fatima tries to redirect the conversation. "I've learned from watching this sport that most players have superstitions. I know Paolo has a few. But I want to hear about yours, Eli."

His father laughs. "Tell her the truth now," he says.

Eli tilts his head at Abe. I recall the evening he busted his Dad about joining a senior basketball league. *Beware the swing of the sword; it cuts both ways.*

"I do have one crazy habit before every game. I started doing it when I was only twelve, but it doesn't make for appropriate dinner conversation."

"Go on," Abe teases. "You're among friends. Not a reporter in sight."

Eli shakes his head and runs his hand down the side of his face; then he straightens up. "OK. Well, I knock twice on my cup after I put it on. There. I said it; the truth is out. It actually feels good."

Not as good as it does to me: I nearly fall out of my chair. Moki is giggling at a high-pitched, rapid-fire speed that brings Mama to tears. She points at him, dabbing her eyes. Darius looks like an old man clasping his chest before a heart attack. Other restaurant patrons, who have no idea what's so funny, are laughing contagiously. I keep trying to calm myself, but it only makes the next wave even less controllable.

Fatima isn't laughing. She's looking around in a desperate attempt to comprehend the joke. She whispers to Mama in Italian, "How and why do you wear a cup?" Sports were never big among the women in my family.

But if Mama doesn't understand, neither does she care. I haven't seen her laugh this hard since before Papa died.

Eli realizes Fatima's distress and raises his hands for quiet. "Paolo, please explain to your sister—in Italian—what a cup is."

I oblige. Fatima covers her mouth. Now it's her turn to laugh. I can't help but wonder if that blush in her cheeks is more than embarrassment.

"You won't need to wear one when Darius pitches to you," she tells Eli.

Darius looks thrilled. Eli looks jealous.

"Well in order not to give you the overlook, Darius, I think I'll wear one just the same. Besides, I'm OCD about my superstition. That's how they work, after all."

"What's OCD?" Darius asks.

It stands for Obsessive Compulsive Disorder. It's a mental state where you can't help doing the same thing over and over again."

"I see. Then I'm OCD too. Every morning when I brush my teeth, I have to place the toothbrush in a glass with the bristles facing the wall. They have to face the wall or it drives me crazy."

"Yeah, that's classic OCD material," Eli says.

"I too have this sickness," Moki announces solemnly. "I bow to 'self in mirror each morning, then wink with left eye, followed by right eye. Then wish 'self good day."

"What the heck..." Eli says. More outbursts of laughter are followed by more of Mama's tears.

When the noise level drops, I hear Darius's cell ring. He glances at the number and then excuses himself from the table. It can't be my great uncle; he'd never be so cryptic about a call from Sicily. His face looked strange when he saw the number. *What's going on with him?* Ever since we arrived in the U.S. he's become more and more secretive. I don't like the vibes I'm getting, while Eli's attitude suggests a similar suspicion. *Did I do right in bringing this guy to this country, not knowing his whole story?*

Chapter 27

Eli

It's another typical day in the Valley of the Sun—though anything but ordinary for Paolo and Darius, who are scheduled to play a few innings in the big league exhibition between us and Cincinnati. Unsurprisingly, they both seem to have a case of the jitters.

We peek into the stands to find our entourage. Fatima flanks her mother, who's beside my Dad, so no surprise there. T.P. is still in Tempe.

"What's so damned interestin'?" Mose says as he steps into the home team confines. "You three stooges ready to play ball?"

"Ready, skipper," says Darius.

"Si, Signore," says Paolo.

"Yes, sir," I say as I snap on the rest of my gear before I'm good to go.

The starters for both teams reach their pitch count limits after four innings—none too soon. Mediocre pitching has given way to "stinky cheese" pitching followed by my-grandmother-can-throw-better-than-that pitching, and finally to Stephen King horror film pitching. Before we reach the I'd-rather-eat-shit-and-die-than-watch-this pitching, Darius, mercifully, takes to the mound. Wholesale changes in the lineups carry a distinctly minor-league feel, except for me and my opposite number. I notice both Silvana and Fatima squirm nervously in their seats when Paolo trots to center.

After the final warm-up toss, I lift my mask and stride to the hill. I smack the ball into Darius's glove, advising him, "Just stay within yourself and follow my signals."

He does.

The first batter goes down on strikes. The second hits a chopper back to the mound which Darius easily fields and throws to first. The third takes a seat, quite literally, thanks to Darius's wicked changeup.

I'm still in the lineup, batting fourth. Mose inserts Paolo into the fifth slot. Our turns will come this inning.

I climb on deck and slip the heavy donut around my bat, swinging the weight around to warm up my arms. The club's

Double-A leftfielder enters the batter's box first, and hits a pop fly to right.

My turn.

Cincinnati has their Triple-A ace on the mound. I think it's time to welcome him to the Big Leagues. My 20:10 vision recognizes the pitch just in time for me to whack a double off the wall. It wasn't a bad pitch—a swing and a miss most likely at Triple-A. *But this isn't Triple-A, dude.*

I rest on the second base bag, watching Paolo strut to the box. He considers what he's about to be thrown. The pitcher looks fairly pissed off that I managed to handle his best fastball. Paolo is smart enough to sense that this guy will likely try another to a former superstar with back trouble.

He guesses right.

BOOM! It's like thunder on top of lightning, on top of hurricane force winds. I'm surprised there's no earthquake when it hits the ground. Silvana and Fatima are screaming like rollercoaster addicts. The entire place is abuzz, even Cincinnati's dugout.

But as Paolo joins us on the bench I notice him wince. The skipper sees it too. He's put on ice for the rest of the afternoon.

•••••••••••

My father has been back and forth from New York several times, due to business, but he left today for good. The next time I see him will be our opener in the Big Apple. He was a huge help to me at the beginning of camp, back when the press flak regarding my stance on the team logo was coming hot and heavy. I'm grateful it's become mere background noise compared to all the excitement in camp over Darius, Moki, and Paolo.

With Dad and T.P. both away I guess I'm a free agent tonight. Fatima and Silvana have been touring California again. They were due back late afternoon, but I haven't heard from her since, and it bugs me that it bugs me so much... After all, what difference does it make? I can't seem to score time alone with her anyway. I'm beginning to suspect her of using her mother as a guard dog.

My favorite dance club is next door to this restaurant. The bouncers slide me and a couple of the other guys past the line. Inside, the song is a raunchy number for the bump-and-grind set.

On what I know is a stupid whim, I recognize a blonde who hit on me last week and start shouldering my way through the crowd toward her.

Oh shit! There's Fatima and Paolo, along with Darius and Moki. I dial down my naughty boy, but it's too late: the blonde is all in. *Dammit. What the hell is Fatima doing here?* This is no place for someone contemplating the convent. It's so loud and flashy—so not her.

I'm busted. She sees me.

So what? We aren't a couple. But I hate that she's whispering into Darius's ear...

When the song begins its interminable segue into the next one I kiss my dance partner on the cheek and beg off. I head straight for Fatima.

Paolo seems distracted by beauties both left and right. Ignoring him, I greet Moki and Darius and immediately ask Fatima to dance.

To my surprise she agrees. To my even bigger surprise she has no rhythm.

Meanwhile I feel Darius's dark heat targeting me like a missile. *Too bad, dude. Welcome to The Show.*

Paolo still has more attention than he can handle. Oh, how kind. He's sharing. The disco version of our tune has carried on long enough for Paolo, Darius, and Moki to sweep onto the dance floor with babes of their own.

Moki hops and bops like a battery bunny gone bonkers, while his partner whips around him in a fit of giggles. Soon everyone is stopping to watch. I whoop and clap, encouraging Moki all the more.

Having acquired a rapt audience, Moki decides to crank up the interest. He begins unbuttoning his shirt in a mock striptease. Mercifully, the song ends before he drops his drawers. He bows twenty times in a circle, as his admirers celebrate his nerve. I reach around the rookie's shoulders and quietly suggest he slip his shirt back on.

Darius doesn't let his opportunity slide, and asks Fatima for the next dance. He's definitely a quick study, dammit—and not just in sport, either. As Moki and the others stroll off center stage I decide to stay and watch my competition.

The song is only halfway through when a furious commotion in the general direction of where Moki and friends wandered is followed by the crash of shattering glass. Perhaps used to this, the DJ merely raises the volume. Darius leaps onto the stage, while I scoot toward the noise. A couple of cowboys, hats and all, are shouting and pointing at poor Moki. He looks helpless, having been pushed against a table full of what were formerly full bottles of beer now reduced to wet shards of glass.

I jump in to mediate, holding my hands in the air, stalling for the bouncers. *Where the hell are they, anyway?*

Clearly the cowboys are tiring of my voice of reason. One of them taunts me with a thick poke to the chest. Paolo slips behind the guy and backhands his hat off his head. (Probably not a good idea, but that's Paolo for you.)

The dude and his partner in crime are whirling around seeking the culprit when first one and then the other is slammed in the crotch by UFOs from the direction of the stage. *Holy crap.*

Falling to their knees in search of breath, they curse their unknown assailant. They wail in that kind of pain that makes every man in the room nauseous and every woman secretly pleased.

Moki and Paolo raise their arms aloft in triumph. Atop the stage stands Darius, legs apart and arms crossed like the King of Siam as the other partygoers go nuts. He's floored the cowboys with a couple of fastballs.

The bouncers finally show up to mop up. They motion Darius down from the stage and wrangle the cowboy dudes who are reduced to a hatless, hobbled pair of baldies, embarrassed by the entire scene.

Darius tries to leap down, but is diverted onto the outstretched arms of the mob and body-surfed toward us. Moki instigates the chant: "DAR-I-US, DAR-I-US!"

Fatima is smiling, but more in a proud, familial kind of way—at least, that's my hope. *They lived in the same house for several months in Italy, right? Maybe he's like another brother?*

I don't know. I'm jealous, and I hate it; this is unfamiliar territory for me. *She's* unfamiliar territory for me. Sometimes I think I need to wash that hair right out of my head! After all, the possibility of father with mother, son with daughter is something I can't quite get my brain around. And then there's that other issue: that such competition between teammates never ends well. *If I'm going to burn a bridge with a teammate over a woman, it had better lead to the altar...*

She's talking to Darius, but I can't hear her words. I can't even read her lips, because that luscious mouth of hers is distracting me. No matter how I try to shield my heart, it's no use. I'm hooked.

Chapter 28

Darius • Zebulon, North Carolina, April 2015

"Oh, y'all are I-talian," says the hotel receptionist.

"No, no, just him. I'm from Syria," I say.

"Ohhh. I see," she says that last part under her breath.

We've been assigned as roommates. Neither of us is pleased, but as the strangest foreigners on the team we've decided to stick together for now. First we check out the grocery store in the shopping plaza down the street. There we scan the produce department, in order to load up on fruit. A man nearby is jawing and spitting into a paper cup. Judging from all the tobacco fields we saw on the drive from the airport, I assume he's an informal ambassador for the mainstay of the entire local economy... I didn't even know what those plants were, until I overheard one of the coaches pointing them out. During Spring Training there were several guys who also liked to "jaw a chaw." Others preferred to suck and spit sunflower seeds. Mose himself didn't do either. When I dared to ask him why, "Bad habits I never want to start," was his response.

The man chewing in the grocery store appears to be talking to us, though I can't even guess what he's saying. Between his accent and the chewing tobacco, Paolo and I are both stumped. We just smile and nod, hoping like heck he isn't offended, because this guy must be one of the biggest human beings I've ever seen, not only tall, but wide. Suddenly, around the corner, comes my new pitching coach.

"Hey, Tiny, whaddaya say, my man!" He greets the tobacco chewer enthusiastically, slapping him on the back and giving him a warm handshake. "Isn't this yer wife's job or she finally leave ya?"

"She refuses to buy my tabaccy. Says it'll gimme cancer." He spits the whole hoard into his cup, giving me a chance to finally figure out what he's saying.

"I was just askin' these here fresh recruits if they's players. Spanish, I'm guessin'?"

"No, actually Paolo is from Italy and Darius is from Syria. Boys, say hello to the Mudcats' number one fan, Tiny Tonkert."

"It's nice to meet you, Mr. Tonkert," I say, shaking a fleshy hand. Paolo follows my lead.

"Mr. Tonkert is my Daddy and he's been pushin' up daisies for pert near a decade now. Ya'll just call me Tiny."

Tiny's cell suddenly rings "Reveille."

"That'll be the missus. See ya 'round the yard, boys," he says with a wave, scooting toward the checkout.

"That, my friends, is the richest tobacco farmer in eastern North Carolina and the biggest supporter of our ballclub, in more ways than one," Coach tells us.

I'm as shocked as my father was the day he was mistaken by an old woman for someone whom she claimed had cheated her. Coach shakes his head adding, "His wife doesn't want him chewing tobacco. That's like asking a plumber to use an out-house."

•••••••••••

The clubhouse is hopping. A pop Latino tune is blaring while several players from Mexico, Puerto Rico and the Dominican Republic are singing to the beat. My locker is beside the one belonging to Juan Diego Garpeza, whose family hails from a small town near Mexico City. He has a poster in his locker of the statue Fatima bought in Tucson.

"The mother of Jesus?" I ask, pointing to the image.

"You know about her?" Juan asks. He looks at me like I'm an alien, but continues, "The entire Spanish-speaking population of the planet knows Our Lady of Guadalupe, and that's a sizeable chunk. But I never figured an A-rab would know."

"Muslims believe in the virgin birth of Jesus too, and Mary is one of the most revered women in all of Islam."

"Get the heck outta here! Seriously?"

"Seriously."

"Then, why don't you believe Jesus is the Son of God?"

"We believe he was a great prophet who announced the coming of the last and greatest, Prophet Mohammed. We don't agree with the concept of the Holy Trinity. There is only one God, and to attribute human qualities to Allah, such as being a father or a son, to us is blasphemy... But I'm curious about this notion of Mary having appeared to people in different parts of the world. What's the story behind this particular image?"

"I'll tell ya. In 1531, Mary appeared to an Aztec peasant at the Hill of Tepayac, a stone's throw from the village where my parents were born: I'm even named after him! She performed a miracle there, which is still celebrated to this day, inside the Cathedral. She wanted the peoples of the New World to recognize her son as God and to follow His example. Google it sometime... All I know is, five hundred years later, we have a Pope from the Americas, and that to me is way cool."

Google it? I'm immediately reminded of Sister Colleen. I remember her telling me to google the Lady of Fatima story. I'd seen her several times before we left Sicily, mostly trying to help out with translating when Peppe wanted to take a break from baseball—and, perhaps, to do his bit for the refugees, as well. Suddenly I miss her tremendously.

Juan speaks Spanish, but with a Texan drawl. He lived in the U.S. until he was eight, when his father, the oldest son, was summoned back to Mexico to work the minuscule family farm, due to his grandfather's illness. After his grandfather died, the family returned to the U.S., where both parents between them were able to earn enough money to send Juan to college. Juan was drafted last season as a shortstop, but has since converted to second base. He's an acrobat at the position.

"You speak better Spanish than any of these coaches," he tells me. "Where'd ya learn?"

"I learned Italian, and there are similarities."

"If that's so, then why can't ol' Paolo speak Spanish?"

"He's concentrating on English for now."

"Yeah. I noticed. And he's hilarious sometimes."

Another song blares, apparently a favorite, converting the clubhouse into the set of *Dancing with the Stars.* Paolo prances in from taking extra hitting practice, wiggling his hips with his hands in the air.

"You calla dat a dance?" Juan mocks Paolo's accent. "My dog's got better moves than that!"

"*Si, signore,* but your dog can no do this." Paolo plays along before spinning into a fairly decent imitation of Michael Jackson's moonwalk, producing cheers so loud that the manager, Billy B., exits his office in order to find out what all the noise is about.

He stands, arms folded, shaking his head and snickering, "There's a club I know in Raleigh that could use you, Paolo, if this baseball thing doesn't work out..."

Billy B. is a former big league catcher whose career ended prematurely due to an off-season car accident, after which he was never the same. He's 41, blond-headed, blue-eyed, and bad-assed. No one blames him for his temperament: they all fear a similar fate.

•••••••••••

I'm No.1 in the rotation, so the duty of opening at home falls to me. I don't plan to disappoint.

Tiny Tonkert roots between almost every pitch, but his words are lost in a jumble of mouth mess and Southern twang. But I can still see him: who couldn't? It'd be like trying to hide a hippo in a bathtub. *I didn't think our team's T-shirts came in that size.*

So this is what it feels like. Wow. It's a heady experience—the first game I've ever played that actually counts. I vow to stay in my zone despite all the clanging of cowbells.

Seven innings later I reach my 100-pitch limit—seven plus innings of bloody bells, mostly wrung from the hands of a black woman in the third row behind the home dugout. She's with a group of African-American fans, who cheer even louder every time J.T. Polerton comes to bat. She hollers at her hero, who hasn't had a hit all game. "J.T., darlin', you better watch yo' back, or Billy's gonna have that I-talian movin' up in the batting order to your spot." J.T. gets the message and promptly spanks the first pitch for a double and drives in the game winning run.

We're on our way.

•••••••••••

We sit at the bar and order the special. When the waitress asks Paolo how he'd like his eggs, he's confused. He looks at me for an answer, but all I can do is shrug. So he turns back to the girl and answers, "In a dish." But English words spoken with a thick Italian accent are more than she can handle. She retreats to the kitchen for help.

The cowbell lady herself bursts through the swinging wood doors to find her two new favorite players. Knowing we're foreigners, she quickly grasps the problem and proceeds to explain the nuances of egg-making in America.

Paolo's embarrassed, but has the grace to laugh at his mistake. We all do.

"I'll be gettin' a lot of mileage outta this story!" she teases.

She asks us to hang around until the breakfast rush is over. To ensure we stay, eggs and home fries are followed by pancakes, cheese biscuits, veggie omelets and, of course, grits. We tell her she's our new best friend.

Once the kitchen can manage without her, she joins us, steaming cup of coffee in hand. Turns out she loves to talk baseball. But I prod her for her life story instead.

Miss Juliet owns this breakfast-only diner, serving America's egg-related favorites from 5 a.m. to 2 p.m. every day except Sunday. She's raised five kids, mostly on her own, because her husband was "no damn good." Her granddaughter, the girl who took our order, is dating our team's J.T. Polerton. She's the only one in the family willing to work with Juliet, and Juliet hopes the girl will soon take over the adventure she's turned into a goldmine. Miss Juliet lives in a gracious, sprawling property two miles down the road.

Then she grins and teases us that her granddaughter's friends already have crushes on the two of us. It's her mission to learn if we have girlfriends of our own.

"It's Darius's misfortune to be in love with someone he cannot have, and mine that I can have all I want, but cannot choose only one," Paolo tells her.

She laughs—a loud, glorious, deep-from-the-gut laugh—and resolves to "stick a fork" in her mission. But I'm not laughing. I feel the blood rising to my cheeks at Paolo's revelation. *Is he right? I want his sister with me every minute of every day, but I haven't thought these feeling through. Maybe I should.*

Instead I say, "This America is an even better place than I realized. A black woman alone with five children would be destitute in most countries."

"Here too, believe me, black or white," Juliet tells me, very seriously. "But I had two things goin' for me. One was my sheer determination to stand on my own two feet. The other was Tiny Tonkert. He used to eat breakfast every day at another place in town where I used to cook. One day he asked for the secret to my grits. So I says, 'Help me open a place all my own, and I'll tell ya.' I paid him back in three years."

As if summoned, Tiny himself strolls in and covers the two stools beside Paolo. The four of us talk baseball until the lunch rush arrives. That's when Juliet tells Paolo he's a natural-born cleanup hitter, and me that I have the best change-up she's ever seen.

High praise. Paolo quickly does his voodoo thing.

Chapter 29

Eli • Cleveland, Ohio, May 2015

"They want me to rehab with our Single-A affiliate in small-town North Carolina. Can you believe it—not Triple-A or Double-A in 'big city' Ohio, but North-freaking-Carolina. Are there any Jews there, I ask you?"

"You sure is riled up today. Ya need to calm down. This re-aggravatin' of your shoulder will pass. It's only May; the season's still got a long way to go. A little sacrifice won't kill ya."

"I still think the main reason they're sending me there is to work with Darius. I suppose if a Muslim can survive in North Carolina, so can I."

"Don't be hatin' on my home state," T.P. says.

" Well, did it ever treat you like a favored son?"

"No, but that ain't the point. It's the place I was born, the place I fell in love, first with golf, then with my wife; the place where my kids got made. Time has worked its magic. I choose to remember the good over the bad."

"What town are you from, anyway?"

"Zebulon. In fact, my wife's still there, with some of the kids nearby in Raleigh."

"You're kidding me. That's the town with our ballclub!"

"My oh my, now ain't that a surprise. Well, even if there ain't no Jews there, the town's name oughta make ya feel right at home. Everything in this life happens for a reason."

"Maybe the reason is so you can come with me and face the music, meaning your wife?"

"I was just thinkin' the very same thing. Life sure is curious, ain't it?"

He takes the palm of his hand and smooths back his hair, which doesn't need it. He sits up straighter in the chair. He's already picturing a reunion with his wife.

Elvis looks at me like he doesn't know me. He moved closer to T.P. the minute I started ranting.

"T.P., let's do a little retailing. It calms me down. Besides, we gotta get you lookin' all cool jazz for the Mrs., right?"

•••••••••••

We arrive in time for Saturday brunch. The Holiday Inn is close to the ballpark. We might as well eat here before I head to the yard.

T.P. says, "See that diner across the road? That's where I first popped the question. C'mon, I'll buy ya lunch. I'm flush after givin' all them golf lessons before leavin' town."

"Whatever's handy. I just want to get to the park earlier than usual, since it's my first day."

Crossing proves to be a jaywalking nightmare. *The whole town of Zebulon must be "headin' to the Walmart down yonder."* Still, we manage to dodge all the pickup trucks and make it to the parking lot of Romeo's unscathed.

T.P. admires the neon sign. "They changed the name, sure hope they changed the grits. I got a serious hankerin' for the one thing this place *didn't* do well. If not, I can always fall back on my ol' standbys."

Bells jingle as I open the glass door for T.P. I practically ride up his backside on the way in. *What the heck? Move along, my friend. Surely he must have felt me bump him. Why doesn't he move?*

Then I get it. A tall, thin, black woman with white-rimmed glasses and matching diner-dress faces us, a full plate in each hand. The good old boys seated in front of her spin around on their stools, to see what's distracting her from serving their breakfasts.

I squeeze around T.P. and then take a step backward, suspecting that my presence is unwanted.

"Hello, Juliet," T.P. says. "I take it by the name of this place that you're the proprietress. I always figured ya for an entrepreneur. Risk never had no claim on you."

She sets the plates in front of the men, but T.P. is clearly more interesting than "the usual." They're all staring him down.

"Some risks pay bigger dividends than others," she says flatly.

The scorn in her eyes doesn't appear to scorch my friend. *He's been burned so many times that he's practically fireproof.*

Darius and Paolo enter with a man who has to turn sideways just to get through the door. The big guy recognizes me and says, "Well, lookie here, sports fans. If it ain't the hero of the parent club come to strengthen his weary shoulder on even wearier pitchin'. Good thing you won't have to face the likes of this guy every day, or you'd be headin' back to Little League for rehab." And with this he slaps Darius hard on the shoulder. I feel the ouch in mine.

Paolo makes the introductions and suggests the round booth in the corner. A waitress brings a chair for my new best friend, Tiny (I still can't believe that's his name), and places it at the opening to the booth. The rest of us scoot in on either side, T.P. in the middle, with a direct view of the restaurant, and of everything Juliet does.

The guys soon fill me in on life in Zebulon. They share the scouting report on tonight's opponents and order brunch from a mocha-skinned maiden who has eyes only for T.P. When she brings our meals, he asks who her parents are.

"Why Grandpappy, can't you guess?" she says.

Ten hands stop moving and five mouths stop eating. It's like some Star Trek movie where everyone's been zapped. All except for T.P., that is.

"Darlin', you're as pretty as my Posha was at your age. I've missed your Mama and the chance to know ya more'n—well, more'n you can ever imagine!"

"Well, Grammy's pretty aggravated you're here, but I'm jus' aggravated it took this long fer ya to come."

"That's all my fault, sugar, but it stops today. You can tell your Mama and all the rest I come in peace. Whaddaya think your brothers and cousins would say to that?"

"They're mos'ly like me." She puts down the last of three plates in front of Tiny. "Go on y'all. Eat it 'fore it gets cold. Grits ain't meant to be tasted chilled."

"Mmm," T.P. grins. "Your Grammy always made the greatest grits."

"I know, but she still won't tell any of us the secret. She promised she'd only tell the one who stepped up to take over the business, an' I'm almost done with school. She promised to teach me soon as she hangs my diploma up in the kitchen."

"Good for you, sweet pea. And if she reneges, you come see me, 'cause I'm the one who taught her." Sweet pea's eyes grow as wide as the coffee cups she fills, as he adds, "That's right. The recipe is actually my Mama's."

"You don't say," says Tiny, whacking his fat palm on the formica. "Folks come from all over these parts for a taste of

Juliet's grits. Not that the rest of her cookin' ain't fine. It's fit for kings. But her grits are fit for God Hisself."

We linger until it's time for me to leave. Tiny labors up from his seat, which squeaks gratefully.

"You know, T.P., my daddy was a member of the Country Club back in your day. He loved his golf and always complained his game was never the same after you left. Claims to have voted against it. Told me the vote was close."

"So I'd heard, which made it all the harder to bear."

"Ain't nothin' I can do 'bout them days, any more than I can 'bout these ones. My ol' man was a fan o' yours, as I'm sure that you recall."

"I do recall, Tiny. What you might not know is that he carted me off to my first A.A. meetin'."

"Well, I'll be! Can't say as he ever mentioned it, but I ain't surprised. He felt pretty guilty. He stood up to the Klan in these parts, but only 'cause, as the richest man in the county, he could get away with it. My Mama was another story. Her friends shunned her, and she never forgave my father for it. My brother took her part, and I took my Daddy's. It was me who fronted Juliet the money for this place. She paid me back in short order, no pun intended."

T.P. smiles at this.

"While these young'uns do their baseball thing," Tiny continues, "How 'bout we hit a round? I play purty bad, but you look to be in good shape fer yer age. Whaddaya say we stir it up over at the Club?"

"Well, as this seems to be my day for stirrin' things up, why not?"

The old-fashioned cha-ching of the cash register dings prosperity five times over.

T.P.'s granddaughter gives him a long hug. To my surprise, however, he sheds no tears. Instead he says to the owner, over her shoulder, "I know you was always a ball fan, Juliet. See you at the game tonight?"

"There's lots o' seats in that ballpark, T.P., so just make sure you park your seat as far from mine as possible," she answers.

When we're out the door, he whispers with a wink, "She still loves me."

Chapter 30

Darius

It's my first autograph session. I find it odd. I've never been the target of hero worship. I'm fighting anxiety on top of guilt, but I smile so as not to disappoint the old ladies and young children in line.

One pretty girl asks Paolo for a kiss instead of his signature. Paolo is fine with this until Eli grabs him by the arm and whispers, "Hold your horses, Valentino. This isn't Italy. You don't know how old she is or if her mommy or daddy's a lawyer."

TP watches us from a seat behind the dugout. I find him to be a very interesting man. He gives me hope. He's overcome his own demons, after all. He's talking to his wife and granddaughter, who are probably waiting for J.T. Polerton. I can't believe my favorite woman in Zebulon is married to Eli's favorite man. *Maybe if they can manage a little detente, Eli and I can too.*

My cell vibrates. *I hope it's Fatima.*

Instead, my shadow wants to meet, after Paolo and Eli leave for the party scene. I'd like to go with them, but I never do, and, of course, it's the best time for my caller to reach me. Tonight will be our first face-to-face contact.

Maybe it'll be more comfortable than this autograph business, but I doubt it.

•••••••••••

The city park is deserted this late at night, except for a pack of teenagers raiding the playground. I wait, as instructed, under the magnolia tree. Its scent intoxicates. I drift to a dreamland of Eid celebration—breaking the fast of Ramadan with all of my favorite foods. I can almost taste the halal skewers of lamb kebobs and—my mother's Persian specialty—*fesenjan*, or chicken simmered in a pomegranate and walnut sauce, with saffron and turmeric. Paolo tells me I'll find my foods in Cleveland. It's a stronger push to hurry my progress than any pay raise.

"The night is cool," he says.

It isn't. It's a coded greeting. Like announcing, "I'm the one."

He's not as I expected. He's blond, blue-eyed, and under 40. But something in his face doesn't...I don't know...doesn't quite fit, odd as that sounds. Not only that, but his presence feels vaguely familiar, in a spooky sort of way.

But how can that be? Blue-eyed blonds are not exactly common in Syria—or even in southern Italy, for that matter. This man gives me 'the creeps,' as they say in this country.

"Let's get down to it before those kids become curious," he says, matter-of-factly. "We have reason to believe your mother is alive."

I inhale so deeply that he grabs me by the arm, as if afraid I'll faint. Does he think I'll forget to release the air from my lungs? *Oh, Allah, be merciful. Is this a ploy?*

"How can this be?" I ask.

"We believe that the photos you saw were faked, so that you wouldn't attempt to free her from a marriage made against her will."

"Nooo! My biggest fear in those days was that my mother would be raped. Ever since I'd heard of her death, I'd consoled myself with the thought that, at least, she'd been spared that. With one sentence you give me hope; with the next you steal its joy."

My anguish, however, is entirely lost on my informant. "I'm sorry," he says robotically, "But we need you to remember why you're here. If you want to see her again, stay focused."

"Don't talk to me of focus. I've been a monument to focus this last year. I want to see a photo. I want proof."

He has come prepared.

The image is certainly of her...a down-trodden, worn-out version of her...yet the spectacularly beautiful woman my Sunni father once referred to as his Persian Princess remains, under a layer of what I'm sure are exhausted nerves and—perhaps—far worse.

"Where've they taken her?" I nearly spit.

"We think she's still in northern Syria, near Raqqa, but it's hard to say. Spies switch sides daily in this war."

"How long ago was it taken?"

"Two weeks, a month, tops. Iraqi and Kurdish forces, backed by the U.S., are bombing the area daily. I'm not going to give you false hope. She's still in all kinds of danger."

He's so cool about it that I feel my skin on my back literally begin to crawl. But something else in his voice disturbs me. I can't nail what it is exactly, but the skin crawling is getting worse. "Who is the bastard that married her?"

His pause is a chasm. He doesn't have to tell me.

"I think you can maybe guess. But look at it this way, because he's a person of such importance she has a better chance of staying alive. She's said to be his favorite."

How could a conversation that began by resuscitating my heart have squeezed the life out of it so quickly? I felt more alive when I'd thought she was dead!

He passes more information, which I'm to unravel. He leaves without saying good-bye.

No. No, no, no! I sprint toward my apartment at a speed of which I wouldn't have thought myself capable, attracting shocked glances from every side. When these attacks hit, though, it's the first thing I want to do... At this moment it's possible, and I'm grateful. I have to concentrate so hard on catching my breath once I reach our neighborhood that it steadies my nerves a little... It's 5 a.m. in Italy, but I have to call Fatima. I can't tell her any of this, but I'll think of some other reason. *Or do I even need one? She always seems so glad to speak to me.* I tap her number on my cell. The moment she picks up I feel my breathing calming.

What would I do without her?

Chapter 31

Eli

This is one bar where a recovering alcoholic like TP is safe to sit. Juliet cracks a smile for the first time. It's been ten days, but tonight we leave for a weeklong road trip. Hopefully the ice between them is breaking at last.

Tiny, my teammates and I give T.P. and her a little privacy, while T.P.'s granddaughter delivers our juice. I ask why we haven't met her mother yet. The sound she makes is somewhere between a laugh and a grunt.

"I finally blasted her this morning before church," she tells us. "I said, 'Ain't no use o' you joinin' us, Mama. You must a been sleep-walkin' through Sunday service all these years. How else to explain such lack o' forgiveness?'

"And?"

"And she let me have it right back, but I could tell she got the point. I overheard her talking with Grammy later on."

Darius pokes at his food disconsolately. He's grown mean the last few days. Every question is a demand, every answer curt. Nothing much said in-between.

Paolo thinks the news from the Middle East is killing him. He seems to have become obsessed with blogs from the region. Every so often, too, he gets a call or text that provokes a sinister reaction. I find myself watching his every move. *What if he's being brainwashed, or radicalized online?*

After last night's game a reporter asked him if he was following events in Syria. I thought our boy was gonna reach down the guy's throat and pull him inside out. But his response was what I can't shake out of my head. He said, "Every minute of every day my thoughts are with my people...even when I'm on the mound." *I trust him even less than I did in the beginning.*

Yet it hasn't affected his play. He's throwing lights out. Leyland thinks the three of us will be elevated during the road trip. If so, T.P. will have to find his own way back to Cleveland.

What am I worrying about? He's a big boy.

Juliet delivers Tiny another helping of grits and says, "Well, should we tell 'em?"

"Nah, let 'em hear it from the skipper."

"Hear what?"

"See. I told ya they fall outta bed and into my diner before checkin' the news."

Tiny grins while Juliet continues, "While you boys was out shakin' yo groove things last night, the Tribe's centerfielder broke his wrist crashing into the wall on a ball there was no need to run that hard fer. Anyone with eyes coulda seen it was gone. Meanwhile the ace in the rotation has come down with a case o' shingles, so the trickledown effect is about to begin. Even the lamest Mudcat fans can figure who're the most likely candidates to trickle up."

Paolo grabs the pepper shaker and his water glass, then swiftly orders a grape juice. "That's mighty high praise," he mocks. "I'm not taking any chances with a compliment like that."

Juliet's eyes pool. "I ain't never figured on gettin' so attached to an A-rab and an I-talian, that's fer sure."

Tiny raises his glass of O.J. "Now don't be forgettin' us little people once y'all make it to The Show."

"*Little* people?" I joke, and Tiny laughs the hardest. Then T.P. asks if he can speak to me in private. His eyes match his wife's.

"Son, like Juliet, I ain't never figured on gettin' so attached to a Jew boy. But I imagine the club will be havin' you tag along with those two. So looks like this is where we part company. Juliet and I have decided to start fresh."

I'm not surprised. In fact, I'm thrilled. I take his white palms in mine, just as he says, "I only wish you'd consider doin' the same with Darius. You two are carryin' a world o' history on your shoulders like a badge o' honor. Why don't you give them ol' Greek philosophers a try and offer an olive branch instead?"

"Wow. You really did 'get you an education.' Greek history was one of my favorite subjects at Stanford."

"Well, your Daddy could o' saved himself a boatload o' money if you'd just got yourself a library card. But that ain't the point. Point is that the Olympic spirit mighta started out pagan, but it's meant for everybody. When people o' disparate backgrounds spend enough time together, they begin to 'preciate their similarities more'n their differences."

"I'm not so sure. Remember also that, although every four years they quit making war for three months, the peace never lasted... Like German and Allied forces cuddled up one Christmas Eve during WWI, but they went right back to killing each other the next day. I appreciate history more than you might think, T.P. And what it's taught me is to reach out with one hand while carrying a weapon in the other. Look at what happened to the American natives, and then the slaves—let alone all those Confederates and Yankees. Darius is up to something, I tell you. I can almost smell it."

"Why'd you reach out to me on that sidewalk, if that's your attitude about people?"

"It's not my attitude about people. It's my attitude about *Darius*."

"Son, your upside is so high it's a nose bleed. But you keep cuttin' off that nose to spite your face where this young man is concerned—sometimes with that award-winning ego o' yours and sometimes outta sheer fear... Look, I'll never be able to pay you back for all the good you done me. Only thing I can offer is the wisdom of old age. So believe me when I say, do good to this kid, 'cause if you do bad, you'll not only carry the scars the rest o' your life, but you'll pass 'em on to others, like a communicable disease."

"I appreciate your sincerity, but it's hard for Christians to appreciate what Jews understand. Think of it as something simply outside of your experience."

"There's that ego talkin' again."

"Must you slam me every time we disagree?"

"Hey, I only do it to the people I love."

A lump begins to swell in my throat. "Well then let's agree on that much, T.P., because I love you too."

Chapter 32

Fatima • Sicily, May 2015

Nonna rifles through the drawers in her mahogany dresser, giving orders with military efficiency. She's decided her brother will be more comfortable in *her* bedroom, so we're doing the switch with the guestroom today. Zio finally waved the white flag last night, after weeks of pleading with her to let it be. At 82, he's still her baby brother, plus he's a priest, topped by the fact that the old ways are engraved in her DNA—so, it's happening.

I ask where she wants me to store the high-heeled shoes she never wears. She doesn't answer. Then I notice that she's weeping.

"Nonna, are you all right?"

She's clutching an old Rosary with a shiny medal safety-pinned to the loop from which the crucifix dangles. Upon closer scrutiny, I realize that it's actually the medal that has her so moved. I put my hand on her shoulder, saying softly, "What is it, Nonna?"

"How could I have forgotten?" she whispers. "Sit down, my little love, and let me tell you an old story."

I take my place with pleasure.

She sits in her "princess"' chair, the one she still uses when brushing out her hair. She begins with a deep breath, as if the weight of her tale will be heavy.

"One day long ago, during the furious war years of my youth, my mother sent me to the town of Conflenti to barter goods with the women there. It was a long journey up and down those hills, so I stopped to rest about halfway. I was sitting on a rock when I heard whispering near my perch. I pretended to be unaware at first, because the voices were those of young children. I guessed they were about to play a trick on me, so I decided to catch them in the act. I stood and stretched, before whirling suddenly in their direction.

"Two youngsters darted from behind a prickly pear bush. I caught up to them quickly and grabbed each by an arm.

"Their arms were so thin I felt guilty to have squeezed; their eyes, buried in gaunt sockets, shouted fear and poverty to me. I realized then that the rumors were true. Women washing clothes at the fountain had gossiped that Jewish refugees from Austria had crossed into Northern Italy and were hiding in forests while moving southward, just ahead of the Nazi advance.

"I remember the poorest widow in town telling how she'd left a loaf of bread and some olive oil near the place where they were rumored to be hiding. An old witch had chastised her. 'Don't encourage them! These refugees will soon be stealing from our farms!'

"The poor widow had shaken her head, saying, 'What you won't miss, they will relish.' But the old crone had snubbed her, walking away.

"Anyway, I released the frightened children and asked if they were hungry, gesturing with my hand to my mouth. They conferred together, nervous about trusting someone who'd snatched them. But their empty bellies overruled and eventually they nodded; I beckoned for them to follow me.

"I fed them bread, olive oil and a bit of cheese. In the end, I handed over the rest of the loaf and a mould of pecorino for others that might be part of their group. I hugged them, wishing them a safe journey, and then continued on my own.

"On my return, I stopped at the same rock. I wasn't there long before I heard a voice from behind me say, '*Buon giorno.*' I turned and found a handsome man holding both children by the shoulders. He thanked me for the food in German-accented Italian. Then he asked me the way to Ferramonte, the site of a Jewish internment camp. He had heard that Jews were being supported by the locals in these camps, but, unluckily, he'd gone right past it. He and his children had walked a day too far. So I escorted them to the nearby American air base instead. He insisted I take this gold medal, in return for my assistance."

"You'll have to show Abe this Star of David, Nonna, before he goes. He leaves again tomorrow. Don't forget. Truly, he ought to see this."

"I have no intention of forgetting, my dear. I can't believe it took this long to recall such a magical moment from my past."

"It reminds me of Bisnonna's old saying... 'Do good and forget about it.'"

"It's the second part of that saying that always stuck with me," she laughs.

•••••••••••

Later that day, Abe wipes a tear away, the pendant in his palm. It's possible that Nonna's story sears him deeply because it touches on his own ancestral history. His Austrian grandmother died of pneumonia during the family's flight over the Alps to Italy. Her grave is likely a sheep pasture. He knew his grandfather had taken his father and his aunt to an Italian internment camp in Calabria. For all I know," he says, "they could have been the very people you fed, Marietta, although I don't recall the story mentioning the help of a young Italian girl—or of American airmen, either."

"I had no idea such camps even existed," I tell him.

He laughs at my surprise and says, "I'm not sure why the Italian camps have received such little publicity—except perhaps because they were nothing like the equivalent horrors in Germany and Poland. The Italians had no use for Hitler's rules; they followed them in their own style. And, although the internees were not allowed to work and had to check in with the local police chief each day, they were otherwise free. My Dad's so-called camp even had a synagogue and a school, contained within a convent. The children played sports; the men played cards; and the women shopped with the money from their own bank accounts... It was only when Italy switched sides in 1943 that things got scary. Locals then did their best to hide the Jewish internees from retreating Nazi armies... And it was only after the war, when my family began a new life in Israel, that they learned how fortunate they were to end up in a southern European country. My father's own theory was that no one wanted to talk about their internment in Italy because it was so much better than others had endured, that guilt played a part. He also said the older sister of one of my aunt's friends openly dated a young Italian deserter—so the social life wasn't too bad, either!"

"The Italians are lovers, not fighters—lovers of life, not only women," Nonna laughs.

Without warning, the atmosphere around me starts to fizzle. It happens as it always does. Nonna, Zio, Mama and Abe blur into the light that muscles its way into my vision. The faint outline of Sister Colleen bouncing a child on her knee morphs into a sketchy image of Bisnonna reaching out to me from a distance: so distant and yet so close! The curve of her head, shoulders and fingertips fade into a strange shape. What is it? A wall?

I feel my eyelids droop and it's all gone: Sister Colleen, the child, Bisnonna, the wall. Everyone is staring at me.

"I've heard about this thing you do, but this is the first time I've witnessed it," says Abe. "Where have you been the last two minutes?"

"With Sister Colleen, with Bisnonna, and at some kind of wall, I think. That last is unclear to me."

"Did you hear anything?" Abe asks.

"I never do, at least not in the conventional sense. But generally I come away with some sort of knowledge or understanding."

"What can you tell us, *cara mia*?" says Zio.

"Sister Colleen said something today that comes back to me now. She has a history degree, you know. People don't realize how educated most of these nuns are. They shame me, really. You'd think a medical degree would be enough! We were discussing her plans to travel to Portugal next October for the 98th Anniversary of Our Lady of Fatima."

"The place of your namesake, you mean?" Abe asks.

"Yes. Mama probably explained it to you. The Sisters of Charity only get a vacation once every 10 years or else she'd wait and visit during the centenary. She believes there's a reckoning coming, not in a dark apocalyptic sort of way, but a reckoning, nonetheless. She's sure that the story of Fatima has something to do with it."

I spread my hands on the ancient table around which we sit and massage it like a genie's lamp. *If a wizard could escape its stone, what could it tell us?*

"It's as if she's a seer—or a saint," murmurs Abe to Mama, in tones not meant to reach me. I glance up at him.

"I have to be honest with you, just because these strange moments happen to me doesn't make me a saint. I'm fairly furious at times about what's happening in the world. I fear today's sufferers will become tomorrow's oppressors... Sister Colleen says some of her friends even think we're living in the end times, but I'm not so sure. Peter and Paul and the other apostles thought they were living in the end times too. Maybe 2000 years is like yesterday to God. I don't know... All I know is this: if someone were to take away my home I wouldn't turn around and do the same to someone else, after learning how awful that experience was. I couldn't inflict the same pain."

"If you're speaking of the Zionist movement, you're passing judgment, Fatima, on people and circumstances that I suspect you don't fully understand. You've never been through it," Abe says, stiffly. "My people have suffered for centuries. I'm sorry to say that your Holy Roman Church carries more than its fair share of responsibility for this suffering. Imagine it. If, in every place you ever lived, you were eventually oppressed or annihilated, would you trust your new neighbors to love you?"

Mama is standing behind Abe. She looks furiously at me. She's biting her hand in wide-eyed anger.

I apologize and excuse myself. He's a nice man; I can see that. I'm sorry to have struck such a cord within him. It's what makes our different point of view all the more frustrating to me.

•••••••••••

The sunset waits later each day. Tonight's performance is no less spectacular than the last. I choose an apricot from a tree and punish the fruit with my teeth.

If my legs were bendable enough to kick my own rear, I'd do it. Why can't I just leave it alone? Look at this place. Could anyone possibly live better? Why can't I just relax and enjoy life? I should marry a hottie like Eli or Darius, become Mama's protégé in the business, bring up a bunch of kids—and quit torturing myself. I can't do anything to reduce the flow of refugees. I can't change the way people think. Jesus couldn't get Judas onboard, so what the heck makes me think that I can convince Abe to see the Palestinian question my way? And why should he, anyway? Who says I have all the answers?

Then it happens. I want another bite of the apricot, but I can't raise my arm to my mouth. I stand, as still as the night air. *Please, God, let it pass.*

It does.

But I've lost my appetite. In two days we fly to the States, where I'm due for another round of tests. Not a moment too soon.

•••••••••••

Dr. Bellini isn't as fun as the cocktail of that name. He's also in a hurry; the Cleveland Clinic is a frenetic place.

"After reviewing the tests we've done, I'm afraid I do need to ask for more," he says, very seriously. "You're showing some symptoms of an incurable neurological disease called Amyotrophic Lateral Sclerosis: ALS for short. In America it's often called Lou Gehrig's disease, after a famous baseball player who contracted it. It usually strikes people during mid-life. It's a difficult prognosis at any age, but especially at only 23."

His words become background noise inside my head. My thoughts scatter: *Why does he speak with almost no accent? How does he remain so calm while my world cracks in chunks? When was the last time he visited Italy? Where's Paolo when I need him?*

He explains the disease, to Mama and to me. I catch edges and shards: "loss of muscle function...quite rapid deterioration...her mind will be fine."

Small consolation, that last one. Quite possibly a curse. I'm scared. *Dio mio*, Jesus, Mary, and Joseph help me!

By the time we leave, Mama's capable of putting one foot before the other, but that's about it. I try to speak steadily. "The tests aren't yet definitive. Stay positive, Mama. And, even if they reveal the worst, it means I'll be seeing Papa again sooner than expected. That's a good thing, right?" *I'm trying to bolster myself by bolstering her.*

But it's as though my sentences ping off Mama's forehead. She's not listening. She looks nauseous. I add, more urgently, "Eli has an afternoon game today, remember? That's why he scheduled the weird mother-father/son-daughter dinner for tonight. Let's not spoil today—for everybody."

I wish Paolo and Darius were playing in Akron, but the Double-A club is on the road. I want my twin. I want Nonna and Zio, Darius and Sister Colleen. I want all my family and friends around me right now. *Mother of God, let this be a mistake! Doctors can be wrong...can't they?*

Abe chauffeurs us to Eli's home, which is only ten minutes away. Mama tells him very little, only that more tests are needed;

but he looks suspicious. I'm sure he'll quiz her more when he has the chance.

Eli's dog, Elvis, greets us like a new toy. I don't know if it's because we're almost the same height or what, but this dog simply refuses to leave my side. Even when I use the bathroom, he lingers for me outside the door. After today's news, he's my protector. I stroke his warm neck while whispering silent prayers. He soothes me.

•••••••••••

Eli certainly has clout. We park in a reserved space in the garage, just behind the field. Oh how much I've missed the excitement of these games!—This is the perfect distraction for me right now. I'd forgotten the electric nature of it: I haven't even attended a game since Paolo's injury, now over two years ago. But I still can't forget the news of the morning, as butterflies of excitement are wing-clipped by the kind of anxiety I've never known before. *Is this what Darius suffers?* I resolve, in that moment, to fight as hard as he does.

This ballpark is so cool. The main entrances are open yet intimate, designed to invite you inside. Most major venues remind me of modern Coliseums, with facades like fortifications. But here, even after you enter, the concourses are open to the action you came to see. The buzz of activity, the celebratory atmosphere, and the sense of anticipation all give me hope that the fears of the morning will pass.

In a luxury suite, we're pampered like royalty. We're advised to pace ourselveses with the fancy food, as a dessert cart is to follow. It's total gluttony, admits our host, but who can resist?

Me and Mamma perhaps. We lost our appetites at the Cleveland Clinic.

The park is packed, though the state-of-the-art audiovisual performance dazzles more than the game, at least at first. The hairy fuchsia mascot with the giant yellow nose is stealing the show until Eli jumps on the first pitch in the bottom of the fifth with a solo home run.

By the eighth inning the score is tied and the "bad guys" have runners at first and third base, with two out. The crowd is hushed for the delivery of the next pitch.

It's slammed toward shallow centerfield. He bobbles the ball as the runner bolts for home. The pinch-hitting speedster on his way to first is a lost cause—the throw has to be to the plate. Eli falls to his knees, stretches his arms in the path of the runner while safeguarding his body from another collision. His sweeping tag on the sliding runner is perfect. The umpire searches for the ball in Eli's glove while 40,000 hold their breath.

It's there.

The umpire pumps his fist for the out, but no one hears his call as the rock-n-roll capital of the world twists and shouts for joy.

My heart is pounding. I'm not a screamer, so the sounds coming out of me feel foreign to my ears. Though it also feels good. I see why people use sport as an outlet for those daily dramas where they have to remain under control...such as my own at the hospital, earlier. Though that drama is still beyond my imagination... *Can I scream long enough and loud enough to deal with that?*

Eli stands at the top of the dugout, waiting for the center-fielder. They high-five to the beat of the music. People are still dancing in their seats. Then Eli unhooks his equipment and steps on deck. I feel his eyes on me, and can't resist waving. As our box is in close proximity to the field, I can see his handsome smile clearly. The only thing missing as he strides to home plate is his white horse. People are still going nuts, all around, and I can't help wondering for a second if he's as calm on the inside as he appears on the outside. *Who am I kidding? I know he's wired to explode.* Too bad science hasn't found a way to bottle this kind of energy. It could light the streets of this city for the next twenty years.

Eli sets himself for the pitch. We hear strike one hit the mitt. He steps out of the batter's box for a couple of nervous hacks before digging in and steadying himself once more.

He watches strike two. This time he only moves his back leg out of the box to regroup.

Mama and I suck in simultaneous deep breaths. *What's happening to me? Am I just overemotional because of the events of this morning? Or am I just trying to convince myself that's all it is? Right now I could almost swear the emotions I'm feeling are Eli's. I want to will myself inside him...inside his bat, inside his soul. I want to give him everything he needs.*

He swings at a bad pitch, chopping it toward the third base side of the mound. The pitcher retrieves it, but is feeling over-anxious, judging by the quality of his throw to first base. Eli runs through the bag as the first baseman rushes the tag, smacking him across the shoulders. The ball squirts from his glove toward the visitor's dugout while the first base coach waves frantically for Eli to hoof it for second.

"Is it my imagination, or did this place just get louder?" I ask Mama, but, of course, she can't hear me.

Eli steps carefully off the bag, drawing a throw. He scampers back easily. It's just a reminder by the pitcher that he's still in control—or so he thinks, after two quick outs. But the Tribe's third baseman powers a base hit to shallow left. Eli, the ball in front of him, stays put at second.

Mose now opts for a pinch hitter. Abe tells us this guy has quickly become the skipper's weapon of choice in the early season—and I can see why. He promptly punishes the first pitch deep down the left field line. Eli is waved home.

Oh my God. Will 'turnabout become fair play' in the next instant? The throw is perfect—but Eli's slide is better. Safe!

The catcher replicates a four-year-old's tantrum. His manager runs out to argue, but the umps are already headed for their dressing room, while the bench swarms Eli at home plate.

Mama manages a smile. Our hands meet and she squeezes mine hard. Our prospects for an enjoyable evening have improved by the inch it took Eli to beat the tag. *I can't wait to be near him.*

Chapter 33

Eli

Showered, changed, and post-game interviews completed, I drive to the East Side like a Formula 1 qualifier. No offense to my big puppy, but going home to Fatima is more motivating, even if—unfortunately—we won't be alone.

Apparently, she heard me coming. As she opens the door, the north coast breeze blows her Medusa curls into delicious dishevelment. She looks fetching in a black and white fitted blouse, dark jeans and red pumps. *What's happened to my future nun?*

She tries to pat down her locks. I wish I could be the one doing that. She greets me in her tradition—a kiss on each cheek. Is it my overheated imagination or is there an unusual warmth in her welcome?

Maybe she's not used to the shoes because she trips over her own feet as we step into the kitchen. I catch her.

"Started on the wine without me, did you?" I tease, yet she doesn't smile. *Something has changed, something fundamental. I can sense it.*

•••••••••••

The autograph seekers have left us in peace; and we can order our dinners at last.

"You're not going to believe the story Silvana's mother told me before we left Sicily," Dad says.

He's right. It makes me feel a curious historical connection between our families.

We drink a toast to Nonna Marietta. Then Fatima asks about T.P. Text messages and phone calls have already testified to his reconciliation with Juliet, but I have yet to reveal the latest news.

"Thanks to Tiny Tonkert and a whole bunch of lousy golfers in search of their swings, T.P. has been made an honorary member of the same Country Club that fired him all those years ago. There're several stinkers who still treat him like the help, but otherwise, he's having a ball."

"It was good for you to reach out to this man, no?" Fatima asks. "His life is changed forever beautifully because you took that risk. *The pride in her voice means so much it scares me.*

She continues, "But people like T.P. can end up changing you more than you change them. *Veramente?* True?"

I think about the last words we spoke before I left North Carolina...the ones about Darius and me.

"True," I lie.

"What do you hear about Paolo and Darius's progress? Will they be here soon?" Dad asks.

"The three of us only left North Carolina a week ago, and Darius has had only one start at Double-A Akron, but Paolo looks like he could jump from there to here any day. The big news as I was leaving the clubhouse is that Moki Fukui is on his way up the interstate from Triple-A Columbus. The only guy not happy about that is the one the club sent down to clear his roster spot. I don't want to jinx us, but things are looking good."

Silvana reaches into her purse. "That reminds me."

She hands me an 18-karat gold neck-chain featuring a lace-gloved hand, over which hovers a single eye.

"Some call it the hand of Fatima, others the hand of Miriam. Either way it defends against the evil eye," she says. "I gave Fatima a bracelet just like it."

Dad beams and squeezes her hand, as I thank her.

I appreciate the gesture, but I'm still ambivalent about her and my dad. There's not a bad thing to be said about Silvana Giobatti, but, ever since she came along, Dad's had much less time for me. This is the first game he's watched me play since we opened in New York two months ago, and his calls and texts have become much less frequent. I don't want a chaperone, but he used to fly cross country every three weeks when I was at Stanford. Growing up the only child of a widower made us a couple. As far as I know, the woman whose letters I found years ago while looking for a pair of his shoes is the only other special female before Silvana. *I wonder if Dad's told her about the mysterious Maryam Salamah?*

I only remember the name because she quoted from a crazy poem he wrote her, something about her name meaning Mary Peace, whereupon he rhymed "peace" with "cease": *Mary Peace, my love for you is holy, my love will never cease.* It should make me gag, but somehow it never did.

•••••••••••

Shaker Lake is empty tonight, except for the three of us. I unhook Elvis to let him do his thing, and decide to take a chance. I reach—and it is a reach—for Fatima's hand.

She looks up at me and smiles, but tucks her palm around my elbow instead. Since women also walk arm in arm in Italy, I try not to read too much into the gesture. I also decide not to push it. Although we've shared a hundred phone conversations, this is the first time we've been alone together. *One victory at a time.*

"Have you spoken with Darius recently?" I ask.

"Earlier, yes; we talk almost every day."

I had to ask. What a *stunad.*

She senses my irritation and changes the subject.

"I'm considering a trip to Portugal in October. I've never been to Fatima, believe it or not, so I'm thinking that it's about time. But where I'd really love to go is to Jerusalem and the Holy Land. Your father says he goes back to Israel every few years."

"That's true; he's about due. I haven't been back myself since graduating from high school, which makes me well overdue... But I'm hoping this October to be knee-deep in championship baseball. How about we plan a trip for November?"

"Good point. In that case I'm hoping October won't be good for you to go anywhere...or Paolo...or Darius."

I tug on my new medallion, for luck. And we both laugh.

"This is the first time Elvis has ever left my side," she says.

"I don't blame him for sticking close to you," I say.

I stop. The moonlight half-fills her face.

"Would you allow me to touch that fabulous head of hair of yours?" I ask.

"Well..."

She's uncertain, but I wait her out.

"*Va bene*, OK," she says.

Each silky lock must be three times as heavy as strands of my own. I wade in slowly, touching only the tips. I can't resist sliding my fingers from her temple past her ear. I do it again, only this time with both hands. She puts her hands on mine and draws them down, clutching them to her chest like a bouquet.

"We left our parents alone long enough. It's time to turn the tables on them," she says. But I feel the rush of victory at the flush in her cheeks and tremor in her voice. She drops my hands and whistles for Elvis. He's beside her in an instant...it's as if he is drawn to her too, in a totally different way.

"Holy crap. Where'd you learn to whistle like that?"

"Some things are just genetic."

My little black "horse" leads us past an empty bench lakeside. I want to lift her into my arms, set her on my lap, and hug her like a three-year-old's most precious blanket.

Her cell signals a text. *Need I ask?* Anyway, I don't.

She reads it and politely places her phone back in her pocket.

I refuse to be beaten. After all, I'm here and he's not. I put my arm around her, squeeze her close, and then take off running, to test if Elvis will follow me.

Nope. The best he can muster is a wimpy bark, otherwise, he's glued to her side. I stop to complain.

"What's wrong with you, Elvis? Who's the one who feeds you, picks up your poop, takes you to the groomer and lets you slobber all over his furniture? Where's your sense of loyalty?"

She's laughing, but I badly want to ask her a similar question. *Where do her loyalties truly lie?*

Chapter 34

Darius • Akron, Ohio, June 2015

Paolo and I are starving. We've certainly earned our dinners tonight, as I made it a quick game on my end. At 9:30 Silvana and Fatima are picking us up for dinner at the Greek restaurant that's become our kitchen of choice. The *souvlaki* doesn't come with as much love as Juliet's grits, but it'll do.

Silvana shifts in and out of traffic like a Roman taxi driver. With the top down on her rented convertible, we have a comic view of horrified senior citizens and enraged middle-aged men.

My damn cell rings. *Can't it wait?* I excuse myself the moment she parks. Usually I check in when Paolo is either bar-hopping or else snoring like a goat. Once in a while, things get hot and I'm needed on short notice, but a call like this is rare. My first thought is my mother.

It's Blondie, alright, and he's in a hurry. "I want to know everything you can tell me about a Libyan arms dealer who goes by a Russian name, we think it's Valeri."

My brain halts. *He wants to know everything I can remember about a guy I'd rather forget.* My escape to Europe turned into a near-miss, thanks to this man. Until Valeri, I never knew that murder has a taste. Blondie may have nothing to fear from him anymore, but, as for me... The sweat begins, at my temples and armpits, the small of my back; my breathing becomes labored. *This is a bad one.* I'm trying, I'm really trying, but finally I beg off.

"I've told you everything I know, I swear it! I've got to go."

I hang up and start running. I know I'm screwed once I let the "flight" reflex take over, but I just can't stop this time. I keep running until I'm completely out of breath. *OK. Relax. Slow deep breaths...*

My cell rings again.

"Darius, where are you?" she asks.

"I...don't...know."

Breathe. Breathe.

"You're having an episode, aren't you?"

"You can't...help me. Just...order your dinners. Just...give me... some time."

Then I jump up and down like a swimmer adjusting to freezing temperature; I stuff my forearm into my mouth and scream.

"I'm in the car," she says. "Tell me which direction."

She means business. "Left," I say, at last, "And keep going."

I finally notice that I'm in the parking lot of a large coffee shop. I tell her which.

She whirls into the lot as badly as her mother might. To see her running toward me is a near rescue in itself. At first, she wraps her arms around me, but I can't bear to be held, not even by Fatima. It's claustrophobic, suffocating; it counterpunches my attempt to outrun my fear.

Understanding, at least in part, she releases me. I pace back and forth, waving my hands and ranting like a jihadi. If I had a gun right now I'd probably blow my brains out. In lieu of that I have to move, and keep moving.

"Let's walk," I say.

But her midget stride can't keep up with the urgency I feel, so I revert to pacing in circles, while she asks, "Who's doing this to you? Paolo and Eli suspect you're in contact with someone who never fails to set you off. Tell me, Darius. Let me help you!"

"FBI, CIA...they're all connected. I call him Blondie, but it's not his real name. I don't know his real name. Something in his voice disturbs me, the way his face did the one time we met. I wish I could reach into the back of my brain and draw out what it is. I have no reason to hate him, yet hatred is what I feel—and fear. Lots of fear."

"Oh, Fatima. Did you really think they'd allow me into this country, no questions asked? Really? They're watching us now, I guarantee... But I can't tell you anything. It's too dangerous—for you, for your family. Just let it go. Let it go, I tell you! Go back to the restaurant!"

Her phone rings, but the look on her face isn't surprise at the sound, but surprise at my revelation. Her mouth is agape. "Answer it," I tell her.

"We're fine. *Mangia.* Eat without us. We'll be there later."

Before she can ask me any more questions, a police cruiser pulls up.

"Good evening," says the cop, more of a warning than a greeting. My nerves increase, but Fatima is calm.

"Good evening, officer," she says.

"I need to see some ID. From both of you."

His hand is on his holster. I've seen my fair share of American television by now, so I reach for my wallet very slowly. He reviews Fatima's passport and my visa. My anxiety is reaching volcano-level when he suddenly says, "Aren't you the guy who pitched the one-hitter tonight?"

"Yes, sir," I answer, feeling my heart lift slightly.

"Cleveland's game just ended, but you're the talk of the post-game show, at least what I can hear of it between the squawking on my box... Look, the reason I'm here is I got a call from these premises that some guy was behaving strangely in their parking lot."

"It's all my fault, officer," Fatima says. "I lost his favorite keepsake from his mother. It's like his good luck charm. What's that word you American's use?"

"Superstitious?" he asks.

"*Si, signore,* my friend is very superstitious."

"Did you lose it here, do you think? Let me get my search-light," he says.

While his back is turned she flips off her bracelet, tucks it behind her and bends down to check the pavement. Now three of us are rooting around the blacktop. This ridiculous charade is the antidote to my anxiety. *How can someone who wants to become a nun lie so smoothly?* I try to hide my grin behind a frown.

"Here it is, Darius," she sings out. *"Grazie, Dio!"*

Leave Allah out of this, I want to tease.

She places her bracelet triumphantly in my palm.

"Mind if I have a look?" the cop says.

I recognize the symbol. I'm not the actor she is, but I recover quickly. I put my hand to my heart and say, "You don't know what this means to me."

"What does this design *mean*?" the policeman asks.

"It's called The Hand of Fatima by most Arabs, the Hand of Miriam by some Christians and Jews. Basically, it's like your American rabbit's foot...for good luck."

His radio crackles and he excuses himself, shaking our hands. "Glad to meet the club's future savior," he says, before speeding off.

The term takes me by surprise. *He's got me all wrong; I'm just a guy trying to survive. The one person I want to save is half a world away.* Bitterness like bile suddenly climbs into my throat. I can't help thinking that it's as if I'm metaphorically castrated—while she is very probably being raped.

Chapter 35

Eli • Clevelad, Ohio

Dad and Silvana are cooking in my kitchen this evening. Saturday afternoon games are rare this time of year, but relished. I'm home early for a change. Fatima chose to watch her brother and Darius in Akron, but she picked *my* game last night.

"They just called to tell us they're on I-77, they just passed the Turnpike split," Dad says, in lieu of a hello. Elvis doesn't even bother to greet me. He's had plenty of attention already.

Silvana kisses both my cheeks and offers sympathy for our loss. Loss is a polite way of putting it. We were destroyed in a ten-run rout in which three of us—me included—behaved more like circus clowns than professional athletes. My error cost us a three-run deficit, and my passed ball late in the game threw gasoline on the fire.

My kitchen, however, has never smelled this good. Silvana orders me to taste her Bolognese. She raises a spoonful to my mouth. *Do I have a choice?* She may be a Sicilian mother, but sometimes she acts like a Jewish one.

Mmm. I'll deal with it. "It's outstanding," I tell her. And it is.

By the time I return from taking Elvis for a stroll the rest of the party has arrived.

"So how'd you two do today?" I ask.

"Paolo went 2 for 3 with a walk and 3 RBI. I had 10 strikeouts, one walk that the umpire blew, but I gave up a dinger to lead off the game," Darius reports. "Paolo yelled at me in Italian from centerfield after the mistake: he told me to forget the audience and focus or he'd kick my butt. This rooming together thing is getting scary. He's starting to know me like a wife."

Dad doesn't answer. He's busy pouring the wine that Silvana had shipped over before leaving Sicily. Suddenly, he clears his throat.

He says, "I have an announcement to make. Marietta has given her blessing, and Silvana and I plan to be married in November."

Darius looks at Fatima who seems pleased, so he offers his honest congratulations. By contrast, Paolo and I are deer caught in a traffic jam of headlights. *I've been playing with Paolo for how long, now?—Yet this is the first time I ever felt on the same team.*

"Papa would want nothing more than Mama's happiness," Fatima says sternly to her brother. "Surely after all this time, you would want the same for your father, Eli." Her tone only recedes an inch when directed toward me.

Her efforts are partially successful. We both mutter congratulations, but Paolo looks as unnerved as I feel.

Over dinner, we make do with baseball conversation, but it's like a whole herd of elephants are in the room. Dad and Silvana leave the dishes to us. They have tickets for the Cleveland Orchestra performance at Severance Hall.

"Sorry to leave you so abruptly," Silvana says, "but this is a show not to be missed. I never knew Cleveland's Philharmonic Orchestra was one of the world's best. Who would have imagined? There isn't an orchestra in Italy that can compare!"

Is her excitement a mask? Does she sense that the dust hasn't cleared from the bomb they just dropped? I wait, almost fearfully, for the next detonation.

No sooner do they walk out the door, Paolo...goes...off.

English won't do for this tirade and much of it is, I think, in Sicilian rather than Italian. He storms back and forth, his arms and hands—his whole 6' 4" body—gesticulating to emphasize the emotional stream of consciousness that flows from his lips like hot wax blown from Hanukkah candles in a gale-force wind.

When he stops for breath, Fatima grabs her chance, pouncing on her brother like her mother's body-and-soul guard.

"What is your problem here?! Do you think she needs to ask your permission? *You,* whom she bore in her womb for nine months, suffered childbirth for, and raised to manhood? *You,* whose bottom she wiped, whom she fed at her breast, and later permitted to work at her side. Do you think in your selfish delusion she owes you that?"

I must admit, these Italians have a manner of speaking that's like passion pickled with a vibrant array of hot peppers. Even Paolo is—momentarily—silenced.

"Or is your problem that she hasn't waited long enough? Is there a rule written down somewhere on how long a spouse should mourn? Or are you really naïve enough to think she won't be feeling the loss of our father until her dying day? Or that Abe won't continue to do the same for his dead wife? The truth is, you can't forgive the two of them for having big enough hearts to find room for each other, alongside their lost loves—lost loves, I should remind you, who have gone on to a better place. A place where there's no such petty jealousy, only sons and daughters of God, or were you asleep that day at Mass?

"Shame on you! She's suffered more than you can ever imagine. She *deserves* this happiness. So I repeat, what is your problem?"

"My problem is that *she'll* have another husband, but *I'll* never have another father!" he yells, and his eyes flare like those of a runaway horse as he storms down the stairs to my basement bar. I hate to admit it, but I sympathize with his anger.

Fatima spreads her fingers across her face and shakes her head.

"Perhaps I was a tad overzealous," she murmurs. To me? To Darius?

"You think?" I say quizzically.

She shoves her hands to her hips and drops her head backward, staring at the ceiling as if Michelangelo has painted some answer there.

"Damn this tongue of mine. When will I learn to control it?" Then she turns to me, eyes pleading. "Darius, would you excuse us just a moment?" she says.

My heart does a stutter step. A second ago I wanted to shout with Paolo: now I want to shout for joy.

Outside, the sidewalk is uneven. Based on that fact, as well as on the little stumble she took on the way out, I feel vindicated in holding her arm.

"Are you really taking this decision as well as you seem to be?" I ask.

"I'm happy to see Mama happy again—and I know, in my heart, that your Papa is a good person."

"He is, mostly, and I'm sure your mother is, too."

"But," she says, with a note in her voice that says she's not convinced.

"But he's such a hypocrite! What you don't know is that he always refused to get to know any girl I dated who wasn't Jewish. And then what does *he* do? He proposes to a Christian—and to a pretty devout one at that. Am I supposed to accept that there's a different set of rules for him?"

"Maybe he realizes his mistake and won't treat you that way in the future?"

"He'd better."

"I see... This isn't your only problem with it, though. You want things your way in every sense."

The warmth of her arm is distracting: I fumble for the right words. "I don't want to share him, and I definitely don't want to fall to number two on his list."

There it is. The words are out. I'm relieved to be rid of them.

Silence accompanies us back to the house. She steps onto the concrete stoop. Thanks to her heels, she's looking down on me. She caresses my cheek and smiles. "I hope that someday soon you'll be able to think of what you've gained and not what you've lost."

The door closes behind her as she slips inside. A long moment passes before I move. *I don't want to lose the feel of her hand on my cheek.* Then it occurs to me that *she's* on the inside of *my* house...with Darius.

My life is getting more complicated by the second. Now she's not only my heart-throb, but she's also my soon-to-be stepsister. And there's more: Darius doesn't know it yet, but he and Paolo are skipping Triple-A and being called up to Cleveland later this week. That means that my most important teammates will soon be my future stepbrother and my arch rival for Fatima's affection—besides the convent, of course.

I think I can give up television dramas.

Let's see what else I can pile on here. How about the fact that Fatima isn't the only competition between Darius and me? There's also all that history that makes the Salamahs and Kohns sworn enemies, even if my Dad did once have some kind of a relationship with a woman with Darius's name.

Fatima and Darius are starting to clean up the kitchen when I enter, with Fatima struggling to move Elvis from just in front of the dishwasher. We finish the job together, with little discussion. I suggest a movie. I scan my collection and choose *Moonstruck.*

Paolo apparently is still thunderstruck. He never comes up the stairs.

Chapter 36

Darius • Akron, Ohio, June 2015

Paolo nearly decapitates the pitcher in his initial at-bat. He stands on first base, hands on hips. I imagine steam coming out of his ears. He steps off the bag for a sizeable lead then bolts as soon as the pitcher begins to whirl, stealing second on a pop-up slide that doesn't even draw a throw.

Nobody's ever seen him move so fast. "What the heck did he have for breakfast?" our manager asks, before giving the sign for the hit and run.

The batter hits. Paolo runs. In a flash, he's strutting to the bench, half-heartedly trying to protect himself from all the head slaps. He plops down on a seat and glares straight ahead, the reason for his silent seething known only to me and to two women in the stands.

•••••••••••

After the game he snubs his family, instead leaving with an outfielder staying in the same apartment complex. I want to choke him for what he's doing to his mother—so much so that I can't stand to even look at him, let alone speak to him. Not only am I unsure whether I'll ever see my own mother again, but she's married against her will to a sadist and stuck in the middle of a war zone. *Would Paolo realize the level of his stupidity if I could only share my mother's story?* Some of the guys keep asking, "Hey, what's up with Paolo?" but I just bite my tongue and shrug. As long as we perform well, they'll leave us alone. But it feels like playacting. How long can I keep faking my own reality? Every time my cell rings my heart leaps into my mouth...but it isn't him. At least, not yet.

The ladies drive me home, and I key into our apartment. Paolo is watching another game. Then our phones start going crazy. It's the skipper: we've both been called up to Cleveland. He doesn't understand why we don't sound happier.

Paolo calls Leyland. Our agent wonders the same.

•••••••••••

"Do you know what today is, Leyland?"

"Of course I do. It's a new beginning for you, Darius. The deal was, should you be elevated to the big leagues by the end of the season, you'd earn a million-dollar bonus. If you made it before the All-Star break, that amount was set to double. It's June 17th and that break is still a month away. Welcome to The Show!"

I wave this away impatiently. "No, listen. I'll tell you what day it is, Leyland, it's the first day of the month of Ramadan—a time of prayer, fasting, and celebration—a time for charity. What am I supposed to do with all this money?"

"Well, you could start by finding yourself a beautiful home."

"But whom do I share it with? I've never lived alone in all my life."

"You're making having your own place sound like a prison sentence."

"For me, it is. On my worst nights, even Paolo's snoring is a comfort."

"Paolo's planning on renting a loft apartment downtown. I know the building, lovely place, and masterfully restored. You could easily do the same. The price is exorbitant, but you can certainly afford it... Also, as I mentioned, I've arranged a meeting for you with the team psychologist, Dr. Levy. After working with him you won't miss Paolo's snoring anymore."

"You make it all sound so easy, Leyland. Everything in America is easy, quick, convenient, comfortable, and readily available to buy. How quickly can you arrange for my mother to come here? That's the person I'd like to share my new, masterfully renovated, ridiculously expensive, conveniently located apartment with! Can you do that for me too?" *My voice is almost a shout.*

Leyland, however, can give as good as he gets. He slams right back. "Just when you think you've seen it all in this business, I'm thrown *this* curveball! Billions of people would kill to be in your shoes right now, yours and Paolo's both, but I've gotten nothing but grief today—first from him and now from you! You want your mother back and he can't get clear of his fast enough—sister, too, for that matter."

It takes more than this to move me. "Sorry, Leyland, you're crying to the wrong person for sympathy. What do you know of grief? 'Billions would kill to be in my shoes?' Well, let me tell you something. I *have* killed to be in my shoes and it gives me no pleasure at all!"

Leyland's is a very chic office. His view of Lake Erie is unobstructed; his desk chair ergonomically sound; the desk itself probably antique and exquisitely carved. The pictures of his wife and kids are plump, smiling, and contented. He grew up in the suburbs, attended the best local prep school and earned a couple of Ivy League degrees. His parents are alive and well and he once told me that he couldn't recall the last time he took a sick day.

As if recalling all this, Leyland sighs.

"I'm sorry, Darius. You're just going to have to believe me. I'm doing the best I can."

At this, the anger seeps out of me: I know he is. The check in my hand proves it. He's a good, honest man. Paolo, by contrast, is selfish, spoiled, arrogant, and temperamental. Yet if it wasn't for Paolo, I wouldn't be in this position—a position to turn my mother's world 360 degrees—if only Allah permits her freedom!

"Anyway, believe it or not, Darius, I *do* know that today is the first day of Ramadan. And the reason I know it is because I received a call this morning from a leading member of the Muslim community here in Cleveland. You're invited to an event this evening at the Syrian Cultural Garden in Martin Luther King Park. They realize it's short notice, but since this afternoon is a day game for the ballclub, you're not working tonight, so I thought we could both attend. I'm sure you'd enjoy speaking your native tongue for a change and meeting others from Syria."

"I'm Palestinian. And most of those people were likely born here and don't speak a word of Arabic."

"You can be as bitter as you like, but we both know this is a good opportunity."

I've punished him long enough. He's been more patient than I deserve. "Thank you, Leyland. You're right; I'll go. I'm sorry to sound ungrateful."

"OK, fine. Now let's talk about the questions you'll be asked by the press in a couple of hours."

•••••••••••

Leyland was right. They did ask about fasting on the job. I said that, on games where I'm the Club's starting pitcher, I would break my fast and eat earlier. It wouldn't be fair, either to the team or the fans, for me not to be at my physical best.

He was also right that I'd be asked the following: the Muslim "role model" question, questions about the U.S.'s involvement in Syria, questions about the latest Jewish and Palestinian conflict, along with questions about my pitching and the team of course. The number attending was probably the most I've faced yet, with news as well as sports reporters present, some hailing from places far from Cleveland. There was a real buzz in the room: the longing to see us win the championship is clear, even among those supposed to remain impartial.

The question that surprised me was, "Do you feel like you've won the refugee lottery?" I flushed in annoyance, but Leyland's instructions were in my head immediately. ("Don't answer any question in anger. If you're irritated by the way a question is phrased, imagine something that never fails to make you smile. Not something from the past that might make you nostalgic, but something from the last year.") I thought of Fatima dancing with no rhythm, and then answered the reporter, "No more than Jesus, Mary, and Joseph felt in Egypt."

That ended the press conference.

This clubhouse is better than any home I possessed in Syria; I'm bunked between Paolo and Eli. "The sons of Abraham" a photographer jokes, taking a picture of the wooden closets with our name plates above. His biblical reference is not lost on me, but the humor sure is.

Little does he know that we'd rather be as far apart as possible. Paolo and Eli are clearly the most popular players among the fans, the press...and also the women. Their mutual jealousy is usually manifested in tantrums by Paolo and lectures by the more erudite Eli, who once won an academic scholarship to Stanford. I wish I could ask for a change of position, but as the most foreign foreigner (and also as a rookie) my rights are limited. I'm on the lowest rung of the pecking order. Meanwhile, members of the club's PR staff figuratively hold my hand just as much as the coaches do. I appreciate it, but it isn't necessary—how could they have any idea of the minefields I've survived already?

At last, a welcoming face bounces into the room. Moki spots me and throws his arms wide. "Hey, man, good to see you, dude!" His pleasure is genuine.

Paolo and Eli arrive soon after Moki. They're done with the press and are wearing their game faces. *Good idea. Battle mode is more my style, too.*

A clubbie hands me my spikes, cleaned to shimmer, and then passes me a note. Surely Blondie wouldn't trust one of these guys with information? I open it, aware that both Paolo and Eli are watching me. The nervousness in their eyes amuses me.

"It's from Fatima," I lie. They turn away, both pissed...

Good. I'm tired of being spied on. There are enough people casing my every move without the two of them piling on...

Darius,

I'm your chauffeur tonight to the Ramadan event at the Syrian Gardens. Leyland has been called away on other business; Eli has a fundraiser and Paolo has begged off (I'm afraid we can all guess the reason) so you're stuck with me. I hope you don't mind.

Abe

I'm so glad it's not from Blondie! Every day I subconsciously suspect that I'm a day closer to figuring out why this man rattles me so... How I wish I was there already!

•••••••••••

The family waiting room is filled with beautiful women and young children, with a smattering of visiting parents and grandparents. We won, so everyone's in a good mood, except for Paolo, who went hitless. He says "Hello" curtly to Abe, and leaves with a young lady whom he introduces to me as an "old friend," a red-headed beauty.

Eli and I flank his father on the way out. It feels weird to be walking as a threesome, but not necessarily in a bad way—somewhere between prickly and snug. Abe discusses a design project his architectural firm landed this morning. Eli and I both congratulate him; then Eli unlocks his convertible. "See you later," he waves, and he's off.

What is it with these people and topless cars? Abe is driving one too. Then I remember the culture shock of the topless sunbathers in Calabria and decide that the topless cars aren't so bad.

Personally I find Abraham Kohn to be an enigma. He's likeable enough. He treats Silvana like a queen. He enjoys philosophical debates with Fatima, and takes Paolo's temper gracefully in his stride. His love for Eli is clearly boundless, but there's a hole in this man. That affability masks an ache.

He makes conversation easily. We talk of life in the U.S., real estate in Cleveland, Silvana and Fatima (having dinner with relatives of Sister Colleen) and, naturally, baseball. He explains that the organizers of tonight's event were hoping for photos of me with Paolo and Eli, but they'll settle for Abe and me with the Roman Catholic Bishop of the Diocese of Cleveland.

•••••••••••

The food is so awesome to my taste buds I'm moved to tears. I work a napkin cleverly to hide my emotions. Perhaps I'm so emotional thanks to all the incredible changes in my life. I see my mother's face in every woman wearing a hijab—although, admittedly, there aren't many. This diversity within unity I see before me is exactly the dream she and my father shared. In a garden alongside a winding road named for Martin Luther King (the man most admired by my parents, along with Gandhi), Shia and Sunni laugh with Protestant and Catholic, Buddhist and Jew, Hindu and Sikh. Back slaps, hugs, kisses, invitations, greetings, and gifts overwhelm me. Leyland had me memorize a short speech for the occasion; however, I can't help but go off script, speaking of some of these things and what they mean to me. *Leyland was right. I'm glad I came.*

After my speech I'm pulled, sometimes physically, from one conversation to another. Everyone seems to want to meet me. I realize that my status as an athlete is the main draw, but I see no reason not to use it to my own advantage—and to the advantage of others who have suffered. I agree to attend two fundraisers in support of the refugees. One is to be held at a mosque, but another is backed by members of a Jewish Temple, which surprises me. Then a Palestinian imam invites me to Jum'ah Prayers, held at one o'clock for those who work downtown. I make an excuse. *As long as my mother is lost in hell, I can't find prayers to Allah.* A bitterness creeps up my throat—the first negative in an otherwise positive evening.

Abe, meanwhile, is working the crowd like a politician. He continues to make eye contact with me though, smiling and nodding, and on several occasions introducing me to people. A few guests ask for my autograph, but not so many as to become annoying.

By the time we leave I'm exhausted. I want to loosen my belt, but I'm not sure how to do it inconspicuously. When we arrive back at the hotel, Abe asks if we can chat for a while, since we've been busy with other guests all evening.

We find a comfy seating area, where someone recognizes me and asks me to sign a baseball. I remind him that I have yet to pitch a game in Cleveland. "How do you know I'm worth it?" I ask, only half-joking.

"You're all anyone has been talking about since Moki Fukui arrived. With a closer like him and an ace like you, we can't lose—especially now that Paolo's back." I notice he's wearing a jersey with Eli's name on it but, naturally, he doesn't realize who Abe is.

"I feel like the golden calf. How did Eli ever get used to all the fans?" I ask, once he's gone.

"I'm not sure he is really used to it, but it's different for him. It's a nuisance more than anything else, while you feel humbled and only slightly annoyed."

"Correct."

"Anyway, it's part of your job; you don't have much choice. Turning folks away generally leads to trouble."

"The thought has crossed my mind, but I'll deal with it."

"You've had to deal with far too much already in your young life. I'm so sorry about that. I—well, I was hoping to hear about your parents, if it wouldn't hurt too much. And if you trust me, of course."

"I do, and I'll deal with it." I smile.

He smiles back. His smile is different from Eli's yet vaguely familiar. *More weirdness.*

I dismiss it from my mind, saying, "My parents met at university, not as students, but as instructors in the language department: She was teaching English, he French. Their fathers had both been educators, as well. Learning different languages always leads to appreciating different cultures, of course—but I think that valuing people as people was always in their DNA. I would argue it's what drove them not only to study languages but ultimately to fall in love with each other, despite her being a Farsi-speaking Shia-Iranian and him being an Arab-speaking Sunni-Palestinian.

"As you probably know, strict-observing Sunni Muslims consider Shia Muslims to be fabricating a faith, and vice versa. It would actually be more likely for a Sunni or Shia to marry a Jew or a Christian than someone from the other branch of Islam, because at least each recognizes Christianity and Judaism as actual religions."

"I believe you. It reminds me of Catholics and Protestants during my dad's youth. Anyway, how did they wind up in Syria?"

"Syria was the place both their families found safety, fleeing war and strife. My father's grandparents fled Palestine during the 1948 war, just after the creation of Israel. In the case of my mother's family, it was out of fear that her younger brother might be "martyred" on the front lines of the Iran-Iraq War. Her brother had become drunk on the words of the Ayatollah, and spoken of longing for military glory and a heavenly paradise: he was threatening to run away to the front where young boys were sacrificed to locate landmines ahead of the soldiers. My grandfather was assured that he'd find work as a teacher in Damascus, and so they fled. It's sickeningly ironic that a country like Syria—a place which has itself harbored refugees from so many countries, including Armenia, Lebanon and Iraq, to name but three—is now bleeding them onto other shores. How can this have happened?"

He doesn't say anything, and I calm down. I'm a little curious about his own ancestors' role in the upheavals of the 20th century. But in another way, I don't want to hear, and he volunteers nothing.

I continue. "They married against the consent of their parents—and were never forgiven for it. The man responsible for that union was an Italian Jesuit Priest named Paolo Dall'Oglio. Dall'Oglio, after ordination in the Syriac Catholic Rite, established an interfaith community at the ancient Monastery of Saint Moses the Abyssinian, about 50 miles north of Damascus. I visited there once and was astonished by the 11th and 12th century frescoes on display. But my parents, years before, had been more amazed by the man himself and by all the clerics and scholars of disparate religions who worked together in peaceful dialogue inside those mystical walls in the hills of the desert. They respected Father Paolo's efforts to build bridges, although the regime later banished him for it and he eventually fell into the hands of the group you call ISIS. I don't know for sure, but I fear that he is dead."

"Did your parents marry in the faith?"

"What wedding ceremony my parents shared is unknown to me, but they never renounced Islam. Our home was what all that a Muslim home should be—a haven of hospitality. Visiting professors from various parts of the world were welcomed with lavish meals. Syria is, was, a modern country with educated masses, no Third World wasteland! It's beyond belief that it's gone this far! What were people thinking?"

Again, Abe says nothing, but I see my own pain reflected in his face.

"Anyway, maybe being outcasts within their most intimate circle made it easier for my parents to endure being outcasts in the wider Muslim world. Being pacifists, they were accused of being weak, selfish, even foolish. But they also had a strong following, and it was that which lead to disaster."

The barmaid takes our drink order. Abe has a Manhattan; I have a Coke. Perhaps the interlude gives me the courage to add, "I'd rather not relive the next part, if you don't mind."

"Of course not. This is a special day for you. You have every right to enjoy it. You also have every right to happiness, as soon as you determine to begin the hard work of leaving your past behind. Which you must do—otherwise you'll die a little each day. Trust me."

He's speaking from experience here, I think.

"I was wondering," Abe says, with assumed casualness, "If your father might possibly have had a relative named Maryam Salamah?"

"Yes, he did! She was my favorite relative. This is a strange thing! Did you meet her?" My heart begins to pound.

"I'm not sure if we're talking about the same Maryam Salamah," Abe says, a little unsteadily. "The one I knew was a very beautiful woman. She had a pair of dark moles, one above the other, just on the outside of her right eye."

"It is the same!" I shoot up straighter in my seat. "She would visit us twice a year. She was extremely smart, my father always said, and had a very important job in the U.S. She was so kind. I can still summon up the tones of her voice, as she used to read to me for hours when I was a child... She seemed to love children. Was she your colleague, then?"

Mr. Kohn has slumped forward in his chair. Alarmed, I squeeze his limp forearm. "Mr Kohn? Abe? Are you all right?"

"I'm fine," he says, at last, but he doesn't sound fine. He swallows so hard that his Adam's apple bounces.

"I did indeed work with Maryam Salamah...about twenty years ago. Your father was right. She's an amazing woman. We lost touch, however. Can you—can you tell me what became of her?"

"I'm sorry to say that she died of cancer, when I was fourteen. Until the war, I never knew such loss."

His eyes fill, but being of that generation, he blinks the tears away, stands heavily and walks toward the bar to ask for the check. I can only see his back, but I can imagine his face. *He must have cared for her too.*

As we're walking out, I thank him for the drink and for taxiing me.

He hugs me and whispers in my ear, "You have nothing to thank me for, son. I've been honored with your confidence." There are still tears in his eyes as he says, "It's been an astonishing evening."

My priest friend called me "son" on numerous occasions. Now this Jew does the same. Isn't this what my parents would have wanted for me?—to live in a world where people with strongly held differences care for one another, regardless? Most everyone at the event tonight could not have been more thoughtful... *These signs should give me hope.*

I watch Abe circumnavigate the revolving door out of the lobby. Tomorrow I'll dress for work next to his *real* son...the one I trust about half as far as I can throw.

Chapter 37

Fatima • Sicily, July 2015

Nonna watches me do it. Then she wrinkles her face, trying to understand how I could drop a tray of filled wine glasses.

"What's wrong?" she says, in that don't-you-dare-lie-to-me tone.

I tiptoe over the mess to hug her. I hold back nothing. It's impossible to dam the flood of my tears. The woman is as strong as The Rock of Gibraltar. She encircles both me and Mama in her formidable arms.

"I always knew God was keeping me alive for a reason," she says. "How I wish it was a different one!"

She calls to Zio Peppe. He is stalwart. He's a good brother to her, a wonderful great uncle for me, and the best priest I've ever known. His prayers will carry weight.

Of course, Nonna had guessed that something was going on. Tongues were apparently wagging while we were away. I'd been seen at Dr. Dante's office twice in back-to-back weeks. Then I'd "disappeared" to the U.S. The word was hissed in that slanderous way people speak of unwed mothers.

Nonna says she dismissed the gossip outright, after considering the source. It was the woman Nonno Pietro was meant to marry before Nonna came into his life.

"Some hatchets are never buried," she says, "They just keep chipping away."

My cell rings. It's Paolo.

"Pronto? Chi parla?"

"You know who it is, Fatima, but I suppose I deserve that jab. Is everything OK with you?"

"Everything, except my brother let his mother and me leave without even wishing us farewell."

"All right, all right. I apologize, but I'm having one of those weird twin moments. I feel like something bad is happening to you."

It *is* weird, but it's not the first time it's happened, although I'm usually the one with the premonitions. I go from pissed to touched in the time it takes Mama's Testarossa to go from 0 to 100.

"You sure everything is OK?" he repeats.

The truth is: everything is not OK. We received the final test results the day before we left. It's ALS for sure. Dr. Belini tried to encourage us with news of all the money raised by the Ice Bucket Challenge and how those funds already are leading to encouraging developments, but it was small consolation. I told Sister Colleen the other day that I'm trying to take heart in my prayers, but I'm struggling. She reminded me that I now have a powerful new tool in my prayer arsenal, which is to offer up my suffering for a higher purpose. *I don't know if I'm up to it, but I'll at least try.*

Mama and I had made a pact, however, not to worry the rest of the family yet. That idea crashed and burned with the wine glasses, as far as Nonna and Zio go, but I'm trying to keep casualties to a minimum. I take a deep breath and lie to my twin: "I'm fine. Better than your batting average."

"Ouch, that hurts. You manage to kick me in the *coglioni* across an ocean! Are we even now?"

"We are, but you'll never find your swing until you apologize to Mama."

He knows that already. His sigh tells me so. "Put her on the phone," he says.

•••••••••••

Each morning, the people of Villa Multicino watch the game Zio recorded the previous evening on satellite TV. We zip through the commercials and those incessant waits between pitches and pitchers. Every time a batter steps out of the box to adjust this, that, and the other, or a pitcher huffs and puffs around his mound, Nonna curses. "They're like little boys, trying to make a big show. And for what? Can't they see that Darius and Paolo never do that and they're far more successful? You'd expect the others to follow their lead and get on with it. *Stunads!*"

The boys are successful though...on the field at least. Off the field: not quite so much.

One day I talk to Paolo and he's cursing Eli.

Another day I talk to Eli and he's fishing for affection I have to fight not to give. With my condition—and its terminal prognosis—it's for his own good, but he doesn't know that, of course. Having this disease should make it easier for me to focus on myself, shouldn't it? Yet oddly enough, I find focusing on Eli, Paolo, and Darius is a help.

I had one of my lost-in-the-light-episodes earlier: a blessed escape from all this worry. It was as though I became a sunburst...a zillion sparkling rays melding into another more powerful explosion of hot bright glory. I wish I could have stayed there.

But at least I returned from that place to enjoy a more grounded conversation with Darius for a change. He told me that Paolo appears to have lost his touch with the ladies, of late. He said, "Paolo's spit-in-the-wind frustrated, slipping-on-black-ice humiliated, and, worst of all, toilet-seat-up-when-it-should-be-down shocked. He's in virgin territory, a dodgeball rookie, naked in the frozen food section of the grocery store singing the wrong words to an Adele tune."

We both laughed so hard I wet my pants. It gave me hope for Darius, as, the last time we'd spoken, I'd asked him if he was happy after his last start—which they'd won—but he only said, "Happy? What is happy? I don't even know that word. How can I be happy? Your brother and Eli are so suspicious of my every phone call that they can't decide whether to be relieved or pissed when they find out it's you I've been talking to. The city of Cleveland has been surprisingly welcoming, but the daily news from the Middle East is not. Would this city be so generous to me if I wasn't helping it live vicariously through a winning ball club? My teammates have no idea what's happening outside of baseball. I wish I could enjoy it the way they do, but my anxiety hits me at 3 a.m. every night. I'm so grateful that it's 9 a.m. in Italy and you are there."

I let him vent, and then ask, "Isn't Dr. Levy helping you?"

"A turtle makes better progress each day than I do with Dr. Levy."

And so it goes with the last of the "Sons of Abraham." That's what the press dubbed the three of them, after someone snapped a photo of their names above their side-by-side lockers.

I feel their pain, but I have my own. I'm worried about my disease, and working with Sister Colleen I hear hellish tales continuously.

I'm wearing out my Rosary beads.

•••••••••••

Mama tosses a newspaper on the patio table, a tiny grin creasing her lips. Nonna, Zio, and I are enjoying peach sodas—it's a muggy day. Three familiar faces peer at us from the front page. Television news too has been gushing in its praise.

Even Italian journalists and broadcasters are traveling to the States to cover the group; they've become the talk of *Italia*. Little boys are playing wiffle ball in the streets of Catania, courtesy of a clever promotion from a brand Paolo endorses. It strikes a chord: like Puccini on his best day. A Roman journalist shoots a video of the kids in Piazza Duomo and asks them why they're playing.

"I want to be a star in America, like Paolo Giobatti," one says.

The Italian League actually holds a tryout camp for refugees. Football Federations throughout Europe steal the idea; and three young men from Eritrea sign contracts.

Mama is continually besieged with requests for appearances by Paolo and Darius. She has to hire someone to assist or she'd have no peace and no business, though she's very proud. I've overheard her talking to her best friend on her *telefonino* about Paolo's batting prowess and recent triumphs.

Abe visits—for the second time since our return. He's amazed by the sensation the boys are making in Italy, but their new appeal in the Middle East is potentially even more astonishing. The club has had to make playoff-type media arrangements, in order to accommodate the entourage from abroad. We have some idea of what that entails from our phone conversations with the boys.

Eli is fast becoming an even bigger household name in Israel than Paolo is here in Italy. Luckily, Abe's administrative assistant is a pro at fielding all the media bombardment coming his way.

A plan for a baseball exhibition (concocted by Leyland's marketing agency) is also under consideration. Abe tells us it could be big—provided hostilities overseas don't turn a honey of an idea into box-office poison. Sporting goods, apparel, and footwear brands are hoping to jump on the bandwagon in order to boost sales abroad. We'll learn more when we see him in New York.

•••••••••••

For the first time since the 90s, Cleveland has the "horses" to ride to another Championship. By the third week of August, Paolo is on a 30-game hit streak, drawing comparisons between the Italian native and the legendary Italian-American, Joe DiMaggio, amongst all the rest of the buzz swirling around the team.

Cleveland is playing in The Big Apple. *The NY Times* headline reads: *UN Battles Yanks*. This is probably because the Cleveland club recently added an Aussie and a South Korean to go along with Moki, Darius, Paolo, Eli, and several Spanish speakers, including Darius's friend from Zebulon, Juan Diego. Leyland considers New York the perfect launch-pad for his proposal to promote harmony through baseball which stands in stark opposition to political discourse. He's meeting with the Commissioner of the league, a taxi ride away, just as Mama and I land at JFK.

Leyland finally explained his plans to us and the boys, in a conference call before we left Sicily. His firm has created a complete package they dub (not surprisingly) the "Sons of Abraham" Tour. It includes stars from around the world represented by his firm in a baseball skills competition. Top sporting goods, apparel, and shoe manufacturers are already fighting for exclusive sponsorships. Operations, marketing, and logistics are outlined. The tour venues include Rome, Dubai, and Jerusalem—the last being dependent upon a lull in the ongoing clashes between Israelis and Palestinians.

The Rome venue is the most intriguing. The vast parcel of land beyond the Coliseum and Palantine Hill (where the Circus Maximus once stood, with its 300,000 attendees) will be transformed into a sports venue once more, though a temporary one. The vision of home runs being launched from a modern sport venue into an ancient world is spectacular.

Leyland admitted that security is a concern, and also that slating the feat for this November is a pretty crazy time-frame, considering that All-Star Games are usually years in the works for any host city. But he's confident in the abilities of his organizing team. After covering expenses, the proceeds will benefit the International Rescue Committee and PeacePlayers International. I'd never heard Leyland so excited.

Now he prances into the palatial lobby of the Marriott Marquis on Times Square. He's glad to find us greeting the guys before their departure for the stadium. Autograph seekers hover like vultures, trying to gauge the polite moment to interrupt, but—this time at least—they're ignored.

Paolo hugs Mama tight. That's so typical of him after one of their blow-ups—they've been raging and reconciling all my life, always ending up closer than ever. He asks about our trip. "Gloriously uneventful," is her reply. They confer briefly about this year's grapes and expansion plans for the winery. Darius corners me by speaking in Italian, irritating Eli, who's barely listening to his father's news of relatives in California.

Darius asks me how long we can stay. Two weeks, I tell him. The grape harvest is looming and, although the staff is completely capable, Mama remains Queen of the Harvest.

It's time for the team to board the bus to the Bronx. We kiss good-bye, but not before Eli reminds his father that our tickets for the game have been left by him. I smile and say, *"Grazie."*

It's so little, yet it means so much. Eli beams; Darius frowns; Paolo, of course, is oblivious.

Chapter 38

Darius • New York City

The media spotlight in the media capital of the world is utter madness. The growing appetite for the "Sons of Abraham" has now swallowed up Mose, along with the rest of us. Not that he seems to mind: he understands the power of the pen and respects the job required by reporters. He also understands the need to meet deadlines with something unique, compelling, or scintillating. Personally, I think he feels sorry for the club's PR staff, with the double whammy of a Championship race, coupled with the herculean effort required to meet the demands of a growing foreign press. Add in Paolo's hitting streak and circumstances are pushing them all to the point where hair loss meets stomach ulcers. But Mose remains excited. He said to me only minutes ago, "Son, this is what it's all about." Then he went back to the League's PR team, whipping up reinforcement and tactical support.

Our skipper is assigned Japanese, Italian, Arabic, and Korean interpreters. As he shuttles with us from one pre-game interview to another, between the stadium media room, field, visitor's dugout and clubhouse, I'm impressed by the number of meaty questions he's asked. Mose just eats it up. His coaching staff thinks he's nuts; but I think it's the reason why *he's* the manager and *they* aren't. Listening to him has become a lesson in PR 101.

He's developed an especially good relationship with two journalists: an Italian sportswriter and an Arab TV personality from Al-Jazeera. They lack a common language, but share a mutual respect. Mose is fascinated with his opportunity with détente, after 50 years in the game. I witnessed them sharing drinks in Boston. He told me their English is good enough for socializing, and that they both fully understood those three magic words: off the record.

A young woman from the club's (recently augmented) staff of interns escorts Paolo and me to join Mose, who is ensconced with the Italian media. I instantly pick up the signals Paolo is practically shouting at her and—to be honest—I can't blame him. She's an extremely attractive red-head with bright, almost exotic, green eyes. She's having none of it, however. Smart woman. *What is it with Paolo and redheads, anyway?*

Mose's new friend, Michele of *la Repubblica*, jumps in first. "Mose, how has Paolo changed from the player you managed two years ago?"

"He grew a pair of ears in the interim. It's amazin' what happens when a young man starts listening to his elders."

We all laugh, including Paolo, though rather unwillingly, I suspect. But he can charm, as well. "A year with Mama bossing me around the family business made me appreciate my coaches," he says.

More laughter.

Ahmad, an Egyptian with Al-Jazeera, asks, "What do you see in Darius's demeanor when you remove him from a game?"

"Relief," Mose jokes. Then he smiles at me and says, "Seriously, I have yet to take the ball from this young man's hand feelin' there's nothin' left in the tank. He's never ready to leave, but he knows that his pal Moki's fully gassed and ready and eager to drive the bus home. It's unusual these days for a pitcher to go eight innings regularly, but Darius is special. His demeanor is businesslike, and he's conscious that every person on the team has his role to play. He's done *his* job, and Moki's comin' on to do his—that's that. Besides, there's no need to tax his young arm. He only turned twenty less than a month ago."

Ahmad seizes his opportunity. "Darius, how did you celebrate that birthday?"

"What is there to celebrate when your family is not with you?" I smile to take away any tinge of bitterness. "Everyone was very kind. The boys had an American-style cake delivered to the clubhouse. The clubbies put candles in it and everyone sang the American birthday song and told me to make a wish before blowing out the flames. I realize many Muslims don't celebrate birthdays, but in my family my mother always made a special meal... Since the next day was a start for me, I also chose to review some game film and scouting reports from the advance crew."

"Darius prepares more than anyone I know. And when a game situation intensifies, he and Eli are an island of cool in a boiling ocean," Mose adds.

Paolo is frowning, probably due to jealousy. *It's certainly a description nobody could use of him.*

Another open door for Ahmad. "Much has been made of the Arab/Jew, pitcher/catcher duet of you and Eli Kohn. How do you manage, considering your bloodlines are killing each other over disputed homeland?"

I've been schooled to avoid loaded questions.

"We both want to win. We both like to study. We both come from families where hard work, preparation, and discipline were highly valued. We want the same thing and we both go after it with patience and determination. Yes, our religions differ, and it is true that we were born in different lands. But because those other core aspects are the same, we fit 'hand in glove,' as you Americans say."

I'm speaking about baseball competition, but thinking about Fatima, wondering what the coming weeks of *that* contest might bring...

•••••••••••

Days later I have the answer. It's war. I think I trust him even less than I trust Blondie.

Eli invites Fatima to a fundraiser for the Temple he rarely attends—the same day that I ask her to teach me how to drive.

Fatima is content to do us favors, as she calls it, but always avoids committing herself, something which must be as obvious to Eli as it is to me. However, just before we leave for a three-game road trip to Toronto, she confesses to me that Eli is having me followed. He thinks I might be involved with some highly unsavory characters.

Is she baiting me? Does she think this too? Well, in a way, based on what I've told her already plus her own brand of off-the-chart instinct, to admit otherwise would be a lie. I tighten my lips, but before I can respond, she is in the middle of one of her spaced-out moments. Her face is still her face, yet isn't exactly: it's too peaceful, all the mischief is gone... Uneasily, I check my watch. Paolo and Silvana always time her when this happens. With neither here, I do the same. Her lips are slightly parted. I want to touch them, but don't dare disturb her. Her eyes appear to be focused somewhere beyond the ceiling. Three minutes later she's back, only to hastily excuse herself. *(Why? What did she see?)*

I could care less what Eli thinks, but to lose her confidence... *Breathe, breathe...don't think of this now...release it. Breathe: focus.*

I need to run.

•••••••••••

Game one against the neighbors to the north is *my* start. Over the first five innings I give up too many hits, and two runs. I don't like the game Eli's calling and shake him off continuously.

Mose bolts to the mound in the top of the sixth, after another rerun of the same lousy show. Eli has to hurry to reach the hill in time to join us. The skipper whistled for him the second he was out of the dugout, just as he always does when highly ticked-off.

"What the heck's goin' on here? We're damn lucky to still be in this thing and no thanks to your swing either, which seems to have gone MIA," he snaps at Eli. "I'm about as tired as a one-legged rooster in a king-sized hen house of the wordless bickerin' goin' on between you two."

The home plate umpire joins our pow-wow in time to hear that last part. He's trying not to snicker as he politely suggests moving things along.

"That's precisely what I'm tryin' to do here, Brian, but these two knuckleheads seem determined to stretch nine innings into five hours!" With that, he storms back to the bench.

Eli trots back to the plate, frowning. He squats into position, throws down two fingers and pats his inner thigh.

I decide I'd better oblige—unfortunately, not very skillfully. The ball sails over Paolo's head so fast he barely runs and mostly watches.

"Go get that kid before I make a scene ESPN'll never forget," I hear Mose yell to our pitching coach. Then he screams at Eli, "Your ass is next, even if I have to get out there and catch myself!"

I wisely take a seat as far away from the skipper as possible.

It's my first disastrous outing. I choose to take it like a man—no glove-slamming for the TV cameras or hustling off to hide in the clubhouse. I sit there, glaring straight ahead, pissed, but, with a little luck, with some dignity still intact.

Eli settles down and calls an improved game. He even ekes out a walk before it's over, but it's not nearly enough to overcome the opposition.

I calm myself before facing the press.

•••••••••••

As it turns out, the press is the least of my problems. Eli and I, like misbehaving schoolkids, are ordered to the principal's office. Mose implodes.

"My given name might be *Abraham* Moses, but I ain't nobody's daddy. There's times when I've wondered what it'd be like to have kids of my own, but after livin' with the two of you, I'm thankful to have been spared that pain in the ass.

"Don't think for one second that I don't know what's goin' on here. That pretty little missy from the Mediterranean is gonna be the downfall of the both of ya if y'all don't learn to share. I may not be an expert on children, but I know a thing or two about women after bein' married to three of 'em, and I can tell ya, sure as the sun's gonna come up tomorrow, that girl ain't gonna choose either of ya. She's neutral territory if I ever seen it. So, the sooner you get over it and negotiate a ceasefire, the sooner we can get on with winning this thing. Don't you realize what's at stake here? This could be the biggest year of your entire careers, for God's sake!

Now get the hell outta here before I reach across this desk to spank the both of ya."

Chapter 39

Paolo • Toronto, Canada

My hit streak stands at 35 games, but it's Darius and Eli's failures that make the headlines. I toss the newspaper toward Fatima across the table in our hotel room, Mama having already gone downstairs for breakfast.

"Darius and Eli are stinking it up and the reporters are all over it. They may not know the source of their problems, but I do. They've barely spoken to each other since New York, not that they were ever bosom buddies. They haven't argued either, but then what's there to argue? Neither has a claim on you. You tease them with your kindness, which only makes matters worse. Instead of my hit streak making the headlines, look what they're saying today!" I stab my index finger at the front page of the sports section.

Fatima doesn't even look. "Does your selfishness know no bounds?" she says with quiet but savage intensity. "Is that what this is about for you? You don't care if their feelings are torn, or mine for that matter. You don't even care if they play badly. You only care that the spotlight which feeds you is shining elsewhere! Don't worry, dear brother, I'll be gone soon. They'll bounce back and the moon and stars will once again align for you!"

She storms from the room, but trips on the way.

"Good," I yell. "I hope you hurt yourself! That's what your words have done to me!"

She shakes her head, picks herself up, and leaves without looking back.

Chapter 40

Eli • Cleveland, September 2015

It's a glorious day for baseball. The usual diehards dot the seats. Others, with their balls and pens in hand, line the rail. The dugout security cop makes certain they behave like school kids on a field trip. The air is warm, but crisp; the lake breeze brushes my cheek.

But it doesn't soothe. I feel like I'm acting out a scene from the same horror flick as yesterday, and the day before, and the day before... *I can't even remember how long it's been since this monster slump to end all slumps actually began.*

Today, Mose opts to remain in the dugout rather than stand in his usual spot, directly behind the batting cage. Reporters are there instead—they're everywhere. Today's game is the first of three at home with the boys from the Bronx. *Could the timing of this debacle possibly be worse?*

Our bullpen coach is serving them up to Paolo. I think: *you Italian pain in my ass. The worse I swing the sweeter you do. It's like you're sucking the life right out of me...*

Paolo catches the jealousy in my eyes as he stretches a leg backward, arching to re-grip the bat. He glares at me as he digs back in. We have a perfect view of each other. I'm leaning on the first base side of the cage, directly across from the batter's box. Daggers are flying between us. Probably, everyone can see it. I picture the players, coaches, and reporters nearby collectively tucking in their chins, for fear of getting caught in the crossfire.

Paolo doesn't miss the opportunity. He strokes the next toss toward the centerfield picnic area. Someone from the group sales staff yells, "Incoming!" Fans scramble to retrieve the souvenir.

He's tempted to grin an in-your-face smile, but even he won't stoop that low. It's a jinx. Slumps are no laughing matter to any player. *Oh God, I can feel my confidence seeping out my shoes.*

"That's it!" the coach who's pitching yells. "Eli, get in the box."

I take a deep breath and stomp my right cleat into the ground, desperately looking for a toehold that will become the first step to ending this madness, once and for all. I settle in, though I can sense desperation in my fingers and palms. I feel as though I'm on an adrenalin overdose. I tell myself to calm down, to breathe. I jiggle my head.

In sails the first pitch. I swing and barely miss belting it, instead fouling it straight back so hard everyone around the cage flinches.

"Close," Paolo murmurs.

Bastard. *Why does he have to stand just where I can see him?*

As if telepathic, Mose shouts at Paolo from the dugout. A member of the marketing staff is standing beside the skipper, gesticulating the universal sign for autographs. Paolo remembers his promise to schmooze a sponsor and saunters from the cage.

I spit on the ground as I watch him go. A gull squawks overhead. *I don't believe it.* A flying plop of poop streams past, landing next to the spit I just hawked. The gang around the cage cracks up.

"That was close, Eli. Maybe your luck is changing," someone with a New York accent quips.

But I know better. It was Paolo who taught me that being dumped on by a bird was actually *good* luck to Italians.

But I'm not Italian. So maybe my luck *is* changing. This is ridiculous. What's happening to me? My brain is fumbling for anything it can grasp, just to get me out of this fix. *So shut up already.*

I'm beginning to fear for my sanity.

Nine more pitches come and go, without a solid smack to be had among them. When the coach yells for the next guy to take his turn, the relief is wonderful. I trudge, like a wounded soldier, head down, toward the dugout. I rub my right elbow and roll my shoulder.

The truth is that I feel fine—physically. I just can't stand for the fans nearby to believe I can perform that badly of my own volition. I step down toward the bench just as a returning Paolo sneers, under his breath, "Faker!"

A hot poker of fury prods me, all the way through the tunnel and back to the clubhouse.

The room is empty, except for a couple of clubbies cleaning spikes, when I thunder in through the doors. They immediately register my animal fury. They plead with their eyes for me not to destroy the room they've scrubbed immaculate. So I decide to shit on the plumbers instead. As I burst into the cavernous bathroom my scream echoes like that of a sci-fi robot gone berserk. I level the first wood-chop of the bat still clutched in my hand straight down onto the sink and faucet nearest the door, pounding and pounding until the bat is reduced to its handle. Tossing it aside, I grab Moki's jumbo bottle of men's cologne, hurling it across the room like a French missile. It disintegrates into a musky splat on the back of a toilet stall.

Wheezes lurch from my throat, coming in waves like a drunken puke. I bend at the waist and stomp my feet on the ground as if it could force another strange chortle from my mouth. A clubby peeks fearfully around the door—which stokes another performance.

I fall to the floor and giggle like a six-year-old prankster with his first whoopee cushion. Tears stream down my face, but what's happening? I stop in an instant and sit bolt upright. I'm shocked my wails are sobs.

Yeah, yeah, a voice jeers sarcastically inside my head. *I've seen the movie. There's no crying in baseball.*

From my spot on the floor I find myself eyeballing a pair of pant legs and socks of a teammate, but which one? It occurs to me I'm wearing my spikes on the tiled floor. *Stunad!*

I pan from the interloper's shins to his hips, where both hands rest in disgust, like a mother catching her son in the act of swinging the family cat by the tail. I dare look no further to ID the character. The bastard's sexy accent gives him away as a string of Italian cuss words flow from Paolo's lips like an operatic libretto. I don't know their meaning, but can guess. Even cussing sounds melodious in Italian which pisses me off, all over again, as I'm trumped by Paolo once more. He even cusses better than me!

I spring to my feet, but my spikes slip. Paolo catches me by the arm and jerks me to his face. He growls in English at the clubby picking up shards of wreckage to leave them be, then continues to me, "You make my heart sick. It bleeds with the knowledge of your stupid arrogance. It's beyond that of the Caesars, and just as destructive!

"There should be a measuring stick for arrogance in this game. If there was, you'd break the record. You kill me and everyone else around you with it. Have you seen the lineup card for today yet, eh?"

"Why should I? I'm sick of seeing my name at the bottom of the order!"

"Then look again, asshole! You're batting cleanup today."

He might as well have slapped me across the face. That's how shocked I am.

"That's *corretto*. Just before me. I could use an RBI or two, if you can get you sorry butt on base for a change. You think you can do this for me, eh?"

My head is reeling. What kind of game is Mose playing? Is he trying to boost my confidence or does he actually think I'll do better under this kind of pressure?

"It's New York today, Eli, on national TV," Paolo continues, as if I didn't know, already. "You think you can handle it? Do you even remember how? They're throwing a 'September call-up' from Double-A. Not even Triple-A. Double-A, Eli. So I repeat. Can you handle it?"

Paolo punctuates every sentence with a poke to my shoulder, taunting me with eyes squinted so tight they nearly snap with each jab of his finger. He then lowers his voice, but not by much.

"This stupidity has gone too far...ever since my sister's last visit. You think I don't know your problem? Your problem is that you think every woman should fall for you. I don't have to be a shrunk to know this!"

"Shrink, Paolo, the word is shrink."

"Shut up! I don't have to be a head doctor to know how to help you! Listen, and I'll help you fix this sloomp."

I can't even laugh at his pronunciation, so I sneer, "Oh great, here we go. Some kind of Sicilian voodoo, I suppose."

Paolo drags me by the arm and shoves me onto the toilet of the cologne-saturated stall.

"Sit!"

Curious and desperate, I slouch on the john, like a punished child.

"Now just be quiet and hear me out," he says.

This is a switch from his cursing and screaming. I'm touched by his pleading tone, so I shut up and listen.

"Your swing is a mess, because your head is a mess. I actually respect this. It means you have a good soul. If you were no good inside, you would bat .500 when a woman gives you trouble.

"I once knew a guy in the *Italiano* League, his name was Bino Malatesta. You know what this last name means? It means 'bad head.' But Bino was not just bad in the head; he was bad to the core. The more screwed up his life was, the better he played. The more people he made sick, the more power was in his swing. Scouts drooled for him.

"One day he no show up to the yard. We play without him and we lose. The next day, they find him in a small street...alley... in Catania, his eyes wide open with a bullet in between. But that wasn't the worst. The worst was they stuffed his *come si chiama* in his mouth."

Paolo grabs his crotch for me to get his full meaning. "He slept with the girlfriend of a Mafioso from Palermo. What a *stunad!*"

I inadvertently cross my legs. "Did you really have to tell me that last part? I got the point a minute earlier!"

Paolo snorts.

"Forget her, Eli. I told you long ago my sister is not for you."

But he doesn't know how she let me touch her hair...how she speaks to me, cares about me. He just doesn't know...

The youngest clubbie nervously enters the room, to tell me a package has just arrived with my name on it. This is highly unusual.

Paolo shrugs.

I walk out the bathroom and back into the lockers area of the clubhouse behind Paolo.

"Surprise!"

Oh. My. God. It's a chorus line of *Playgirl* rejects...a baker's dozen of bare butts spelling out, 'Happy Birthday.'

How self-absorbed by this stupid slump could I possibly be to completely forget my own birthday?

I laugh so hard it nearly sends me back to the scene of my crime to pee.

Letter "H," a.k.a. Moki, stops laughing when I break the news, "You better send a clubbie over to Macy's, my friend. Sorry to tell you this, but you're out of cologne."

•••••••••••

The girls are back in town, but the news is not good.

The text from Silvana is to all three of us: *Fatima fell. Leg broken. At hospital. Wait for us at Eli's.*

Dad is waiting with Elvis when we walk in the door.

He explains Fatima's spill at the ballpark. The story destroys my appetite instantly. I mention my own experiences with her falls. Darius does the same. Paolo confesses how he berated her misstep at the Toronto hotel.

Dad's face is pain-soaked. I remember that look. My brain does a moonwalk back in time to an accident when I crashed my bicycle and ran home screaming, blood gushing from my elbow. Dad studied the gash and, spotting bone, whisked me away to the emergency room. But the worry on his face before grabbing the car keys was one I'll never forgot. It's there now.

"What's going on with Fatima?" I growl. "Don't treat us like little boys, we're grown men." Paolo lowers himself slowly onto the sofa. Darius joins him, rubbing his stomach as if trying to hold its contents in place.

Dad scans our intent eyes and says, "She has ALS."

I boing like a jack-in-the-box at the proper note, but my expression is nothing like that of a clown. Paolo and Darius turn to each other in bewilderment.

"No! No! No!" I fist the air, but no amount of crazed fury can erase his words.

Paolo and Darius plead pitifully for understanding, in voices that contradict their questions. They don't really want to hear the answers. They appear utterly trapped, torn, and disbelieving.

"But there must be a cure, or at least some treatment!" Paolo keeps saying, over and over.

There isn't. It's not a common illness—thank God—but I know all about it. I pace back and forth as I explain: "When I was a child, my baseball hero was Cal Ripken, Jr. I didn't fully understand then the illness that had allowed my idol to break the "consecutive games played" streak set by Lou Gehrig. Nor did I grasp why for Gehrig it had ended at that number, giving the Ironman, as he was called, the dubious honor of having this nightmare ailment named for him. But it *is* a nightmare. Nobody on earth has ever recovered from it."

Paolo is full of more questions as if he can free his sister from this ball and chain if he asks enough or the right ones. Darius, by contrast, presses his palms against his temples as if he's trying to escape the blackness closing in on him, tension in every line of his body. Just as Silvana's rental car pulls into the driveway, he bolts. He reaches the passenger door and throws it open... Dad calls out as we all rush the car. Fatima reaches out gently toward Darius, who is weeping. *Am I wrong to believe it's me she cares for? Have I been wrong about everything, all along?*

Darius hugs her tightly, then releases his grip, as if afraid of injuring her. He helps her from the vehicle and embraces her again with a tenderness that stings.

"Why all this concern?" she asks lightly. "I'm fine."

"No, you're not." Paolo, at least, is still capable of anger. "When were you going to tell me?" He glares at his mother. Silvana wrinkles her brow at Dad, who shrugs.

"After the season," he says simply.

Paolo pushes past Darius to embrace his sister, kissing her forehead possessively. She's wearing an inflated boot for mobility without crutches, which makes her tiny foot look huge.

"It's only a hairline fracture," Silvana says, to everyone...to no one...to the breeze.

Paolo and Darius between them cradle Fatima, helping her inside. She smiles meekly at me, recognizing my frustration, accepting its multiple meanings.

I gulp down the cry in my throat.

Chapter 41

Paolo

The day is gray, the ballpark empty. A chill already spices the Cleveland air. I think of fishing with my father in the wee hours before dawn, trawling with nets in liquid stillness.

I sit alone in the dugout. A large gull from the lake a few blocks north, lands on the warning track in front of me. It waddles closer to the edge, cocking its white head sideways.

"What are you looking at, bird of the sea?"

The bird squawks: a long loud reply that both startles and intrigues.

"Do you bring me news from the heavens you roam?"

The gull hops down the steps with an easy flap of its wings. It squawks again in choppy clucks.

I'm oh so still, not wanting to startle my new friend. But the urge to touch this little creature overtakes me—so powerful is the connection I perceive between us. I slowly lift my bronzed arm toward the pale being, my palm beseechingly upward.

As if in slow motion, with one puff it airily lands on my perch. Does it sense the energy pulsing down my shoulder to the place it now stands? Did it intuit my almost holy desire to feel its weight in my palm? Does it realize the need I have to be caught, to be saved from a freefall into despair?

Now *I'm* the one with a head cocked in curiosity. "You've snatched my heart from plunking into the abyss?" I whisper.

We peek at each other in awe, breathlessly connected: a shared knowledge, a sudden peace.

Sounds of the camera crew starting their day break the silence, jolting both man and bird. The gull returns to the clay track before flying the short distance to home plate. It steps on the pentagon and screeches back at me, in a language I can almost understand. Next it hops to the pitching rubber and jabbers at me once more. Then it jets into centerfield, where it loops the area in an effortless show, before soaring above the left field scoreboard and back to the waters from whence it came.

I stretch to my feet, watching him go, tears slipping down my face. "Thank you, Papa," I say.

Paolo

•••••••••••

As I enter the hallway for the clubhouse I see Darius push through the metal doors into the underground service corridor. Something makes me decide to follow him.

Utility carts, forklifts, and people are scurrying in every direction in preparation for tonight's game. Darius isn't scheduled to pitch. He's left to battle his distractions until his next outing. I've seen these phobic attacks before, and I suspect that another is creeping around the edges of his well-being. I suggested that he speak to Dr. Levy again, but he told me he doesn't need any help. He's survived the loss of his family and can manage this scare too. He doesn't realize that this new tragedy—Fatima's—could trigger suppressed anxieties from the old ones.

I've been to the head doctor myself. And I know.

I call to him. He turns. His eyes are frantic; a nervous flutter deforms his voice. I put a hand on his shoulder, "Talk to me, bro. You going to be all right?"

"I'm not your bro, and she is not my sister," he murmurs running his hands over his face.

I curb my impatience. "Let's walk," I suggest.

Instead, this new, manic Darius begins to jog. I have to work hard to keep pace with him as we work our way through the concrete corridor to the giant garage. TV trucks are parked in place and another semi, delivering concessions, is being unloaded. We dodge the vehicles and run up the ramp from the entertainment underworlds of the ballpark and the arena next door.

The avenue, which runs between E. 9th and Ontario, behind the scoreboard and along a parking garage, is speckled with baseball diehards. Miraculously, none of them appear to recognize us in our shabby sweats – or maybe it's more that they'd never expected to see us there. Past the statue of the pitching prodigy Bob Feller, to whom Darius is often compared, we cross the gateway to downtown Cleveland, entering the E. 9th Street cemetery.

Its creepy black iron gates surround a grassland of monuments of all shapes and sizes, shaded by leafy trees. Frankly, I don't care for American cemeteries. I prefer the mausoleum villages on the outskirts of town that we have back home. There, the dead are placed on top of each other, which seems far less lonely. Also, our cypress pines are green all year, and point to heaven. These trees rustle the breeze in ghostly whispers. *Stai zitto*, shut-up I tell them.

Eventually, Darius stops running. He steps left, then right, forward, back, every which way to nowhere, gesturing in a futile rant. "I don't know what's happening to me... I don't understand. I feel like I want to scream, run, hit... kill."

"I know what's happening to you, Darius. It's normal. You're going to be all right. Let me call for Dr. Levy. Really. You need him, man." I text the skipper to send reinforcements, while Darius stares at me, as if he's never seen me before. I say—and I don't know where the words come from—"Listen, Fatima's illness is reminding you of the deaths of those you have yet to mourn. How could you? You've been too busy adjusting to life without them. Self-preservation had to take precedence."

Darius breathes heavily a few moments before responding. "M-maybe, yes. Yes, it's true. You're right. But how can I mourn them?" He flails his arms through the air and spins to display the surroundings. "Where are their graves? Where can I mourn them?" He begins to tour the stones around us. "Let's see, who do we have here? Rebecca Cartwright, born 1889 and died 1920," pointing to a monument, "and Thomas Cartwright beside her, born August 1, 1920, died August 2, 1920—mother and child no doubt—victims of birth.

"And who lies behind them under this puny rock? Joshua Taylor, born 1898, died 1918 in the Great War. The Great War! What was so great about it? Twenty years old, same as me, gone in a war they called 'Great'—thinking, like fools, that no war could kill more.

"How stupid can people be? Had to top it, didn't we? Our enemies become our friends, then our enemies again. Sorry, Joshua! Rebecca and Thomas may have fared better. But even you, all of you," he shouts, as if to wake them to ensure they hear his point, "all of you are luckier than *my* family! My relatives were blown to bits by their own kind! Into bits, I tell you—tiny bits, or maybe some large parts and scattered bits. Or maybe burned to dust, I don't really know. I don't know because I wasn't there—I was in another hell, trying to save myself from the same fate!"

I'd thought he was winding down. Instead, he's just getting warmed up.

"I held no funeral for them. I ran away to a foreign land. I became a slave. But then *she* came along. Fatima. Can you believe her name is Fatima?" he says to the monuments, not to me. "She made me want to breathe again, to laugh, to play. And so I followed her wishes for me, all the way to America—land of the free. But in the end, what does it matter? Slave or free, war or peace, we all die!

"Now *she's* going to die they say. But that's not enough. First she's going to suffer—a lot—for years maybe. Even my father was spared such a curse!"

By now his tears are raining down a river, his voice choked. He turns from the stones toward me and reaches into his pockets. He withdraws a ring of beads from each and waves them in the air. "How many prayers, Paolo? How many prayers will it take to save her? Only one, perhaps, if my faith was strong, but I don't even know what I believe anymore. Yet here they are—in my pockets—not a word to God spoken on one of them in over a year! This one was a gift from my mother and the other my Aunt Maryam. Every night they stand guard beside my bed, every morning I place them in my pockets. Why do I bother? Why can't I just completely let go? There's no hope! "

He begins to sob pitifully.

"Why?" he cries softly, clutching the beads to his chest.

I struggle for the right words. *Dear Lord, help me to help him*, I beg.

My prayer is heard. The words illuminate like halogen field lights...slowly brightening...until at full force they make green grass shimmer silver in the breeze. *Could my dugout visitor have released something in me?*

"Zio once said that fathers teach discipline, but mothers teach faith—and that faith, once learned from a mother, is never forgotten. I believe these beads to be a reminder of that faith. To let them go would be like letting go the memory of your mother. Mothers are the ultimate givers. They carry us in their wombs and suffer our births to teach us, in that very act, the true meaning of life—that life is about giving, no matter what the cost... You know how strong Fatima's faith is, don't you?"

Darius nods.

"She inherited it from our great-grandmother, a woman who suffered the ravages of war, but who never lost hope. To do so would have led to despair, despair to desperation, and desperation to a selfish lack of caring toward everyone and everything—ending in destruction or death.

"It's true that we all must die, but a death induced by *taking* brings hell to those left behind. Death of those who *give* is like a seed planted. Fatima is a giver not a taker. By the time her days on this earth are done, she'll have left a vast garden in her wake. You and I will live in that garden, and, if we're smart, we'll ensure that it grows to feed as many as possible. We'll never miss her because she'll be present in every root, every bud, and every fruit borne.

"The fact that your family has no grave is immaterial. Cemeteries aren't for the dead; they're for the living. They exist for those who need to be reminded of someone, or of something that the dead one represents, or to show their loyalty. You don't need that, Darius. You won't forget.

"You know what I see when I look at you? I see a guy still holding tight to his faith, no matter how much dust his prayer rug is collecting. Your faith will continue to sustain you, as it did from Syria to Italy and from Italy to here."

A calmer Darius moves his gaze from me toward someone who's emerged to stand right behind me.

"You may have another calling, Paolo," says Dr. Levy.

•••••••••••

Eli parks his sleek car in the players' lot. He's surprised to see us trekking the sidewalk toward him. He waits as we pass the security gate before saying hello. Darius and Dr. Levy nod to each other and head inside.

"How're you doing?" I ask.

His effort to formulate a response is evident. Yet the words don't come. I resolve to put my new-found calling to use once again. I imagine a blur of thoughts bumping, colliding and whirling around his brain. ("There can be no future with her. Why do the most significant females of my life die so young? How can she smile, knowing that it's incurable... How can I bear to watch her suffer and die! ... I could give a shit about tonight's game.")

At last he answers, “I feel dead inside.”

We walk to the below ground environs in silence.

“Your mother stopped by to see me this morning, after dropping Fatima at The Clinic,” he tells me. “At first I assumed she was there to see Dad, but apparently Fatima’s compassion is an inherited trait. She cooked breakfast for us, telling me stories about Fatima’s childhood. How did she know that was exactly what I needed?

“One sentence she said keeps replaying in my mind. ‘Fatima is like the sun and the moon together—a constant presence of light to shield you from darkness. If this disease should take her, I will but look to the orbs of the sky to see her smile.’ It was said in that beautiful Italian way. It made me wonder at the strangeness of a life that would steal one mother while giving me another. My eyes must have been an open book to her, because she took my face in her hands and smiled at me, smoothed back my hair, and kissed my forehead before she left to return to the hospital.”

I should be jealous, but I’m not. Fatima’s scolding on the night our parents revealed their plans is still fresh in my head. *I know my mother’s heart is big enough to love more than two children.*

Eli continues: “I had a long talk with Dad after she’d gone. I’ve been oblivious to the load he’s been carrying, keeping her diagnosis secret. He had a business associate who’d died of ALS, and, although he mentioned it only in passing, I could see those thoughts terribly disturbed him.”

As we near the door to the clubhouse where reporters hover, the flurry in my brain gives way to my game face, as if in response to the ring of a soundless bell. Darius and Dr. Levy are just ahead, moving toward the trainer’s room. Local reporters, aware of Dr. Levy’s specialty, take note.

Eli and I undress and put on our uniforms. I face my locker until my game pants are belted over my cup and undergarments, jersey fully tucked in, and stirrups and socks in place. As I turn and sit to fasten my cleats, Eli does the same. For the first time I feel we share a bond, of mingled grief, sorrow, and hope.

Odd, that last one.

Chapter 42

Paolo

Leyland's dugout suite at Progressive Field is headquarters for the family. From there Fatima meets our gaze for nine passion-play innings. Eli is so close when catching that he speaks to her, upon occasion. This is the first time the obvious connection between them doesn't bother me. Meanwhile, Darius sits at the farthest point of the home team dugout, as if seeking an unobstructed view of her face. I decide to use my pain to advantage by venting in Sicilian during every at-bat.

As a right-hander, I can see her easily, but go about my business as if yelling at the wind. At first the umpire and catcher are puzzled, until I put them at ease.

"I'm speaking words of love to the *bellissima signorina* with the crazy hair beside the visitors' dugout," I whisper.

They snicker, but, thanks to the masks over their faces, their smiles go unobserved. Thus begins three hours of debate in the broadcast booth, thanks to the sound mikes clipped to the protective netting behind the batter's box. My whisper was incomprehensible, but my Sicilian comes through loud and clear—except that no one in the broadcast booth or TV truck knows a word of it.

They wonder what I could possibly be saying that doesn't get me tossed, or provoke the masked men to hush me or chat with me either? With each trip to the dugout, the clubbies keep me informed of the television drama I'm producing.

My first at-bat is a single and an RBI. My second, a double, is the only hit of the inning. My third, a towering home run, lands in the back of the centerfield monuments. It brings most of Northern Ohio to its feet, jumping and cheering so powerfully the ballpark itself seems to rumble.

But in my final at-bat, anticipation of a triple and 'hitting for the cycle' for my first time sends Fox Sports on a mission. Sportitalia, the network carrying their video feed in Italy, is summoned for translation of my monologue at each at-bat. But what they learn is all the more confusing:

At-bat (1) "Watch me as I punish this ball as I would your disease."

At-bat (2) "I'm done with my anger at God. I remember what you taught me. I'll descend on this pitch instead with all the fury in my soul."

At-bat (3) "Like lightning, I'm going to transfer all that's inside me to this pitiful sphere, wishing so desperately for the power to cure you instead."

They find it all quite the opera—as it's meant to be. But they need help to understand what it's about. By my final stroll to the plate, calls have been made back and forth from the press box, ticket office, Leyland's agency, and the underground parking spot of the broadcast's control room—until all the sleuthing eventually pays off. The commercial break in the middle of the eighth inning is a beehive of activity. At the end of two minutes and 45 seconds, all systems are go.

I have to see this. I run back to the clubhouse. I'm up third in the inning, so I have time for the show. The booming voice of Luciano Pavarotti under video replays of each of my previous at-bats, subtitled with my outrageous words, are spliced with live shots of Fatima, each time panning closer to her in Leyland's suite. The talking heads introduce my twin sister to the world, "Fatima Giobatti, recently diagnosed with ALS, aka Lou Gehrig's disease." The camera then pulls back again to include Mama in the shot, "their widowed mother who's found a kindred spirit in" (the camera drawn yet further) "Eli Kohn's father, a widower since Eli's childhood."

The gods of hype couldn't have scripted it better. It's reality TV at its most melodramatic. But for the actors of this drama, it isn't TV—just reality—and reality at its most gut-wrenching.

Then it hits me—like a bat flying from a hitter's grip and thumping me up the side of the head: *I've served up my sister on a platter.* The media will no longer be satisfied with me and Eli; they'll be relentless in pursuit of Fatima as well. *Stunad!*

I choose not to speak in my last trip to the plate: I've done enough damage with my mouth. I decide to let my bat drop the blows instead.

It isn't the triple everyone was hoping for. Bombs like this one used to be clichéd as 'rainmakers.' Eli and Darius are the first to shower their congrats at home plate.

Chapter 43

Fatima

"Did your brother unnerve you last night?" Zio asks quietly. He called as soon as he could, given the time difference.

"He meant well. It probably helped his play, but, afterward, the media scrum was ridiculous—and very embarrassing, too."

"Oh *bella*, I ask the dear Lord every day why not take His old servant instead and let you live a long and beautiful life!"

Zio's a man of powerful faith...but still a man. Moments of doubt don't run from him just because he wears a cleric's collar. I've heard some in his line of work even murmur of it as worse for them: how better for the devil to win the war for this world than to fell the leaders of God's own army? It's a thought that gives me pause, but not one I care to consider at the moment. Instead, I have something important to ask him.

"Zio, I've been thinking: could you possibly travel with me to Fatima, Portugal? I've wanted to visit there for as long as I can remember. I know you've been to Medjugorje, but surely Fatima is even more alluring, especially since the Church has sanctioned *those* apparitions."

"Yes, it is indeed alluring—perhaps even more than you might think. I was there in my youth. In fact, it was the place where I answered God's call."

"Really? I had no idea! Tell me!" I'm wholly intrigued.

"I was already in the seminary, in Naples. A group of us had traveled there, first by train, then on foot, hitching rides when we could to the little town. It was 1949. Europe was still rebuilding after WWII, and many believed that one of the secrets the Blessed Mother had given Lucia, the little shepherdess, had predicted these terrible events. Needless to say, though times were tough, the place was still teeming with pilgrims.

"My classmates each had a special request to make of Our Lady for her intercession before God; these they shared with the group. But I didn't even dare to mention mine. How could I tell my friends I was thinking of leaving them? I'd fallen in love with a beautiful young woman. We'd been seeing each other in secret for two months when she finally told me. 'You must choose. It's either me or the church.'"

I'm astounded. "All these years, Zio, and I've never heard a word of this!"

"There never was a need to mention it, was there?...Anyway, while my friends and I were in Fatima, I met a family, a mother and her three children. Because of my mother's devotion to Our Lady of Fatima, I had chosen to study Portuguese at the seminary, a choice that allowed me to communicate with this lady and her little ones.

"She was very poor. Her husband had been killed in the war and her youngest son suffered from polio. Their clothes were mostly rags, yet she offered me what little food they had—some bread in a basket. For some reason, she confided to me that her husband had wanted to be a priest, but had chosen to marry her instead. She secretly feared that she was being punished for stealing him from God.

"I told her I didn't agree, that God has given us all free will for a purpose, and that our collective wills affect each other. Our fates are not pre-ordained: instead, they are affected by the choices we make, as well as the choices others make.

"She didn't like what I had to say. She criticized me, saying that I would make a very bad priest, because my words gave little consolation. So, instead of praying for guidance that I would make the correct choice for my life, instead I prayed for this woman and her children.

"The day we were leaving town, she spied me from inside a restaurant and ran out the door, napkin in hand, flagging me down. I almost didn't recognize her; she looked so different, dressed in fine clothes and with her hair styled prettily. She took both my hands and apologized for her insult. I'd been right and she'd been wrong, she confessed. My words had burned inside her, causing her to pray for guidance. The following evening, when she and her children were short of food, she'd noticed a family with a brimming basket and resolved to sneak a loaf of bread from them while they were receiving Holy Communion. But when the opportunity arose, she'd heard my voice in her head and chosen to remain hungry.

"After the outdoor Mass had concluded, another prosperous family had waved to the one she'd been considering robbing; the two families had mingled together, chatting loudly. That's when she'd heard someone mention the name of the small town where she'd been born, which she'd left at a very early age. She decided to introduce herself and to ask if they knew anyone with her family name. One of the wealthy families turned out to be her distant relatives, who immediately took pity on her and her children. One cousin even had a brother who worked as a doctor in Lisbon and promised to arrange for the best possible treatment for her son with polio.

"The joyful peace that swelled through me at that moment was greater than any other emotion I'd ever enjoyed...even with my sweetheart from Naples. My decision was made—the life I truly wanted chosen.

"So, yes, my child; I'll certainly accompany you to that fateful place, in hopes that you will find the same peace that I did."

•••••••••••

We watch the game from Paolo's apartment. The team loses. Only Abe sits in suite D1 with Leyland's other guests, garnering more than his fair share of TV coverage.

Mama decides it's true—TV does add 20 pounds. Our laughs are tinged with tears.

It's a close game, lost on a close call, but the umpires get it right. (Mose puts on such a show before and after being thrown out of the game that Mama remarks, "Are you sure he isn't part-Italian?")

Laughs and tears merge into soundless light; and I'm in the middle of it. Safe. Calm. Loved. I see a vineyard. Eli is there, and Darius, and Paolo. A wall—the same wall?—looms in the distance. I linger dreamily before the images fizzle and blur. I blink to find I'm gazing at the exposed brick of Paolo's loft.

"Where were you?" Mama asks.

"In a spectacular vineyard... It made ours look unremarkable in comparison. The boys were there, and a wall, in the distance."

"A wall again. You mentioned a wall last time, didn't you?"

"I know, but it's no less of a mystery this time."

Mama holds me tight, but not tightly enough to keep me from where I have to go.

Chapter 44

Eli

Darius's cell phone is on fire, and not with calls from Fatima, who has returned to Italy with her mother for the grape harvest. His mood runs the gamut, from white-water rocky to still as a dead sea. My level of suspicion having temporarily waned, I had cancelled the private detective I'd hired to follow him, but now my fears have risen to alarm status. The moment I see him move, I'm following him.

Not that his playing has been affected: we won tonight, mostly thanks to his exploits. He was unbelievable. Detroit's ace was awesome, but Darius was even better. He said all the right things in his post-game interviews, too. But the call he received before we left the clubhouse turned sweet to sour in an instant. Instead of staggering off to my favorite watering hole I'm casing his route to his downtown loft.

Except that he heads off in a completely different direction. I keep my head down in my hoodie, moving swiftly, hoping not to be spotted by a fan. An odd-looking guy lurks by one of the guitar monuments in the middle of the plaza in front of the Rock Hall. (The museum itself closed hours ago.) The space is desolate, as all the action this time of night occurs uptown. I keep my distance, as there's no crowd in which to lose myself. *What could bring Darius here?*

Another guy approaches Darius. He's blond-haired and clean-shaven as opposed to guitar man, who frankly looks like a poster child for terrorism. *I need a reason to be here, or they'll notice me for sure.*

I spot a lone woman, dabbing her eyes and nose with a tissue. Perfect.

"Are you all right?" I ask her.

We chat. No sports fan, she's at least ten years my senior and would be prettier in the glare from the street lights had she not let herself go in her distress. It seems her boyfriend of fourteen years has admitted that marriage and kids were never on his radar screen. Part of me does feel sorry for her, but my focus is on Darius... I listen, while mostly tuning in to the gathering at guitar row.

Then a shout causes both of us to turn. Darius is thrilled about something. He shakes hands with both men and runs away, electrically fast, punching the sky with his fist. The blonde and the guitar terrorist instantly split, in opposite directions. *Are they working together?*

I politely extricate myself from Miss Bleeding Heart in an effort to shadow my teammate.

Darius slows to a trot then winds down to a stroll past the Great Lakes Science Center, heading toward the football stadium. Eventually he enters his apartment building uptown. Since tomorrow is a day game, I decide that Darius has the right idea. But sleep is as far from my mind as is the woman I just met. *What's up with this guy, anyway? Who are these characters he's involved with? Is it political? Drug-related? Gambling-related? Can he really be trusted?*

•••••••••••

The next morning, after an unquiet night, I arrive at the yard earlier than usual. I've decided to tell the head of ballpark security what's happening. He's a good guy, an ex-sheriff with an even temperament and a wise way with people. I've seen him bust up more than one argument before it escalated, using a combination of humor, reason, and laid-back threat.

"Jamie, can I bother you for a few minutes?" I ask. He always cases the player zones before most of the players arrive.

"Sure, Eli. What's up?"

"I want you to know that what I'm about to suggest isn't easy for me. But we live in crazy times. Sometimes we have to be vigilant in our own crazy way."

"Just spit it out, Eli, you don't need to make excuses to me. What have you seen?"

"OK, well, it's Darius. Ever since I've met him I've had my doubts. He takes these phone calls that afterward morph him into Mr. Spooky. I realize that's not much to go on, so I trusted my instincts and followed him last night, after we left the park. He had a big win, a good time with the press, and then one of those mystery calls. He suddenly turned 'right ugly,' as my pal T.P. would say... So I tracked him to the Rock Hall where he met two guys, one a bearded menace and the other a blond All-American. Go figure. But when he left them he was whooping and shouting like we'd won the Championship already... And what I'm thinking is, couldn't you guys confiscate his cell phone while we're on the field? You know, dismiss the clubbies for a while and investigate his locker?"

Jamie laughs, then shakes his head. "I appreciate your concern, Eli. Really I do. But believe me when I say you have nothing to fear from Darius."

"But how do you know? The guy's a walking time bomb! He has these emotional meltdowns, and he won't tell any of us about his past. Somebody needs to be keeping tabs on this guy!"

"Eli, listen. Did you really think he could have entered this country so quickly without agreeing to be totally transparent with us? The authorities are well aware of Darius's situation—and I've probably already told you more than you need to know. Let it go. It's cool."

Jamie leaves the clubhouse. The slam of the metal double doors behind him unplugs me. *I was so damned sure! Or am I just jealous because of his connection to Fatima?*

But what's his secret? I have to know.

•••••••••••

The Jewish New Year celebration of Rosh Hashanah culminates today with Yom Kippur, the Day of Atonement. Dad is with me; our fast began at sundown last night and will last until after sundown tonight. It's a work day for me, though, and a key one at that. A win tonight would clinch the Division Championship, guaranteeing a spot in the playoffs, which begin in just over a week. "You know who" is pitching, too.

Dad drops me at the ballpark after the solemn service of the morning. The dirges are still filling my head and weighing on my heart. We hug, and he hands me a loaf of the round Challah bread, traditional for breaking the fast. He offers it with a wink and a smile as I tuck my prayer shawl and yarmulke into the glove compartment. *In some ways, I'm still his little boy.*

•••••••••••

The clubbies are almost finished cleaning up the celebratory mess. They've removed the plastic from over our lockers, but the place still reeks of champagne. Darius is still here, having finished icing his arm in the metal tub in the training room. So's Paolo, drinking straight from a bottle of his own wine. I'm nursing a bottle of bubbly. Darius, as usual, sips a soda. Unusually, the three of us are alone.

In the spirit of this holiest of days I am prompted to do something I never imagined I would: I apologize to Darius for my suspicions—and with Paolo there, too.

Paolo is shocked to hear the lengths I went to—hiring people to watch Darius as well as following him—but Darius doesn't seem to be. Instead, he sighs deeply, and says, "Maybe it's time I tell you my story."

Paolo seems as anxious to hear it as I am. He even puts down his booze in order to concentrate better.

"My gift for languages is also a curse. When Daesh...ISIS... ISIL...whatever you want to call them...captured much of Yarmouk Camp, my parents forecast that our days together would be few. You understand: they were both prominent opponents of violence. They expected to be arrested and murdered, but they made me promise to try to stay alive, no matter what I had to do—and I promised. Sometimes, I wish that I had not.

"With the camp surrounded and in shambles, we were all starving. This was probably deliberate, as Daesh recruited soldiers by offering salaries. Many joined, but my family all refused.

"They killed my father outright. They broke into our apartment and shot him dead before our eyes—my mother's screams will never leave me, never." His composure is faltering: he speaks as if sucking air between sentences...fighting tears.

"In the time it takes for your next breath, he was gone. Then they took my mother and me north from Damascus to their headquarters in Raqqa. They offered to take care of us if I became an interpreter for them. If not, my mother would be abused for her beauty and I would be beheaded."

"Nice," Paolo says, frowning. He's trying to be sympathetic, but I shush him.

“In Raqqa I saw and heard many things,” Darius continues. “Some of those things have been helpful to the U.S. in their fight against terrorism at home and abroad.

“The blond man you saw me with, Eli, has been my contact ever since our press conference at Spring Training. I met him once in North Carolina, which is when he told me my mother was still alive. I had been told before that she was dead.”

“Oh my God,” I say. Paolo is equally shocked. We hope his next sentence won’t dash our hopes for him.

Daesh made me believe she’d been killed in a drone strike. They’d even doctored photos, in order to ‘prove’ it to me. Then they gave me a big, fat raise. However, because I believed them, and because I believed that my mother could suffer no more, I also began to plot my escape. I was sent to a meeting with arms dealers in Libya, which is where I first came in contact with some people smugglers.”

“Scum,” says Paolo briefly. Darius half-nods.

“Some of them were certainly scum, but others were in it to feed their families. The worst would extort from the most destitute... Mostly, the darker your skin the worse you fared. Sub-Saharan Africans would give money to a smuggler, only to be kidnapped by another one, working in concert with the first. And then, they’d occasionally starve migrants, extorting more and more money for an attempt at crossing to Italy by sea. Some, especially children, were sold to human-traffickers, others to militias. As for me, I made a deal to cross in return for information. I was extremely lucky I wasn’t double-crossed for my double-cross...

“Anyway, Blondie—I don’t know his real name—finally admitted that my mother had not died in the drone strike. Instead, she’d been chosen for a wife of a leader of that criminal caliphate, a man infamous for brutality, particular to women.

“But here, just the other day, he told me she had been freed! Kurdish rebels attacked the home where she was living—if you can call it living. She and her so-called husband tried to escape. She was shot while running to their vehicle, and he—the coward—left her for dead and drove off.

As she could speak the dialect of her new captors, she gained their trust during her debriefing in hospital, and was assured that she would be used kindly. Imagine her shock when a radio in the room carried a news program about me. She'd had no idea that I had even survived! The Kurds believed her and contacted American officials who had her lifted to a military clinic in Frankfurt, Germany. I've spoken to her every single day since."

"That explains the new Darius," Paolo says.

"Yes, she can't get here soon enough. I want to give her every comfort this country offers—and that's a lot!"

We can't help but join his merriment. His smile is brilliant.

"I take it she's recovered from the bullet wound?" I ask.

"There were two. One was in the lower leg; it shattered the bone. Another grazed her temple, causing great loss of blood. She won't be able to fly for a while, but she's in great spirits."

"I'm so happy for you," I tell him.

"Me too," says Paolo. So happy that he offers the last swig from his bottle to Darius.

To my amazement, he takes it.

"*Tante, auguri!*" Paolo shouts.

"*Shanah tovah,*" I answer, in the spirit of making the year ahead as good as it can possibly be.

Chapter 45

Darius

It's on. The Sons of Abraham Tour is happening, even though it sounds more like a retail promotion than a baseball exhibition. Still, it'll take us to Rome, as well as to Dubai and to Jerusalem, all places I've never been. The three of us use an off day to fly to Philadelphia for a private meeting with the Pope during his visit to the U.S. He asked a rabbi and imam to join him with Paolo, Eli, and me in private prayers. For the first time in his life I think, Paolo was humbled. He kept lamenting it should have been his twin there instead. The rabbi was a friend of Eli and his father's. He and Eli were in deep discussion regarding the Jerusalem tour stop.

I received an express letter yesterday regarding the tour stop in Dubai. It was from an Eritrean refugee who has become a cricket star in the U.A.E. He looks forward to meeting me when we play at his home field. He even attributes his good fortune to my own, in that the cricketing scouts offered a chance to several refugees.

The best news of all, however, is from my mother, who will be meeting us in Rome! She can travel by train from Frankfurt without fear of blood clots, apparently. Eli jokes that we need to hurry up and win this thing so he can meet her. For some reason he seems almost as pleased as I am myself... Tonight Leyland has invited the three of us to dinner at an intimate *osteria*. It is low-light and extremely discreet: no one bothers us.

"I have some news," he says. "The league and its tour title sponsor have co-opted a TV commercial to be shot between rounds one and two of the post-season, in order to promote the Sons of Abraham Tour. I've got the script here." He pulls three pages from his briefcase. "You're to speak in your native languages—well, actually, it's Hebrew for Eli—while outfitted in the sponsor's gear."

Eli is already under contract to the brand. He simply nods to Leyland and thanks him for the bonus. Paolo grins like a Powerball winner, and takes back every rude remark he ever made about Leyland to his face or behind his back. I, however, feel pensive. *More guilt for the migrants I left behind in Libya and for the refu-*

gees from Syria. My hope is that I can donate my way out of these conflicting emotions.

The 30-second spot is designed with a moody, almost epic, tone. It features the three of us training, with tight shots of gear, equipment, sweaty grimaces and pulsing muscles. These images, which will apparently be in black and white, will be jump cut with images in color of famous crusaders, warriors, and gladiators readying for battle, mixed in with real-life baseball highlights. In the end, we'll stand together at home plate, wearing the special uniforms licensed for the event—Eli in shin-guards, catcher's mask in hand, Paolo with his bat on his shoulder, and me tossing a ball up and down with my pitching hand. We're to speak our lines, turn, and walk away together toward the outfield as the music crescendos and the scene morphs into sounds and images of a blissful Eden.

The problem occurs as we read our lines. Eli skews a pucker to one side of his face. I purse my lips; Paolo bites his.

Eli is the first to comment. "I'm not going to say that, Leyland; I don't care how much they pay me."

"These words—they have no soul," Paolo objects, in more Italianate English than usual.

"I know they have things they want to sell, but to us this event is about far more than money," I add.

Leyland lifts up his hands. "OK, OK, I get it. Write your own lines, and I'll fight that battle later... But it won't be an easy sell. The ad agency has already been tasked with a production straitjacket—and now this! I only hope your talents aren't limited to baseball."

•••••••••••

Paolo is the hero of Game 1. His at-the-wall robbery to preserve the club's one-run lead for Moki to close, lock, and seal is a highlight-reel winner.

For Game 2, however, a circus ensues, with Eli as ringmaster, Paolo as trapeze artist and Moki as clown. We score six runs on four hits by Eli. But the craziest part of the night comes at the finish, when Paolo stretches through the air "with the greatest of ease," landing, ball in glove, to preserve the save for Moki and a

6-5 victory for the team. Moki enjoys Paolo's catch so much he twirls off the mound with a funky Kung Fu kick-punch. The rest of us on the bench stay put initially, wrapped in hysterics, rather than rushing the field. I'm snorting so badly by the time Eli reaches the bench that he falls into my arms. The two of us are caught on camera in a jubilant embrace that sweeps the sporting world. Scribes declare the squeeze reminiscent of the one between Larry Doby and Steve Gromek after the 1948 World Series Championship, when their cheek to cheek mirth shocked a black vs. white world.

In Game 3, I shine like a freshly scoured stainless steel grill on a sun-soaked holiday. It's a 7-0 route and a clean sweep. We advance to round two.

•••••••••••

We're standing shoulder to shoulder in Eli's living room with only Leyland and Elvis for an audience. Leyland's obvious tension turns to relief. Even the dog barks contentedly...and we're off, to my TV acting debut. I'm feeling slightly guilt-ridden, but committed.

We arrive to find that the clubhouse has been transformed into a film set, along with the field, tunnel, weight room, and cages. Catering is set up in the press room and makeup utilizes the trainer's tables. Paolo and I are aghast. A member of the crew notes our amazement and explains all the equipment as well as what will go on in the edit later. We had no idea what went into the creation of 30 seconds of TV.

Leyland pulls aside the director, a tall, bald, skinny man in constant need of a cigarette. He lowers the hammer. The man commences to cuss and moan, arms flailing and bald head turning rosy red. Luckily, when Leyland shows him our revisions his flush recedes like a thermometer.

The account executive and creative director want to know what the fuss is about. Leyland strolls away. His work is done.

The crew appears braced for us to behave like prima donnas, but we prove to be, at least according to the director, "a delight," taking direction without griping, patiently delivering take after take until League rep., Sponsor rep., and director are each satisfied, and it's all "in the can." It's a full day's effort, though. Frankly, I'd rather pitch 30 days in a row than go through all that again.

•••••••••••

Our round two opponents prove only slightly more difficult to dismiss. I win Game 3, but only because Eli knew the hitters' tendencies so well. In post-game interviews, I'm effusive about his game calling, while he praises me so gloriously that it causes a stir in the Middle East press.

So much so that, the next day, before leaving for the ballpark, I receive a call from the imam I met with the Pope. He tells me Eli is receiving a similar call from his rabbi friend. They want to warn us of the social media buzz in Arabic and Hebrew before we're asked about it by reporters. *It's good to be warned.*

Mose's friend, Ahmad from Al Jazeera, waits for us as we step off the bus. "You two have caused quite an uproar among your countrymen. Many think you both went too far in praising each other last night. What do you have to say to those who are calling each of you a 'traitor to his people?' "

We stop in our tracks, pretending shock: but thanks to the tip-off, we're immaculately prepared. Eli answers, "Darius Salamah is my teammate, my friend, and a good Muslim. He's also one of the most exciting young pitchers this game has ever seen. Most athletes, whether they pray to God, Allah, the Great Spirit, or whatever name they use for the Almighty are thankful and humbled by their God-given talent. So when we praise the talent of a teammate we're really praising the One who gave all that talent. Why it was given to this simple Jew and Muslim is not for you or anyone else to question. It's simply for God to be praised."

I couldn't have said it better, and don't try.

We clinch in Game 4.

After a long hiatus, the road to the World Series Championship once again travels through Cleveland.

Chapter 46

Eli

It snowed in Cleveland during the Indians 1995 and 1997 World Series opportunities. This time Mother Nature seems far less forbidding. Games 1 and 2 and, if necessary, 6 and 7 will be warm—unseasonably so for late October in the Great Lakes Snow-belt. Of course, our opponents from Pittsburgh will enjoy the same weather pattern, only two hours down the turnpike.

There are peaceful protests on the plaza between the arena and ballpark, some for keeping the "Chief" logo and some for retiring him—but the whole debate has faded to background noise compared to the clanging gongs for world peace being emitted by the Cleveland clubhouse, although the Department of Homeland Security has partnered with the League to play it safe. *Time* magazine has been given the OK for a cover photo-shoot of the three of us. It's heady stuff. I can almost forget our constant worries for Fatima—almost.

I.M. Pei's magnificent glass jewel of geometric dichotomy, The Rock and Roll Hall of Fame and Museum on Lake Erie's shore is transformed into the site for Cleveland's Baseball Gala on the eve of Game 1. Players often avoid the event because of the sheer volume of media people seeded between league sponsors and their guests, but not us. Darius and Paolo even help me coerce Fatima into joining the fun. She's happily spent by the time we leave.

At 3 a.m., I imagine her fast asleep, treasuring memories of the evening in her dreams while three young men cry in their beds, fearing the nightmare she'll eventually endure.

•••••••••••

No wonder all the world loves sport. It's uncontrived reality TV, with villains and heroes, behind-the-scenes melodrama, and—at least at the professional level—competition on a plane that most mortals can only dream of. And, just when you think you've seen it all, something ridiculous happens to remind everyone that, after all, it's just a game.

For example, Game 1 features an errant throw from Pittsburgh's right fielder on a play at the plate. The ball thwacks the sound mike clipped to the backstop, shocking everybody's eardrums as it breaks into pieces. It's that kind of night for the black and gold: Cleveland takes Game 1.

Game 2 is highlighted by our mascot Slider, a fuchsia, fat, furry character, who had decided to feign a re-enactment of his right field wall fall during the 1997 playoffs. Instead of tumbling the creature is conked by an aspiring home run that ricochets off his noggin while he hangs over the fence into the field of play. The ball serendipitously falls into the glove of the same Pittsburgh fielder, with the player concerned going from zero to hero in 24 hours. It's that kind of night for the red and blue. To our annoyance and amusement, Pittsburgh takes Game 2.

In Game 3 in Pittsburgh, just before the first pitch of the bottom of the eighth inning, I flip my catcher's mask to admire the bridge beyond centerfield, one of many along the three rivers that make this city so unique. On one side of the Fort Pitt Tunnel, it seems you're in no place special, only to emerge amidst great bridges and skyscrapers—lights, camera, and action all around.

Squatting down, I give Darius the sign for the first pitch. As soon as it rolls from his fingers I know it's a mistake. I'm sure Darius does too. I imagine him flinging his arm at it like a lizard's tongue, longing to sling it back inside his palm. Instead he drops his head and clutches his knees, refusing to witness a shipwreck of his own making.

Mose pops out of the dugout, signaling immediately for Moki. Our ever-smiling friend will have to work three more outs than usual to preserve what is now a mere one-run lead.

Mose and I reach the mound at the same time. "Don't sweat it, kid. You've had a good night," he says, taking the ball from Darius.

"Moki needs the extra screen-time," I joke. "Rumor has it he's auditioning for Japan's version of *The Bachelor* in the off-season."

"No way," Mose says. "Moki? Our Moki? He can't stay serious for two seconds!"

Moki bounces up the slope into a ring of laughter.

"Wha so funny?" he asks, his accent making me smile.

"You man, you so funny," I tease.

"Just try and be serious for six more outs," Mose says, dropping the ball into his glove.

Inquiring minds worldwide want in on the joke.

Pittsburgh finds Moki to be quite serious enough. We notch Game 3.

Paolo and I forget to eat our Wheaties the next day. We strand a total of seven men between us. Pittsburgh gobbles Game 4, but chokes in Game 5 by committing four nauseating errors. The Series moves back to Cleveland.

•••••••••••

Old-timers who can still remember the Indians 1948 championship assert that nothing matches the insanity of this time around (though 1995 came close).

The November issue of *Time* has hit the newsstands, as well as our lockers. The cover photo features Mose sitting on a stool, flanked by the three of us. Dressed in "road" uniforms with the Cleveland script across the chest, we each wear gaudy gold chains, mine featuring a Star of David, Paolo's a crucifix, and Darius's the star and crescent moon. It's a tight shot from Mose's chest on up, with the caption, *Cleveland's Sons of Abraham.* Now everyone who'd forgotten can remember Mose's given name.

Darius stares at his own face smiling back at him, then at the chain around his neck.

"The weight of this day lies heavy on me," he says, maybe to himself, but I'm next to him. "I haven't come this far only to disappoint my team, my people, and myself." He twists the beads in his pockets then reaches for the prayer rug in his locker and a bottle of water.

Curious members of the media as well as a few players follow him as he marches through the concrete tunnel. *What's he up to? It's hours before the gates open.* When he emerges from the dugout, the grounds crew is prepping the field under sunny skies. I hang back with the others, sensing that something important is about to occur.

I'm keenly aware of all the eyes, human or mechanized, surrounding Darius—but he seems totally oblivious. He unrolls a little red carpet with an image of Mecca in the center, and places it on the grass beside the mound. Then he opens the water bottle and pours some into his palm, splashing the contents on his face, neck, and arms. Finally, he removes his shoes and begins his Salat, kneeling in the prescribed direction, while high-speed lenses click like cicadas. He recites his prayers only to himself. Some of the members of the camera and grounds crews working nearby stop what they're doing out of respect. A few cross themselves. A man in a yarmulke bows his head, lips moving, praying words of his own.

Little do most people know just how long that prayer rug has been gathering dust, but it's obvious that Darius isn't pretending. When he finishes, several media types ply him with questions, but Darius only smiles and shakes his head as he moves swiftly away.

As we approach the clubhouse it's obvious from raised voices that something's going on. Juan Diego spies our confusion and comes over to us. He slaps Darius on the back, saying, "Hope you're feeling strong tonight, my friend. Looks like it'll be your turn to have Moki's back."

Moki's in front of his locker ranting and raging, his right hand bandaged like a giant cotton ball. It's so uncharacteristic—not just the bandage, but the fury—that everybody wants answers.

"It seems our smilin' savior got roused by a reporter from Tokyo in a club in The Flats last night," Juan explains. "They was Kung Fu fightin', man. Wish I coulda been there to see it, but the Mrs. has me on a short leash. Anyway, the reporter dude resorted to flailing a broken bottle of saki that the Mokster was too dumb to keep away from his right hand. Don't they teach pitchers in Japan to lead with their non-pitchin' paw? Anyway, his season's over and we need you to go nine. No pressure or anything," he matter-of-factly concludes with another whack across Darius's upper back.

Darius winces, more from the words than the slap, I think. But I know he can do it.

•••••••••••

The weather gurus called it right. It's May in October, so when the game reaches the ninth inning, nobody wants it to end. The pitching duel is so close that only two hours and 20 minutes have elapsed. Darius has been near-perfect all night except for a homer in the third inning, courtesy of his nemesis from Game 3.

I supercharge the fans with a double in the bottom of the eighth to set the table for Paolo to break the 1-1 tie. I'm so jacked, I shout at Paolo from second base, "Ship my ass home, Maserati Man!" It's his favorite nickname, newly acquired, courtesy of an Italian journalist.

Paolo launches the first pitch off Larry Doby's monument, God rest his soul. Maserati Man becomes Maserati Missile. Pittsburgh's hurler regroups and finishes the inning with us up, 3 to 1.

Darius has thrown 101 pitches, but his speed still looks good to Mose and me. The skipper asks him how he feels.

"Like a hungry wild boar," he tells him.

The look in his eyes gives Mose the confidence he needs to send his ace back to the mound for his first ever ninth inning.

Now it's Darius's turn to listen to me yell. *Am I high on adrenaline, or what?* I've never acted like this before, but considering that I've never been this close to a World Championship win, I feel vindicated. "Let's finish this, man!" I yell at him, smacking my mitt like a prize fighter.

I have no fear of over-pumping Darius. His control has been beyond belief for the last six innings and he's been throwing 98 mph consistently. He can go higher; I've seen it before.

My strategy is for batter No.1 to see 100 mph on the scoreboard radar, to make the guys, both on deck and in the hole, tighten up, try too hard, and—with luck—make mistakes.

The strategy works. The first two outs come and go, on three swings and misses apiece. I imagine a TV camera panning our faces up the middle of the field from home plate to pitcher's mound to center—and beyond the fence to the monuments directly behind Paolo and then jump to the blimp shot for what is expected to be the most watched game ever. The whole world seems to be holding its breath.

The Pittsburgh cleanup hitter dips a toe-hold, glaring fearlessly at Darius. I drop the signal, and Darius delivers the pitch. The ump rings strike one. The scoreboard radar registers 102 mph. That fastball was a blur; senior citizens with hearing aids might be in trouble.

The man in black and gold retreats to re-grip his weapon, then again settles into his stance. I drop the signal. Darius again delivers; the hitter swings and misses. It was another fastball, but too high in the strike zone for this hitter to kiss at 99 mph.

The batter again two-steps through his routine. I point and pat the signal for what I hope is the last time this season. Darius puts his glove over his face: to focus, to stay serious.

I'm so glad Father Peppe is here to see the changeup of his dreams.

Jackpot!

I have to hurdle the hitter, who's screwed himself so firmly into the ground he could blow a disc. Darius leaps into my arms. I've never seen him more excited. He pumps his right fist in the air—then he's swamped. It's a red, white, and blue tidal wave of arms and legs, discharged caps, dropped mitts and a feeling of communal ecstasy by the 36,000 in attendance that's downright spiritual. Sixty-seven years of somebody else leaving with the Homecoming Queen are finally and irreversibly over for the city on the nation's north shore, thanks to a Muslim, a Christian, and a Jew who just led a band of baseball brothers, Indians fans, and believers around the world on a magic carpet ride to sports nirvana.

Chapter 47

Fatima

The Indians World Series Champs Parade along Euclid Avenue is barely hours old when its main attractions scatter. Abe escorts Eli to New York where, as the event's MVP, he'll work the morning show circuit. Paolo is off to Rome for advance publicity of the first leg of the SOA Tour. Leyland and Darius will soon follow, but not before meeting with Mr. Powers and his staff, who want to begin contract negotiations with their ace pitcher. Meanwhile, Mama, Zio and I are packing for Portugal.

Yes, it's really happening. I'm going to Fatima.

•••••••••••

The square between the old and new cathedrals in Fatima, Portugal is wide open after the half-million throng of three weeks ago for the October 13th anniversary has disappeared. Zio regrets having so narrowly missed it, but the events in Cleveland were compensation. He's so pleased for the boys—and for himself, too, I think. He worked harder than his old bones wanted to admit during Darius's early training on the farm.

The day is clear and lovely, as a November sun whitewashes the Basilica and its flanking colonnades. Zio points to the left of the grand tiled plaza where sprouts the weathered oak tree that bore the apparitions, a small open-air chapel by its side.

Mama and I stand listening, entranced, as 62 bells clang from its tower. In a niche above the Basilica's main entrance, a sculpture of Our Lady of Fatima by American priest Thomas McGlynn gives me pause. *Is that what she really looks like?* We're told McGlynn collaborated with Lucia herself (by then Sister Lucia), in order to fashion it. So maybe the likeness is accurate, or as accurate as human skill can achieve.

We kneel in prayer for 90 minutes inside the massive church: it feels like ten minutes, the atmosphere is so peaceful and glowing. Later we tour the tiny stone peasant dwellings of Francisco, Jacinta, and Lucia before enjoying a picnic dinner in the scenic countryside. Best of all, I'm completely uplifted in the evening by the candlelight services in the magnificent plaza.

Mama and Zio are happy I haven't stumbled the entire day. *I'm simply happy to be here at last.*

•••••••••••

During the flight from Lisbon to Rome, I withdraw from my pocket a postcard of the Basilica which I'd purchased while waiting in the airport. I take my time with the words. Each is a challenge to first script in my brain before writing on the page.

When I've finished, I address it to the boys and give it to Mama to put in her purse. I'm not carrying one of my own. I rarely do.

Chapter 48

Darius • Rome, Italy

Leyland leads us on a tour of the Roman venue for Saturday's Sons of Abraham event. Due to the shortness of the notice for the Dubai and Jerusalem stadiums, this will be the only SOA event occurring on a weekend.

In the shadow of the ancient Roman Coliseum, on land where once stood the largest sports venue in history, we're treated to a display of modern American marketing virtuosity. Styled with the sleekness so beloved of Italians, the venue, dubbed "Baseball della Max" in a nod to its famous location, is capable of seating 20,000 with standing room for at least 5000 more—which is still less than 10% of the capacity for chariot races at the Circus Maximus 2000 years ago.

The title sponsor has spared no expense. The event will include a Milan-style fashion show of its latest sports apparel and gear, along with massive, high-tech displays and retail hubs on each end of the valley between Rome's Aventine and Palatine Hills. Opera staging pros have been flown in to design a stage looming twelve feet into the air above the oblong-shaped space where stars from all around the globe will launch balls into the 2000-year-old ruins next door. The Home Run Derby is scheduled to be the climax, preceded by radar-displayed pitching performances against those Italian baseball players and even football stars curious enough to take on Darius and Moki. Fielding tricks will also be on display, while Italy's top sportscasters will act as Masters of Ceremonies and interviewers alongside some of the country's top comedians, actors, and vocal artists. Security precautions for fans and athletes, tricky sightlines, multiple translators, and audio visual enhancement make the entire project a challenge that only the best of the best could consider tackling—precisely those folks tagged to make it happen, within the heart-attack time frame.

Despite the difficulties, the ethos behind this project has had event gurus and celebs jumping at the chance to participate. The TV show will also employ roaming cameras and interviews with fans, staffers and producers in order to make the experience as exhilarating on TV as it should be for the spectators. The afternoon program will air live for Europeans, but delayed, on baseball's own network, in the U.S. The whole event will conclude with a star-studded sponsor's gala.

Leyland is beaming; I'm so happy for him. He's happy for me as well, or so he told me earlier.

He wasn't speaking of the tour, or the championship, or even baseball. It's because—I still can't believe it—tonight Mama arrives at last!

•••••••••••

Our boutique hotel was booked by Leyland at the kind of price it takes to bump already scheduled guests. We should feel guilty, but no one does. I'm just so grateful to be able to share this experience with my friends.

The Mercedes limo glides in the front entrance. I've been waiting an hour...almost two years...since forever. My legs propel me through the door so fast they feel winged.

She's radiant...older in appearance, but no less lovely. Our grip on each other some compensation for all the months of being parted.

Weeping, she kisses every inch of my face. I laugh and cry and squeeze and whisper every word of love I know from every language I can speak. Our audience cheers and claps, sharing our joy.

I proudly introduce her to everyone, but when I finally get to Eli, my mother looks stunned. She looks again at Abe, and again at Eli.

"I'm sorry," she says. I'm a bit deaf from all the shelling I have experienced. Please, what is your name again?"

"Abraham Kohn," he says quietly. "I don't know if Darius ever mentioned it, but I was once a friend of your husband's cousin, Maryam Salamah."

At this her legs buckle; Eli and I both rush to catch her. Somebody quickly finds her a chair in the tiny lobby. There she asks for a glass of water. She takes her time drinking it, trying to smile, trying to apologize. Then she asks for another chair for me, so that I can sit beside her.

Ours is a dramatic heritage, yet even among our kind her reaction seems excessive. For whatever reason, I'm trembling too. She takes my hands in hers, and begins to speak low and softly.

"My son, forgive me, but the life I've led since our days together have caused me to lose interest in such civilized matters as politeness, tact, or spinning fables simply to keep others at their ease. I have learned that the truth is never to be feared, if we are not to waste a precious moment of what remains of our lives."

She brushes my hair from my brow and cups my cheeks in her slim hands.

"You loved Maryam very much, didn't you?"

"Of course. She was like a second mother to me!"

She stares at me for a long moment that feels like a lifetime. Then she says simply, "She was your first."

Abe drops to his knees, so close that she reaches out to pat his shoulder sympathetically.

"Oh God, oh God," he says over and over. "I had no idea. None." Tears pour from his soft brown eyes. *My eyes, I see for the first time.*

Eli puts his hands on his father's shoulders—our father's shoulders—and grips hard, bowing his head.

"She didn't want you to know," Ummi tells Abe. "She wanted you to marry her for her alone and not the child she was carrying. She was a woman of great love and compassion. She refused to take the life of her baby and she felt great sorrow for her cousin and for me, who were ourselves unable to conceive. She gave Darius to us, freely, never imposing herself, and never telling anyone what she had done. I'll never be able to repay her for the piece of heaven she placed in my arms that day!"

I can see nothing through my tears.

"She even let me name you," she tells me. "I chose the name of the king who ruled Persia at its peak, 2500 years ago, a name meaning, "He who holds firm to good." He promoted religious tolerance and forbade slavery. He practiced an early form of monotheism known as Zoroastrianism, which holds that, in the cosmic battle of order versus chaos, light can overcome darkness through thoughts, words, and deeds. Remember always, my son, Maryam's son, that you are my gift of light!"

To Abe she continues, with growing warmth in her voice, "Maryam kept her pregnancy a secret from everyone. She went back to Bethlehem after we adopted Darius. She used to tease me that her hometown—a place which means so much to Christians—would never accept an unmarried pregnant Muslim carrying the son of a Jew... Later she moved to America, where she died of cancer, when Darius was fourteen. She only allowed herself a visit twice a year, though she loved him dearly. Yet she was always happy that she'd given him to us, out of the generosity of her heart."

Abe is sobbing uncontrollably.

I'm in shock. I feel almost faint, yet somehow unutterably relieved. *Perhaps I always suspected this, on some subconscious level?*

"It's my fault," Eli says suddenly.

"What are you talking about?" Abe asks.

"I accidentally found some letters from Maryam to you, but I never dared ask you about them... Anyway, I had no idea what my behavior as a kid cost you. I don't remember her, but apparently I lobbied hard in my own childish way to keep you to myself. Until I met Darius, I thought you'd lost a love, a potential wife and step-mother for me. After I met Darius, I was surprised by the resemblance between us, and haunted by his last name, which matched Maryam's. I couldn't wait to see your reaction to Darius, yet afterward you never seemed as intrigued as I thought you might be. Then the jealous nagging in my head started to ease."

"I've heard everyone speak of the resemblance between you and Darius, but I've never seen it myself," Abe says. "When I looked at Darius I only saw Maryam," he sobs. "Yet I never imagined the *whole* truth. I thought it was just a family resemblance, the way cousins can resemble one another... Even when I realized it was the same woman... How blind I was!"

Silvana, deeply moved, curls her arms around his shoulder.

"Oh, Silvana, I don't deserve you," he says.

Fatima takes Eli's hand in hers, and reaches for mine with the other.

"When our parents marry we become one family. No matter what other people say or do, we must never let that bond be broken. Never, never."

Paolo grabs Eli and me around the neck and squeezes us together.

"No more Cain and Abel shit. I pledge right here, right now, before our parents and Zio, to never let it begin again. Now, you two have to promise too."

"I promise," I say.

"Me too," Eli agrees.

Abe reaches for me, almost blinded with tears. "My son! I have another son!"

I embrace him tentatively, glancing over his shoulder at Eli.

This could take some getting used to.

Chapter 49

Fatima

Saturday's show is a phenomenal success. The first benefactors are the charities tied to the event. The second are the networks, undoubtedly relieved that the juggling act of programming has come off. Advertisers and the title sponsor are the next smiling faces, followed by the League and Leyland's agency, both euphorically relieved that there were only very minor glitches. The city of Rome, as if it needs the publicity, got it anyway. The players, some of whom had been apprehensive about participating, had a blast—as did the children who positioned themselves along the slope of the Palatine Hill, gloves in hand, in hopes of catching long balls sailing toward the ancient ground. Admittedly, they were an added security hassle—but it made for soulful television. Social media is buzzing with it more than with anything else.

We flew Nonna into Rome to join the festivities. A pre-taped address from the Pope, backed by Muslim and Jewish clerics, was broadcast on large screens just before the event. The Pope, his face radiant, called for peace among all people as modeled by the athletes.

How I pray for that possibility!

•••••••••••

With the exception of Abe and Leyland, we were about as prepared for Dubai as cavemen time-travelled to the 21st Century. The stunning modern metropolis, in the middle of the desert, and its landmark Burj Al Arab hotel, blows us away like a sandstorm. "Welcome to the Disney of the desert," Leyland says.

I have never been to Disneyland, but this is no child's paradise: instead, it's a playground for the jet set. This brutal dry heat is causing my leg to itch more than usual because of my soft cast. Abe and Leyland have been to Dubai several times, so they act as tour guides, although a tight advance publicity schedule before tomorrow night's event leaves little time for the boys to explore the man-made islands, state-of-the-art sporting venues, or astonishing malls.

One exception is a visit to Dubai's mind-boggling Meydan horse racing track. Here a real sandstorm blows us away, delaying the start of the races.

The evening proves a paparazzi feast. "I could handle a steady diet of this," Paolo says.

He's all alone on that score.

•••••••••••

The rest of the SOA tour players, having spent an extra day sightseeing in Rome, arrive late in the evening. The Skyview Bar at our hotel becomes the happening place into the wee hours. I'm the first to make my excuses and leave, but Darius and his mother offer to escort me. Darius is absolutely ebullient with her back in his life. I've never seen him look so contented.

We traverse the glittering hallways to our rooms together. Mrs. Salamah's is the first we come to. She kisses us both good night, with an extra hug for Darius.

"This all feels strange to you, doesn't it?" I ask, once we're alone.

"I can't even begin to process it. She's my mother. She raised me. But Maryam... It's all too soon, too fast—and too much. Once this tour is over, then I can begin to think. And this place is so unreal... Unreal too is the thought that, only 135 miles from our next tour stop, is the city I once called home. I can't help wondering if I'll ever see it again."

"And not a word about all your recent achievements! I knew you'd never truly fall in love with baseball." I tease.

"Oh, well, I loved winning the World Series, because I accomplished that with my teammates. To use your words, I loved the sense of oneness it gave me, for that brief moment. But I lack the same passion for the sport that Paolo, Eli, and the others have. I didn't grow up desiring it as they did. My desire has always been to become a doctor—and it still is."

"I can picture you some day, working at Sister Colleen's side."

"What a dream that would be! But I still feel so strange, Fatima," he says, almost to himself. "It's as if all those months ago someone took an ax and split me in pieces. Part of me never left Damascus. Yet, as a Palestinian, part of me was never at home, even there... My journey won't be complete until I return to Syria, recover that part of myself, and transplant it into a place that will truly feel like 'home' to me... But where? My people are walled away in a prison by the other half of what I now know are also my people. How will I ever find peace?"

"I feel sure you will, Darius," I tell him.

"But how? I've been living in a fantasy world with you and your family and baseball. It's *un*-reality, if that makes any sense."

"To someone like me, it makes perfect sense," I say, joking at the expense of my mystical moments.

But he's not in a laughing mood. He says, with intensity, "Worst of all I've come to understand that I can't truly love a person, a job, or a country if only part of me is trying. And yet I think I know what I need to do. It's as clear to me now as the purest water from the purest spring...

"I'll never be able to repay your faith in me, Fatima, when so many others weren't willing to trust a Muslim refugee. Those phone conversations when I was training with your uncle—that time we shared in Sicily—these are memories I'll treasure forever. You've been my crush for so long, it's tough to accept that you will soon be my stepsister. I haven't even come to terms with having a new father yet!

"But having Ummi here has opened my eyes to many things. I think I treated you like a substitute of sorts...someone to hold my hand, in her absence. Can you understand that?"

"I've always understood you, Darius. Why would I not now?"

"True."

"What are your thoughts about Abe?" I can't help asking.

"I've always liked him. I'm sure he loved Maryam...my birth mother. He's as jolted as I am, at the moment, but we'll get there."

"And Eli as a half-brother?"

"I'm glad you mentioned him. Eli is in love with you, Fatima. I think he's known plenty of women, but I sense that they meant nothing to him, in comparison. You may imagine that because of your illness, you're sparing him, but I suspect you might be using it as an excuse."

Could this be true?

"When I was in Portugal I prayed continuously for you, Paolo and Eli," I say, at last. My destiny is separate from yours. I don't know exactly what yours will be, but I do believe that, no matter how far apart the three of you may be physically, deep inside you will be joined forever."

Darius shivers at my words, even though the temperature in the hallway is perfect. I warm him in my arms. We hold each other close – a few moments that in another dimension of time and space lasts for a million years.

I love my soon-to-be new brother.

•••••••••••

The Dubai event proves not quite as successful as Rome, but was not expected to be. Still, cricket stars joined footballers on center stage, which proved a unique bit of fun for those who attended or who watched on TV.

In mid-air, as we fly toward Jerusalem, a storm over the Arabian desert triggers monstrous turbulence. Everyone seems to be sweating—everyone except for me. *With this disease, what would I have to lose in a crash?* By the time we land, sickness bags are in short supply. But there is little chance to rest. The Thursday evening performance means a hamsters-on-a-treadmill schedule.

Abe has rented a house for his new family for several weeks: I sense that he's anxious for the tour to end and the sightseeing to begin. The wedding itself is only two weeks away.

As we drive by Teddy Stadium, Paolo yells, "Look!" There, on the building's façade, is a gigantic banner of Eli, Israel's star baseball player. We urge the driver to swing past the stadium again for a photo op. Eli jumps out for a selfie with his own giant figure as backdrop and posts it to Instagram with the caption, *Ditto.*

Even though the players are ready for this show to be over, pros that they are, they play their parts to perfection. Leyland is ecstatic: the Sons of Abraham Tour is the biggest sporting news over the past ten days, giving a sport that's usually an afterthought by mid-November an extra ten days to milk the cash cow—not bad for a three-month promotional sprint.

•••••••••••

I'm first to the kitchen for this free day on which we've all been waiting. A tiny thrill pulses through my veins, like digital signals through the world wide web. I'm finally able to relinquish the soft cast I've been dragging like a ball and chain since my last fall—which is ironic, considering today I'll traverse the Via Dolorosa: Christ's stumbling path from Pilot's sentencing to Golgotha. The excitement—as least for me—is even greater than it was in Portugal.

Eli walks into the bright, cozy space, "Whoever decorated this place has my kind of taste. The only thing missing is Elvis," he says while trying to suppress a yawn.

Although we aren't alone in the house, my desire for Eli wraps the two of us in the soft glow of oneness. He inches toward me. My eyelids demur, the serene smile never leaving my lips until he kisses it away. He tucks me to him and buries his face in my hair. His athlete's hands are rough on my cheek, but I don't care.

"Finally, as close as I've dreamed," he whispers.

Matching wet streams roll down our cheeks.

"This life is just a tiny speck in eternity, Eli. No matter what happens, we'll be together again, in another time, another place... *per sempre, mi amore.*"

Footfalls on the stairs urge us to reluctantly part, wiping our faces. I open the refrigerator and ask Eli, rather unsteadily, what he'd like for breakfast.

"Dear God, if I could only hear you ask me that question every morning for the rest of my life," he whispers.

"Absolutely anything, as long as you're cooking it," Paolo says cheerfully.

One by one the family joins us in the sunlit space. We eat. We laugh: yes, even Eli and me. We plan our day together.

•••••••••••

Old Jerusalem's stone on stone structures remind me of age-old sites in Sicily, as the sunshine ignites the ancient walls to a sparkle. There's a thrilled anticipatory buzz among our fellow pilgrims, both known and unknown. I feel as if I'm about to burst, like the biblical notion of filling old wineskins with new wine.

Our first tour is of the Western Wall Tunnel. It's where Jesus walked as both child and man— the place which witnessed his confrontation with the merchants. But it's also the route leading to what's left of the temple where Jesus worshipped, a structural remnant called The Holy of Holies which, for Jews, is the most important place on earth.

It also tunnels under the Muslim quarter of the old city, highlighted by the Dome of the Rock, where Darius and his mother plan to pray later in the day. When we finally emerge from ground level 2000 years ago to ground level today, I'm astonished by the archeological science of it all. And everywhere, reverence overshadows us: I will it not to leave.

We plan to return to the Western Wall (sometimes called the Wailing Wall) later in the day. Meanwhile, everyone has agreed to indulge me in my heart's desire, to tread the Via Dolorosa.

Chapter 50

Darius • Jerusalem

"What is it, Darius? You look like you've seen a ghost," Fatima says lightly. But suddenly she looks as if she's just seen one herself. "Whatever you're fighting, I can feel it. I've felt it around you on other occasions," she says, and then, closing her eyes, she begins to make the sign of the cross over and over again on her chest using her thumb. Her lips are moving, but I can't read them. I'm too busy snapping my head this way and that like a startled dove. *Where's the bastard gone?* He's here, in this crowd of pilgrims and a ridiculous array of merchants along the Via Dolorosa to Calvary. Paolo and Eli are investigating a souvenir stall; the senior members of our group are also separated from Fatima and me. *Where is Ummi?*

I can't see him, but I know he's still lurking. I caught only a glimpse, but it was enough to finally realize who he is and why he's here. *My mother! Oh Allah, be merciful! Where is she?* I push and shove this way and that, desperate to catch up with her before he does. *Why on earth did it take me so long to recognize him?* The blond hair, those eyes, that accent...all fake! Surely I've played the role of double agent myself enough times to have known? How arrogant could I have been to think no one but myself capable of linguistic mastery? *Oh, please let me find her before he does* but there are too many tourists, too many natives, and at least one demon inside the walls of Jerusalem's Old City.

"Quick! Over there. Follow me," Fatima says, grabbing my arm. *But how can she know?* Still, I follow.

We dart and weave, skip backward or spin sideways, like footballers en route to a goal. Fatima is amazingly agile for someone who only removed her cast a day ago. *There are too many people... we'll never catch him...we'll be too late!*—or so I fret until, all at once, he appears. Fatima stops and points straight at him with the crucifix of her Rosary. He looks at us, smiling strangely. Are my nerves playing tricks? I could swear his eyes shiver in the mid-day heat-haze like the red hot blaze of hell. *Why is he smirking?*

He turns only his head and suddenly I know. My mother and Peppe are so deep in conversation, they don't see the danger only a step away...too far for me to reach, yet so close to him, the bastard.

Time does a strange swivel back to that day on the beach with the toddler and the wild boar. A souvenir stand beside me is loaded with trashy trinkets of all colors, shapes and sizes, but this snow globe will have to do...

I hear Fatima's scream like the only sound in this frenetic street; it echoes off the Golden Dome and back. Her uncle steps instinctively toward his niece's cry, between my mother and Blondie. He takes the knife deep in the stomach.

My throw is well-aimed but just too late. Blondie falls heavily on top of Peppe. My mother hovers, hands over her mouth, utterly soundless. *Why should she cry out? Death has become her constant companion. All we ever managed was to give her a minor respite from it.*

Tourists are screaming and people crawling up each other's backs to get away, leaving a clear path for Fatima and me to rush forward. I manage to shove that scum off the old priest, but the knife is buried, blood is everywhere and poor Peppe's breathing is already rapid and shallow. Fatima cradles her uncle's head in her lap as I seek desperately to staunch the flow. His body twitches spasmodically but his lips still part in a smile. "Thank you, my children," he says. Then he whispers, "*Grazie Dio* for giving this old priest a good death!" And with a final shudder, he's gone.

Before we can even begin to process this, I see Fatima scream, *"No!"* but I hear nothing. Blondie lies behind me, out cold, or so I'd thought...but, as I whirl around, I realize I was wrong. With a cry, Fatima leaps to shield my mother from the shot. It cuts clean through her neck and grazes my mother—my Ummi's—shoulder. But I only realize this later, much later. After Blondie turns to aim toward me...after the Israeli Mossad agent blasts Blondie, gun in both hands...after it's my turn to cradle a dying loved one...after her initial *"No!"* becomes a relentless chant my heart can't stop repeating...and long after Fatima, eyes already closed, says, "Remember always, Darius, that you are a child of the light."

•••••••••••

The wedding was postponed; we had a funeral instead. And what a funeral! As soon as the news broke, it became clear that the family of Giuseppe Colbino and Fatima Giobatti would have to share their farewells with the rest of the world. The Catholic Church and Israeli authorities worked closely to permit their last Mass to be at the Church of the Holy Sepulchre. Their coffins were laid at the spot where they died and thousands of people, of all faiths, paid their respects to our unusual family.

Nonna Marietta flew in from Sicily and was stalwart as the head of the clan, with Silvana and Abe, my father, by her side. Paolo, Eli, and I, as well as my mother, greeted our fellow mourners for the greater part of two long days of pure torture. I will never forget it. Nor will those who witnessed any part of it, I suspect, in person or on television. Not a single act of violence was committed in any part of Palestine or Israel during all those hours: it was as if that part of the world had paused to mourn with us.

Blondie is now behind bars. I can only hope that his brother, the one who forced my mother into a sham marriage, will soon share his fate. If Fatima was still alive, she would advise me to pray for their souls. I know in my head that she'd be right, but it might take my heart forever to wrap itself around that idea... Let them show remorse first. Then, perhaps, I can try.

I always knew Blondie's face was subtly familiar to me. He had been playing me—and the Americans—all along. Whatever info I fed him was never transmitted, or so it seemed in my debriefing. Judging from the news coming out of Syria, some of what I've told them of late is helping, but the most revolting human I've ever personally met still remains free. He it was who wanted my mother dead, not just to protect himself, but for vengeance's sake—he was so infuriated that she had managed to escape him. She still refuses to talk about her time with him. She says, "Memory wasted on evil is like the sun forgetting to rise: it's destructive of life itself."

Chapter 51

Darius

Three weeks have passed since the funeral, but no one can think about a wedding. Eli, Paolo, and I have tweeted our fans thanks for their prayers. Nonna Marietta appears the strongest of all; she also does all the cooking.

Today Abe sits glumly in front of his laptop; Paolo stares out of the window; I help Nonna to chop vegetables. We're all together in the kitchen when Silvana reaches into her purse for her phone. A postcard flutters to the floor beside her. Eli automatically reaches to pick it up.

"What's this?" he asks Silvana. "It's addressed to Paolo, Darius and me."

At the sight of it Silvana's body lurches as if her last breath is escaping her. "I'd forgotten all about it! Fatima wrote it on the flight from Portugal to Rome," she says. "You know how she always hated to bother with a purse. She asked me to carry it for her."

Silvana reads Fatima's words, fighting back tears.

"You'd think with her illness that in Portugal she would have been praying for a miracle cure. But I don't think it even crossed her mind. I think all her prayers were for the three of you.

"She's written a psalm. She probably planned to place it in the Western Wall. I don't know what to think about anything anymore except that maybe this note fell out just now so that Fatima's prayer could find its proper home."

•••••••••••

The Western Wall plaza is humming—literally, men to the left and women to the right, chattering, crying, mourning, and singing. Thankfully one of the Orthodox rabbis who control the space recognizes Eli. He whispers, "We're so sorry about your friends," and offers us entry. We struggle to find a spot along the creviced stone until a trio of rabbis finish bowing, rocking, and praying. They nod politely as they leave with their Torah as they pass us. Eli touches the wall with reverence. Water trails from his eyes down his cheek, yet he makes no sound.

Paolo keeps wiping his tears and rubbing them onto the wall. Once his sobs subside, Eli slips the postcard from inside his pocket and offers it to me. It's in Italian, so, given Paolo's condition, it is up to me to read her words:

A Psalm for the Sons of Abraham:

In the wind of a stinging desert I hear a siren call of hope. It carries me away from hollow darkness into a cacophony of light. Laughter, crying, shouts, and song fight each other in a race to my lips. I call out to the force embracing me in the sweetness of a mother's love.

At long last I'm at peace—a peace not known since my tiny child's hand rested carelessly in my father's grasp. Dare I name this force? Dare I?

I am no longer afraid to dare, for my soul has taught me your name, oh God. The fear of mortal enemies that walls my heart from the miracle of your love melts away like a dream at dawn, so that in its place can reside the perfection that is You in me, for us, we.

I can't stop my voice from trembling. It's considered blasphemy by Muslims to attribute human traits such as mother or father to Allah; but Fatima, this Christian woman with the Muslim name, is no blasphemer.

I hand it silently back to Eli, who carefully chooses the spot to receive her words. He finds a stony slit at the outermost reach of his fingers. He holds her prayer to his chest a long time, in a desperate attempt to feel her touch once more.

It's hard, even to watch.

•••••••••••

Afterward we walk silently through the streets of the Old City, taking in its narrow cobbled zigzags, with languages from every corner of the world bubbling around us. Amidst the distracting aromas, bartering, vender's cries and general chatter, I suddenly stop, recollection tugging at my soul. I say, "Fatima was mystified by a vision of a wall. Did she ever mention this to you?"

"No," says Paolo.

"Yes," says Eli.

Revelation strikes us, at the same moment. The Western Wall, the place her psalm will rest for all eternity—the place from where she hoped we'd begin to make her prayers reality.

Eli begins to pace. He runs his hands through his hair then squeezes a handful as if he's about to tear it out. "I'm no cleric, but of this much I'm sure—we can't run from our connectedness. But I'm afraid though—I'm afraid of all the hate. I'm afraid it will be too hard."

Then he steadies himself. "She told me this life is over in just a blink of an eye. She promised me we'd be together forever someday. She wasn't afraid to die." He pauses, then looks at us a long moment, saying, "We shouldn't be afraid, either."

The tremor in his voice echoes the ache in my heart.

He rubs his eyes fiercely. "I wanted a life with her so badly! Oh, God! How could you take her from me?"

People are watching. A couple seem to recognize him, and perhaps the reason for his tears. One woman covers her mouth and shakes her head. Others whisper. ("What a shame... Poor young man.")

Paolo embraces him, saying, "*Santa Maria*, forgive me for thinking women are the weaker sex." He says this whacking his forehead with the palm of his right hand. "I'm tired of being shamed by them. Those nuns that Fatima wanted to join, Sister Colleen and all the rest, they're like the oldest olive trees. Their only fear is the unquenchable fire. Your birth mother, Darius, was willing to sacrifice for the happiness of others, and your adopted mother endured the unthinkable, simply for daring to speak out against war! While, as for Fatima... We must do our bit for Sister Colleen and the rest," he tells us, then continues in a more Paolo-like tones, "or I'll have Fatima in my ear every moment of every day if we don't."

Giggles suddenly ripple in the air. They're a glorious salve. Spinning toward their source, we're all struck by the vision of a young Muslim girl tickling a tiny boy, who appears to be her brother. They only stop their play to peddle flowers to passing tourists.

The little girl blinks at our stares. Then she smiles, approaching us with three white roses in her small outstretched hands.

Her dark, overabundant, wild curls are a replica cut and length of the only other human we've known to sport such a mane. She offers each of us one of her prizes. We're struck by the bliss that shines from her face.

I ask her a question in Arabic.

Her single word response is understood by all.

"Fatima," she says.

The End

Acknowledgements

I could paper cut my tongue a dozen times and it still wouldn't be enough self-flagellation to compensate those of you who were so kind as to suffer through the horrible first draft of this novel.

Paul Dolan, Owner, Chairman, and CEO of the Cleveland Indians, your honesty, pragmatism, enthusiasm and kindness I hope will not go unrewarded. Mark Shapiro, President of the Toronto Blue Jays, thank you for introducing me to your Dad. Ron Shapiro, I hope this final version doesn't disappoint. Your faith in the seed of a story that I'd merely thrown a little dirt over at that point meant more than you'll ever know. Thank you also for introducing me to PeacePlayers International.

Cheryl Costner, Mary O'Carroll, Lisa Komara, Valerie Amico, Len Tischler, Aaron Weir, Nancy Scallan, Kathy Roberts, Ken Stefanov, and Sister Suzie Armbruster IHM, thank you, my friends, for the reading you did, the advice you offered, and the support you may not realize you gave. Frayda Froozan, my dear friend, your ebullience is a gift to anyone who knows you. Thank you for all the drafts you read, good advice given, and that ever-present smile. Thanks also to my pal Bernadette Repko, major league proofreader and travel buddy.

Special Gratitude to: Suzanne Fisher Staples, Distinguished Author and Newberry Award Honoree, I am so blessed that someone of your caliber was willing to become my friend. I can only dream of someday being in your league. Your reading, wisdom, and advice were priceless; Dr. Riaz Hussain, Professor of Finance and Imam at The University of Scranton, who was the first to enlighten me of the amazing connection with Mary, the mother of Jesus to both our faiths and suggested the important books by Karen Armstrong; and to Dr. Raymond Khoudary, who took the time from his busy schedule in the fall of 2014 to tell me about life in his hometown of Aleppo, Syria, before and after the war began. I have no words for you, except for the hope between the covers of this book.

Thank you to: Nunzio Botta and his baseball organization near Paterno, Sicily for graciously touring us around your facility (and yes, even for those Red Sox t-shirts); Father Bob Simon for helping me learn about Jerusalem's old city through your eyes; Father Michael Bryant whose enthusiasm for daily Mass was a boost to my morale through this process; and Marwa Gaafer, Father Jim Redington SJ and Sister of Mercy, Kathleen Smith, who each possess a beauty, humility, strength, and enthusiasm I adore. Your enlightenment will never be forgotten.

Thank you Gail Cicerini for introducing me to Dr. Albert Liberatore whose team at Edits Made Easy held my hand through the self-publishing process beginning with that incredibly thorough (slightly painful) assessment of my second and third drafts, and later guided me expertly into the hands of my dynamic, multi-talented writing coach and final editor, Alice McVeigh, whose wisdom and patience with such a novice was a gift. London didn't seem like an ocean away during those Skype sessions, it was like chatting with a friend next door.

Paula Zorc, my best counsel, my guide, forgive me for all those times in our childhood that I wanted to ditch my baby sister when hanging out with my friends. If it weren't for you being at my side every step of this journey, I would have given up long ago. Steve Zorc, you are a good man to put up with not one, but two Arcuri women. Working with you and Paula and my dear niece, Julia, on the cover design was downright fun. Thanks also to my brothers, Tony and Greg—who keep me grounded—and to our Dad, Frank Arcuri, gone since 2009, but whose voice is ever in my ear…pushing, cheering.

Last but not least, to my precious mother, Ida Arcuri, and dear husband, Bill Bonacci, *grazie mille* for your abiding love and fearless spirit, and especially for your lives which show the world every day what a boon immigration is to this great country.

If you are curious about the events that took place at Fatima, Portugal in 1917 you could read:

FATIMA IN LUCIA'S OWN WORDS: SISTER LUCIA'S MEMOIRS, VOL. 2: 5TH AND 6TH MEMOIRS by Lucia Santos and Fr. Louis Kondor

FATIMA FOR TODAY, THE URGENT MARIAN MESSAGE OF HOPE by Fr. Andrew Apostoli, C.F.R.

GOD AND THE SUN AT FATIMA by Stanley L. Jaki

MY HEART WILL TRIUMPH by Mirjana Soldo

•••••••••••

Any errors in religious observances/teachings are solely the author's and unintended. The goal was respect for all.

About the Author

Val Bonacci is a former Vice President of Marketing and Broadcasting for the Cleveland Indians where she spent 17 years from jinxes to joy. Like most players, she paid her dues with a three-year tour of duty in the Minor Leagues (Kinston, North Carolina). She is the Year 2000 Distinguished Alumnus of Ohio University's top ranked Sports Administration Masters Program and did her undergrad work at Ohio as well. She was born and raised in East Liverpool, Ohio and now resides in Scranton, Pennsylvania with her husband, Bill Bonacci. She has taught marketing on an adjunct basis at Keystone College and The University of Scranton.